Welcome to 'Wis' Apothecary

By Andrew Freeman

Lisa

aren't books magical? ♡ ☐ ☐

I hope you keep reading!!

To my loving parents

My supportive sister

All of my beloved brothers

And to my dedicated editor, who was instrumental in making this happen.

You Can Count on Me

"Hmmm…"

I had a tough choice to make. I scratched my chin as I examined the three distinct flowers that were laid on the counter before me. I looked up nervously at my teacher, who was watching me expectantly with cool, lavender-colored eyes.

"Well? Which one is it, Isabel?"

Which one indeed? A cauldron bubbled nearby, anxious for the correct ingredient. I was being asked to make a Dream Eater Draught, a potion more important than most because it was a test—a benchmark of my skill as a witch. Well, a witch's apprentice anyway.

I tucked an untamed lock of my wavy, peach-colored hair back behind my ear, and began reaching for the brightest-colored plant. It had whorled leaves and five-petalled, yellow flowers. But I quickly withdrew my hand as I remembered this was St. John's Wort, which could actually cause *trouble* sleeping. It certainly didn't belong in a potion meant to combat insomnia.

My teacher nodded her head in approval, her eyes twinkling behind a pair of dainty spectacles. I smiled, feeling rather confident that my next choice would be the right one.

My name is Isabel Pirige, student of the great (but… *quirky*) Wisteria Amberfinch. We were in her apothecary, and though potion-brewing usually happened in the laboratory, this particular afternoon we were stationed up front at the counter so we could still tend to customers should they come in, though there was a festival going on in the city of Aramore, so business had been slow.

Sunlight poured into the storefront, bathing the neatly arranged shelves of medicines and tinctures in a warm glow. Cloud, my cat, aptly named for his coat of snow white fur and sky blue eyes, had found the perfect little sun spot, and was lazily lounging out across the worn, wooden floor.

Many of the more expensive and potent potions and medicines were kept behind the counter, along with several tools of the trade. There was a back room where most of our ingredients were grown and stored, and where the lab was located.

I lived upstairs with my teacher, Master Wis as I called her, above the shop. I moved in when I became an apprentice, leaving my family and our orchard behind in the small town of Pommeseed, right outside the capital. Life in the capital city was quite an adjustment, but I'm pretty fond of it now.

I was getting ready to make my next choice when a melding of laughter caught my attention. My apple-red eyes flickered up to the window to see a group of kids my age walk past, joking with one another and horseplaying. I couldn't help but look on enviously, as they no doubt headed towards the city center to take part in the ongoing festivities.

Princess Fleur, King Eilsorin's middle daughter, was getting married and the entire kingdom was celebrating. She was marrying Prince Reynard of the neighboring kingdom of Marza.

The festival would be going on all weekend, with lots of tasty street food, games, music and dance, and special theater productions. It would all conclude tomorrow with the princess being seen out of the kingdom with a procession and fireworks! The wedding, of course, would be a private affair in the days that followed.

But here I was, stuck inside on this gorgeous day, racking my brain over some difficult test. *It's not fair!*

"Isabel! Focus." Master Wis scolded.

"How can I when everyone else in the kingdom is having so much fun?!"

My teacher raised an eyebrow, and shook her head at me. Even when annoyed, my teacher was nothing less than beautiful. Her hair was the color of lavender, and curled down in ribbon-like tendrils at the front. The rest of it was held back behind her shoulders with a large, black bow.

She was a striking witch, dressed in fine robes with a low-pointed hat identical to mine; adorned with a dainty, amber bow at the brim. And while she wasn't particularly tall, she was lifted up by a pair of heels. They matched in color the dark stockings that climbed up above her knees.

Compared to her voluptuous form, I was basically no more appealing than a plank of wood. So I didn't believe her whenever she called me cute. Now, she promises I'll fill out by the time I'm a proper witch, but that was still nearly four years away! At 18, apprentices were eligible to go to the kingdom's capital to take an exam and become officially licensed to practice magic.

A mark of a true witch was the ability to ride a broom! If you saw someone soaring over the city on a broomstick, you knew they were a certified witch. But until that happened, the only capacity I was allowed to handle a broom in was to sweep the floor. Yep, my days were filled with lots of studying, cooking, cauldron scrubbing and other mundane chores. Oh, and tests. Can't forget the tests.

"Master, can we make a deal? If I ace this, can we go to the festival this weekend?"

"Let's worry about the test first. We can talk about the festival later."

"Fine." I groaned, returning to the choice in front of me. Both remaining flowers were pink, and one had to be valerian. If I remember correctly, valerian root had sedative qualities. But which one was it? My confidence was quickly dwindling.

I needed to make a decision. I reached for the one on the left, which had colorful clusters of flowers and narrow, dark green leaves. I had a 50/50 chance, and my gut was telling me this choice was the right one. I dropped it in the cauldron, and the potion turned from a milky white to a dark red. That was a good sign, right? I looked at my teacher apprehensively.

Unfortunately for me, I didn't receive the response I was hoping for. Master Wis frowned, and let out a disappointed exhale. "You just killed someone, Isabel."

"I what?!"

"That was oleander, a particularly poisonous plant." Master Wis explained, as she put her hand over the cauldron. "Every part of the flower is toxic, from the sap to the stem. A single leaf could be enough to kill a man."

"Oh no!" My cheeks turned as red as my eyes in embarrassment. "How could I forget something so important?"

Master Wis had specifically asked me to study oleander a couple weeks before... As I watched another throng of jubilant people pass the shop, I had to admit, my mind was elsewhere.

A ring on Master Wis' finger began to glow, and the oleander began to rise out of the cauldron. The potent solution had quickly begun dissolving the plant, but I watched in wonder as the plant began repairing itself, returning to its original state. The color of the potion also reverted to its initial milky white.

That was the power of an Arcanus. Watching her use the mystical artifact made me realize how far I still had to go as an apprentice. A year and a half had passed since I began training with Master Wis, and yet I felt no closer to earning one. I bit my lip in disappointment.

"Isabel, as an apothecary people's lives are in our hands." Master Wis placed a hand on her hip and her tone turned sharp. I readied myself for a stern lecture, but before she could continue, the door to our shop opened, and an eyebrow-raising trio entered.

It was hard to not notice the two guards first, intimidating men donned in armor and with shields that bore the Aramore crest. But the man they accompanied was even more imposing. He was an older gentleman, with a stern, leathery face and green, piercing eyes. He had a short goatee and well-groomed hair, though there were lots of salty threads transforming his hair from black to white. He carried himself well, and was dressed in fine clothes. Expensive looking fur lined his shoulders.

"Good morning." Master Wis calmly greeted. "Can I help you gentlemen with something?"

"Madame Wisteria Amberfinch?"

"That's me."

What did these scary looking guys want? I gulped, and inched closer to Master Wis.

The official stepped into the center of the store and looked around, before approaching the counter. His gaze settled on me.

"Ahem." He coughed.

I nervously glanced around. "Me?"

"Some privacy please, child."

Child?!

"This *young lady* is my apprentice, Isabel Pirige." Master Wis quickly defended. "I assure you anything you have to say can be told to both of us. Discretion is one of our specialties."

I smiled softly to myself. *Master Wis was the absolute coolest! Take that, Mr. Fancy Pants!*

The official looked uncomfortable, but it didn't seem like a hill he was ready to die on. "Very well…"

"Now then, would anyone like some tea?" Master Wis asked.

"If it's all the same to you, I'd rather cut to the chase, madame."

"Very well then."

"My name is Ambroys LaPannett, Chief Minister to King Eilsorin."

King Eilsorin?! Wow.

"I'm here to ask for your help, Madame Wis. Princess Fleur has gone missing… and we were hoping you might be able to use some magic to locate her."

My jaw dropped.

"Goodness!" Master Wis gasped. "How did this happen?"

"We're not sure… but there were no signs of a struggle. It's possible she ran away on her own…" Ambroys sounded embarrassed. "Whatever the case, we need to resolve this matter swiftly."

"I would be happy to help. Though, I trust you understand my services won't be complimentary?"

"Well, we would have asked our own court mage to handle the matter, but she's in Marza helping with preparations for the wedding." Ambroys grimaced. "With that said, surely you don't doubt His Majesty's ability to pay?"

Aramore shared a border with Marza to the south, separated by a large river. With magic it might have been possible to get the mage back quickly, but clearly asking my teacher for help was the most expedient option.

Master Wis' face lit up, and she pressed her hands together. "Of course not! I am humbled by your patronage."

Sheesh. I could practically see the gold coins swimming in her eyes.

"For now, can you take me to her living quarters? I'll require some of her belongings to cast the ritual I have in mind." My teacher continued.

"Anything you need."

"C-Can I help?" I asked, tugging on Master Wis' sleeve.

6

"Well, this ritual might be a little outside of your ability right now… it requires a lot of precision and magic."

In other words, I'd just be in the way… *Ouch.*

My face fell, and I took a step backward. "But…"

"I'm sorry Isabel." Master Wis placed her hand on my head, and ruffled my hat. "But I need you to mind the store for a while. Why don't you stay here just long enough to make sure no one needs to pick up any medicine, and then after lunch you can take this and go have some fun at the festival?"

She dropped a small but hefty sack of coins into my hands, and looked at me with consoling eyes. "*Please understand,*" they said.

I sighed. Now Master Wis, who was just defending me moments ago, was treating me like a kid? *What gives?!*

I wanted to argue, but I didn't want to cause trouble for my teacher in front of such an important person. The kingdom had quite the crisis on its hands…

So instead I just nodded, and retreated to the counter.

"If that's settled, let's be off at once." Ambroys declared. "I don't want to waste any more time."

The guards opened the door, and Master Wis followed Ambroys out, but not before turning to me and giving me a small wave. "If this wraps up quickly, I'll meet you there. Have fun for me until then!"

***

I'm so bored.

I was slumped over the counter, with my chin pressed against the cool, smooth finish of the wood. My arms dangled loosely to my side, as I drowned in dejection.

That's when I caught a glimpse of myself in our shop's display window, and growled as I unsuccessfully tried to stamp down the stubborn curl of hair that always seemed to be protruding from the crown of my head like an antenna. I don't know why I bothered. It didn't matter what I tried to tame my unruly hair! I've even tried potions.

I was in a mood, and not even Cloud could comfort me. He tried multiple times to jump up on my lap, but I refused to budge from my position and eventually he gave up.

I was stupid. The day was stupid. And the festival was stupid. Why would I want to go by myself in the first place?!

Well… maybe I could have used some company after all. I turned my head towards Cloud to apologize and try and call him back over, but at that moment, the door to the apothecary was thrown open. I sat up from the counter with a start!

A stranger cloaked in a hood dove into the apothecary, and slammed the door behind them. The figure pressed themselves against the door, and peeked out the window as a large group of guards ran by.

"Hey! What do you think you're doing?"

The hooded figure turned their attention towards me, and drew a wand from inside their cloak. They advanced on me quickly, and pointed the wand at my throat.

"Woah, woah, woah…" I backed away from the counter, raising my hands above my head.

"Just shut up and take a seat!" They growled. "Do as I say, and I won't hurt you."

I gulped, a bead of sweat ran down my forehead. Both my hands and knees were trembling uncontrollably. Wands were a bit old fashioned, as most mages opted for the Arcanus these days, but that didn't mean a wand was any less powerful.

If my teacher was here, the criminal would have already been dealt with… but I was just an apprentice. I couldn't even cast a proper spell yet! What was I supposed to do?!

The sweat from my brow was beginning to sting my eyes, and my heart was racing.

Have fun for me?! I couldn't help but chuckle at the irony, as I stared down the length of the wand being dangerously directed at my face. Could this day get any worse?

"I said sit down!!" The hooded figure ordered. Their voice was gruff and artificial, going to great lengths to disguise it.

It might have even been a little funny if I wasn't in such a dire situation…

"Okay, okay!" I hastily replied, settling on the stool behind me.

"Good."

"W-What do you want… anyway?"

"I just need a place to lie low for a minute," they responded, before leaning up against the door and peeking out the window. Though their eyes weren't on me, the wand still was. "Oh, and do you have any amnesiac mixtures?"

"Why…?" I asked.

"You're going to need to drink one. Forget I was ever here."

"What?!" I cried out.

"Shhhhh! Shut up!" They aggressively approached the counter, and once again flaunted the wand. "Just go get one!"

What was I going to do? If I didn't handle a potion like that carefully, I could forget a whole lot more than just ten minutes!

At that moment, my furry companion jumped up on the counter and stood in front of me defensively with a hiss.

"Cloud?!"

"A c-cat??" The hooded figure quickly retreated away from the counter.

Huh?

"Don't tell me… that you're afraid… of cats…"

"Of course not!" The hooded figure quickly retorted. "It's just that… just that… that…"

The hooded individual began staggering and held their hand to their face. Their breaths became sharp and short, and then…

"ACHOO! ACHOO! ACHOO!"

The sneezes had so much force, that by the third sneeze, they completely lost their grip of the wand. It went flying across the shop! We both eyed the wand, but neither of us moved immediately. I couldn't let the stalemate last forever. I went for it!

"No!" They shouted, diving after it too.

My hand grasped it first, but the hooded figure tackled me, and we both went tumbling. We wrestled around on the ground, and somewhere along the way I lost my hat. The assailant managed to work their way on top of me, and tried wrenching it from my grasp.

But… they weren't actually heavy or even that *strong...*

"Let it go!"

"No!"

"Give it back!"

"Get off!"

It continued like this, until…

Snap.

We were both shocked.

"Uh-oh…" The hooded figure gasped.

I used the moment of surprise to my advantage, and using every bit of strength I had, bucked them forward while shoving them to the side. The assailant fell off me, and rolled several times.

"Gah!" They grunted. When they finally came to a stop, we both realized their hood had fallen down!

"W-What?" I shouted, when I got a good look at the face.

"Eep!" She quickly threw her hood back up, but it was too late.

"I… I know you!"

Her hair was long and silky, and looked exactly like the sky on a clear and sunny day. Her eyes were a bright green, though they were more sharply defined than my own. And the tips of her ears were pointed.

With such unforgettable features, how could I not recognize her? She was being celebrated all across the city.

"You're Princess Fleur von Eilsorin!" In my excitement, I pointed the broken wand at her, but I hastily lowered my hand when I realized what I was doing.

Except… *Wait a minute.*

"… Is this just a regular stick?!"

"What? Of course not." She cleared her throat, dropping the fake voice.

I inspected it more closely. Sure, it was made to *look* like a wand, but it was totally just a regular stick!

I couldn't believe I had been so stupid! From her thin build, to the fake wand and her ridiculous voice—how didn't I realize sooner? I was never in any actual danger.

"Are you serious?!" I tossed the piece of junk behind the counter, and Cloud pounced after it. "What's going on?"

"Hmph." Princess Fleur crossed her arms, and turned away from me.

"Okay." I shrugged, going to the door and opening it. "GUAR—"

"Shut up! Shut up!" She scrambled over to me and slammed the door shut. "I'll tell you everything, okay? Can we just go somewhere where... where... ah— ah— ACHOO!"

***

Cloud was crying loudly from the other side of the door, upset that he was locked out from the den upstairs.

Sorry Cloud... He hated being left out.

Princess Fleur sat across from me, fidgeting nervously with an apprehensive look on her face. Now that I was finally getting to take a good look at her, I found myself admiring her beauty.

She looked like a doll. Her skin was completely free of blemishes and almost seemed to glow. And though she was dressed like a servant, she held herself like a proper lady. Her back was completely straight, and her hands were crossed over her knees in a dainty manner.

The immodest dress she wore seemed a little small for someone of her... size.

"What are you looking at?" She snapped, her face turning red.

"Sorry!" I stuttered, unaware that I was staring. "I just uh... think you make for a better princess than criminal."

She shot me a dirty look, but then started snickering, which before long turned into laughter. Then, I joined in, and soon our laughs filled the entire room.

I mean, the whole situation was utterly ridiculous! I couldn't believe I was held up with a *stick*. And I couldn't believe she was thwarted by my cat! Considering how scared I was just a few minutes ago, I couldn't help but laugh.

"Allow me to formally introduce myself. I'm Fleur von Eilsorin." She wheezed, as she wiped tears from the corners of her eyes.

"I didn't expect you to be so young!"

"I'm 23!" She snapped.

"Well, I suppose you *are* an elf."

"Half-Elf." She corrected. "Only my mother is elvish."

"Well, I'm Isabel Pirige. I'm a witch's apprentice here, and 100% human!"

"Nice to meet you…" She muttered.

"But… why are you on the run?" I asked, finally getting to the heart of the matter. "Aren't you excited to get married?"

"Of course I am!" She quickly replied, though she immediately seemed embarrassed at admitting something like that out loud. "But…"

"But what?"

"I'm about to leave Aramore for somewhere new, and…"

"And you're afraid you're going to miss your home."

"I didn't say that!" She snarled. "But… growing up within the castle walls, there's still so much about this city I don't know, and so much I haven't seen. And once I leave…"

I nodded sympathetically. I remembered how scary it was for me to leave Pommeseed to come and live with Master Wis in the city. In fact, there were still times I got really homesick.

With that in mind, it was hard to not look upon her wistful gaze and want to do something.

"You know… my teacher is currently at the castle, working on a ritual to find you."

"She is?" Her expression turned to one of panic.

"Yeah, but don't worry…"

Fleur had a bit of an attitude, but she didn't seem like a bad person. So right then and there, I made a decision.

"… because I'm going to help you!"

"It's not like I asked for your help…" She replied sheepishly.

"Oh, you'll want my help. Because in a single day, I'm going to show you the very best Aramore has to offer!" I declared proudly, once again standing from my seat.

"In a single day? How?"

I grinned broadly. It looked like today was going to be pretty fun, after all.

First, I needed a couple of things from the apothecary…

***

"Hot pies here! Get 'em while they're fresh!"

"Step on up, and test your wit! Can your eyes follow the ball?"

"Giant Boar ribs! Bet you can't finish even one!"

"Want to hear about your future? Find the answers you seek, only a single gold piece!"

In every direction we looked, there was something to fascinate the senses. Whether it was a colorful performance, the tantalizing smell of some delicious treat, or the kind of contagious laughter that brought a smile to your face—the packed streets were truly filled with Aramore's best.

Of course, that's why I brought Fleur to the city's center, so she could experience it all for herself! Pretty clever, right? With the ongoing festival, there would never be a better opportunity to see or do so much.

Aramore was a coastal city, and though the capital's center wasn't particularly close to the port, the cool gusts of wind still carried the savory smell of sea salt—fiercely competing with the festival aromas. It was also a beautiful city, made up of charming cobblestone streets and buildings with colorful, brick facades.

For the festivities, many of the buildings were decorated with either marigolds or primroses, golden streamers or a combination of the three. Even the flags and banners that flew at the castle, which could be seen off in the distance, were changed for the occasion. Now the walls were draped in auric-colored cloth instead of red and blue. All the gold represented new beginnings and was meant to bring prosperity and luck to the celebrated couple.

Not only did yellow and gold dazzle, but the fragrant primroses left a rich scent hanging in the air. And though the city streets were *always* busy, they didn't even come close to the exciting energy that the festival streets held. Everything just felt so much more alive!

"So, what do you think Fleur? Incredible, isn't it?" I giggled in glee. But when I looked to my left, Fleur was nowhere to be seen. "Fleur?"

Panicking, I stopped and looked around wildly. Where was she? When I remembered I wasn't looking for someone with blue hair, I was able to quickly spot her drooling over some rissole skewers.

"Fleur!" I hissed quietly, approaching her and grabbing her wrist. "You can't just wander off like that! A crowd this big has a mind of its own!"

Thanks to a draught I was able to whip up before we left, Fleur's hair was now jet black. It was a crude and simple potion, but effective enough. I was actually quite proud of myself, given the rushed circumstances and my skill level. It wasn't permanent either, which I had to assure Fleur of more than a dozen times.

Having borrowed one of her handmaid's uniforms to escape the castle, we changed her into one of Master Wis' old outfits I found at the bottom of her wardrobe. It fit *much* better.

She was also wearing an old pair of my teacher's glasses with the lenses punched out. And the enchanted bangle bracelet dangling from her wrist wasn't there for fashion, but to hopefully keep her from being detected with magic.

Hehe... sorry Master Wis!

"Isabel, what are those?" She asked, ignoring me and pointing to the croquettes.

"You've never had rissoles before?" I asked, mildly surprised. "They're fried pastries, filled with minced meat."

"Yum!" She exclaimed, snatching a skewer off the cart and taking a big bite.

"Hey!!" The orc tending to the food cart yelled. "This isn't some charity, you know? You've gotta pay for that!"

"Hm?" She mumbled, with a mouth full of food.

It was like being with a child! Was she really so sheltered that the concept of money escaped her?

"Sorry!" I quickly stepped in, and withdrew some coins from the purse Master Wis had given me.

The merchant accepted my money, but continued to grumble under his breath.

"Come on, Fleur." I whispered, grabbing her by the hand and pulling her away.

"H-Hey!" She stammered.

"At least we know your disguise works." I said, as we sank back into the crowd. "I almost didn't recognize you back there."

"I'll have you thrown in jail if my hair doesn't change back to normal before the wedding though."

"Whatever you say, your Highness." I replied with a roll of my eyes. I didn't have the energy to reassure her a 13th time.

Still, it was a little scary how casually she could issue such a threat. I looked on sheepishly as she happily took another bite from her skewer. "Mmmm!"

"Not bad for commoner food, right?" I snickered, as I watched her face light up in delight.

"Urm…" She caught herself looking unrefined, and coughed. "They're not bad…"

I smirked in amusement. "So what do you want to do next?"

"Let's see…" Fleur scanned the street as we continued to walk. "I really can't believe so many people are here! Even our royal balls aren't this crowded!"

Being from a small town, I also had trouble wrapping my mind around it. It was like a raging river of people, threatening to sweep us away in its current at any moment. Subconsciously, I squeezed Fleur's hand a little tighter.

"And everyone here is celebrating you! Isn't that great?"

As I spoke, I plucked a primrose off a nearby flower arrangement, and inhaled deeply. I still couldn't believe how rich and vibrant everything was! It was unlike any festival I had ever attended.

Fleur looked too embarrassed to respond, so she quickly changed the subject. "How about over here?"

"Woah!"

We fought through the flow of traffic, as she hastily pulled me across the street and up to a large and ornate tent. Inside, display cases lined the sidewalls, filled with all sorts of unique and expensive looking jewelry.

"Uh, Fleur... I don't think I can afford anything here." I whispered to her.

"It's fine, it's fine." She nonchalantly replied. "I'll just *look* this time."

However, the merchant inside seemed to have similar concerns. He raised an eyebrow as we entered. "Can I help you girls with something?"

He was a tall, thin elf with a hooked nose and small, black eyes. He was dressed in very polished attire, with a jeweler's loupe affixed to his spectacles. His voice dripped with condescension.

"Girls?" Fleur scoffed. "Is that anyway to talk to your customers?"

"Customers? I thought you were 'just looking.'"

Fleur narrowed her eyes and opened her mouth to give what I could only assume would've been a nasty retort, so I quickly interceded.

"What's this stone?" I asked innocently, pointing at the first pendant that caught my eye.

It was a red, opaque gem that looked as if it were on fire. Various hues of red, orange, yellow and blue shimmered across its surface. It hung from an elegant chain in the shape of an oval.

"You have good taste." The merchant sounded bored, but entertained me anyway. "That's a phoenix opal, set in 18 karat rose gold. Very rare, *very* expensive."

"Isn't it pretty Fleur?" I cooed. "I think my teacher would like it, too."

"Are you a little apprentice then?" The jeweler asked, his eyes settling on my pointed hat.

"Well, I'm not little," I growled. "But yes. My teacher is Wisteria Amberfinch."

"Your teacher is Madame Wis? The apothecary?!"

"The one and only."

The jeweler's eyes widened in surprise, and his bored expression quickly turned into one of delight. "You absolutely must bring her by! A witch of her caliber would certainly appreciate a piece like this! I would be willing to give her quite the deal, too."

"Don't waste her time, Isabel." Fleur yawned. "I've seen prettier."

The jeweler shot her a dirty look and sneered. "I'm sure…"

Though in Fleur's case, she was probably telling the truth.

"And what about this one?" I asked, sliding down the display case.

The next stone to catch my eye was mahogany in color. It was fairly ordinary looking, but its cut caught the light in a way that drew my attention. It was tapered, with sharp, pretty angles. Like the last pendant, it hung delicately from a chain, though this one looked like it may have been silver.

"That stone is a bit less impressive. It's called Aramorite, and can only be found in this region — hence, the name." He explained, though his tone was much more amiable all of a sudden. "However, it can be found pretty *commonly* in this region, so there's plenty of it."

"I haven't heard of it." Fleur dismissed. Though I couldn't help but notice Fleur peering over my shoulder, as if she were actually interested in the stone.

"Yes, well… if you're only around phoenix opals." The elf shot back sarcastically, though he was quick to follow the comment with a smile as if it were a joke.

"So it's pretty inexpensive?" I asked.

"That's certainly one of my more… modestly priced pieces." He replied. "That stone is popular among the working class."

"Oh…"

In other words, just like Fleur didn't eat rissoles, she didn't wear Aramorite either.

"Would you like to see anything else? Is your teacher nearby, by chance?" The merchant asked.

Fleur rolled her eyes, and turned to exit the tent. "Come on, Isabel. There's certainly nothing interesting to see here."

"Uh, one sec! I'll be right there!"

I joined Fleur outside a few minutes later, just as she was starting to go back inside to look for me. "What were you doing in there?! We wasted too much time on that jerk."

"Weren't you the one that wanted to check it out in the first place?" I chuckled in exasperation.

"Yeah, well… my mistake." She sighed. "How about we get more rissoles?"

***

It turned out Fleur had quite the voracious appetite, and the rest of our afternoon was mostly spent sampling different kinds of street foods and sweet desserts.

Of course, we did plenty of other fun things too! We danced until our feet ached, and when it was time for a break, we watched a captivating performance by one of the local acting troupes. We also tried our hand at a game called Thimblerig, which involved finding a ball shuffled between three cups. We didn't win even once, and we were forced to quit when I noticed my remaining funds were being depleted rather quickly.

Honestly, I think the man running the game was a con artist. Surely he was cheating somehow!! Fleur thought so too, and I had to drag her away when her shouting began to attract stares.

We were cheerfully bantering and enjoying a couple of baked pears, when I decided I wanted to learn more about the man Fleur was going to marry.

"Hey, is it true your fiancé is a childhood friend?" It was talk I had heard in the city, just days before.

Fleur's face turned red, but she answered the question. "Yes... It is..."

"Ahhh! That's so romantic!!" I squealed.

"Shut up!" She snapped.

"What's he like?"

"Well... Reynard is... he's... kind, and... sensitive, and strong... and I don't want to talk about this!" She stammered, covering her face with her hands.

"Okay, okay!" I laughed. "But if he's the prince of Marza, how did you both grow up as friends?"

"Well, Marza and Aramore have always been strong allies, and our fathers would often meet for diplomatic reasons." Fleur explained. "So while they would be locked up in the council chambers, us children would often play and explore together."

"Wow!"

"That reminds me... Isabel, if there was somewhere I wanted to go, would you take me?"

"You can count on me!" I happily replied. "Do you want to go now?"

The afternoon was quickly coming to an end, and it was only a matter of time before the sky would begin turning orange and purple.

"Sure, but maybe another one of these baked pears on our way out?"

"Fleur!" I groaned. I didn't know if I could manage to eat another bite! Where was she putting it all?

Plus, I was nearly broke...

Before we managed to get very far, the voice of an entertainer caught my attention.

"Behold! Step inside, and see for yourself the wonders of the deep!" A man dressed in an eye-catching blue houppelande shouted from the front of a large, enclosed tent. The tent was bedecked with lots of flowing fabric and big pieces of coral.

"Oh! Fleur, look!" I pointed.

"Beautiful and exotic, her voice promises to be every bit as alluring as she is! See for yourself the oceanic curiosity that is... Mareena the Mermaid!"

"A mermaid?" I gasped. "Fleur, we have to see this! We have to!"

I had heard many stories about merfolk and even read about them a few times through the course of studying with Master Wis. But never before had I actually seen a merperson. They were supposedly an intelligent and truly fascinating race.

"But... what about the pears?"

"Just come on." I laughed, pulling her with me.

"Good afternoon, ladies!" The promoter bellowed. "You're just in time. Our next show is about to begin!"

I paid the gentleman the admission fee, and we stepped inside the tent. It was then that I realized the tent was actually just an entrance and that we were passing into some kind of small building. Likely, it was ordinarily a shop or something and was just being rented out for the festival.

It was dimly lit, and largely unfurnished. Blue orbs of light danced around the room like bubbles, casting everything in a pale glow. It was magic I was familiar with, a spell I had seen Master Wis perform on many occasions.

22

"Woah…" Fleur whispered, as she gazed around.

Something large was stationed in the middle of the room, concealed by a lavish curtain. I could hear a large amount of water sloshing around from behind it. A handful of other people were already gathered around and waiting. There wasn't much space, so it was standing room only.

Fleur and I joined the crowd towards the back, and exchanged excited glances with one another. Everyone else was excited too, and talking quietly amongst themselves. Suddenly, the curtain fell down and the chattering came to an immediate stop.

Gasps and whispers of awe now filled the silence.

Illuminated with glowing crystals, like those at the apothecary, a tank the size of a carriage was revealed. The light passed through the water and reflected off the walls, creating the illusion of the entire room being underwater.

Naturally, everyone's attention was drawn to what was *inside* of the tank.

I'm not sure what my eyes registered first: Was I looking at a fish? Or a beautiful woman? Though the truth was, I wasn't really looking at either, was I?

Mareena's scales extended past her tail and up the sides of her torso. Parts of her arms and chest were also covered in scales, as if she were wearing a shimmering dress. They were pink, orange and coral in color—with every hue in between. It made her every movement absolutely dazzling.

Her face was just as mesmerizing. It was soft and well-defined, and her skin was like porcelain. Her eyes were almost pink, like pretty seashells. And her hair was a burnt orange, carelessly floating alongside her.

Mareena waved at us with a webbed hand, before spinning around and doing some impressive aquabatics. She swam so gracefully, it was almost like a hypnotic dance. I was completely captivated!

Then she started singing.

23

And... Wow!!

Without even realizing it, I was holding my breath. It was caught in my chest, as her music transported me somewhere else.

The sounds she made were unlike anything I had ever heard. Her song was both otherworldly and mystical, but also soothing and warm. She certainly wasn't saying anything I could comprehend, so how was it possible that I was so deeply moved? It stirred something within me that was hard to put into words.

I was so entranced that when her song finished, I had no idea how much time had passed. It was like waking up to reality after a really nice dream. She had had us all completely under her spell.

It wasn't long after that we all broke out into a thunderous applause! Many in the audience were cheering too, and others were calling for an encore.

I looked over at Fleur, who was wiping the corners of her eyes.

"Were you crying?"

"Don't be stupid!!" She retorted.

Right.

Mareena took a bow like she was on an actual stage and blew a kiss at the audience. In one last dramatic gesture, she suddenly swam to the top of the tank and leapt out of the water!

"Woah!" Came cries from the stunned crowd.

She did a flip in the air before diving back into the tank. Water went spraying everywhere, and the audience members who got wet laughed and hollered gleefully. We all applauded Mareena one more time before the crowd began to disperse.

"Wasn't that incredible?" I asked Fleur, as we headed for the exit.

"I guess it was pretty decent." Fleur replied coolly.

Says the one brought to tears…

"Can we get more salt water in here for Mareena?" I heard one of the assistants ask on our way out.

"It's on the way!" Someone replied.

We stepped out of the tent, and sure enough, the sky was starting to change colors. And with the sun lower in the sky, the air was noticeably cooler.

"Ready to go?" I asked Fleur, raising my hands above my head and stretching. Had it already been a full day?

She nodded, and stifled a yawn. It was probably getting late for her too.

"So where's the last stop then?" I asked, as we started to walk.

"It's a quiet little spot off the riverbank, not too far from the castle. I want to visit one last time before I have to go."

"Excuse us! Coming through. Pardon us!" I was only half paying attention, but up ahead two men were coming towards us, hauling a large container of water through the streets. They were sharing the weight and carrying it on a bar across their shoulders.

Paying them no mind, I continued my conversation with Fleur.

"Why there?" I asked, truly just curious.

"That's none of your business!" For whatever reason, she got really defensive, and her face turned red.

"Hmm?" I smirked.

As we spoke, we stepped out of the way for the men carrying the water so they could get by us.

"Let me guess! It's where you and Prince Reynard first kissed, isn't it??" I teased.

Fleur stiffened, and her face quickly became as red as my eyes.

"It is not!" She shouted, shoving me in embarrassment.

"Woah!" Unfortunately, I was caught unawares and lost my balance. I tripped backwards, and fell right into one of the men carrying the water.

"Oh no!" Fleur gasped.

There was nothing that could be done. The man also lost his balance, and dropped his end of the bar that was supporting the vessel. It spilled everywhere, dousing both Fleur and I, and everyone else who was unfortunate enough to be in our proximity.

If that wasn't bad enough? It was salt water. Yuck!

When the wooden vessel hit the ground, it broke and splintered apart. Water pooled in the street, getting not only people wet, but some of the nearby stands and stalls too. Multiple people started shouting at us and each other, and almost everyone around stopped what they were doing to see what was going on.

"What the hell?!"

"Are you serious?"

"Who's going to pay for this?"

"My clothes!"

It was quite the commotion.

"Fleur!" I growled, ready to chew her out. Then I looked at her and gasped in shock. "Oh no! Fleur…"

She was soaked head-to-toe, and the sudden bath caused her faux glasses to now be dangling precariously from a single ear. But worst of all, her hair was blue again. Unmistakably blue!

The draught wasn't supposed to be *that* temporary! *Surely I didn't mess this potion up too?! I was absolutely hopeless.*

The situation only got worse from there.

"What's going on here?" A male and female guard forced their way through the crowd to investigate the disturbance. "Princess Fleur?"

Fleur's eyes grew wide in surprise, and she reflexively grasped her own hair. "Gah! N-No…"

"Princess Fleur?" People in the crowd started whispering amongst themselves.

"Princess, are you alright?" One of the guards asked.

"The entire King's Guard is out in force looking for you. His Majesty is worried to death!" The other added.

"Erm…" Fleur stepped backwards, but there was nowhere to go. We were surrounded on all sides by people, who were now enraptured. This was bad!

"Princess, can we ask you to come with us?"

"No! Not yet…" Fleur shot me an alarming glance.

The guards exchanged serious looks. "I'm sorry, Princess. Our orders are to return you to the castle, no matter what."

"She said no!" I shouted, startling the guards.

I reached into my messenger bag, and withdrew a small glass bottle. I had hoped I wouldn't have to use it, but it was a good thing I swiped it from the apothecary earlier.

The bottle was filled with swirling black smoke. I threw it on the ground and it shattered, releasing a thick, dark cloud into the air. It enveloped everything around us, so dense nothing was visible through it.

Everyone around us immediately began panicking. Shouts and coughs could be heard as people began running every which way. It was chaos!

"Hey!" One of the guards shouted.

"Everybody, calm down at once!"

"We've gotta run!" I yelled out to Fleur, grabbing her by the wrist.

I heard her shriek.

I didn't even have a direction in mind. I just took off in a mad dash, pulling her behind me. The smoke wouldn't last long, so we had to take advantage of the confusion while we could.

"Stop!" Someone shouted.

We forcefully pushed our way through the throng of people, and soon we broke free of the smoke. An alleyway came up on our right and I swiftly took the corner. I wanted to keep running, but Fleur pulled back.

"I said stop!"

Wait...

I turned around, and my eyes widened in surprise. "Y-You're not Fleur!!"

"Can't you listen?" A young woman shouted scornfully. "Who are you anyway?!"

Shoot!!

I darted out of the alleyway and back towards where I accidentally left Fleur, pushing against the flow of traffic. The smoke had already cleared, but I couldn't immediately find her.

Where is she?!

"No!!" I heard her scream somewhere back towards the mermaid exhibition.

I took off running again, squeezing and pushing my way through the crowd as quickly as I could. I broke free past a particularly tall orc, and finally she came into view.

The guards had her by each upper part of her arm, and were dragging her along between them. I watched as she resisted, before giving up and hanging her head in defeat.

Maybe it was because she was soaked, but to me, it looked like she was crying.

"No..." I muttered.

What was I going to do? I made her a promise that I would take her to the river! And...

"Ughhh!!" I grabbed the brim of my soaking wet hat, and yanked on it in frustration.

I didn't want to break my promise, but now that the guards had Fleur, I wasn't sure how it would be possible to reunite with her. I was out of Bottled Smoke, and I couldn't use magic. Not to mention, the guards were armed and three times my size! Even *if* I had a way to fight them, assault would've been criminal...

"*You can count on me!*" I had told her. But I guess that wasn't true after all.

And it was all because I screwed up that stupid potion. I bit my lip and threw my hat to the ground. *Sorry Fleur, I'm the worst...*

Then, from up ahead I heard someone shout, "Look, it's Princess Fleur! Congratulations, Princess!"

"Congratulations!" Someone else shouted.

"Congrats!" Another chimed in as she passed.

And that's when it struck me: I wasn't out of ideas yet!

***

Because I knew they were going to the castle, I was able to quickly cut ahead of them and stage my ambush without worrying about losing them. The key was to be somewhere with as many people as possible, so I chose a particularly busy intersection where two major thoroughfares crossed.

29

Then, it was just a matter of waiting for them to step into the intersection! I stepped up on a nearby crate to get a better vantage point.

It was a surprisingly simple plan, but if it worked, I'd have Fleur back without so much as touching either of the guards. I couldn't help but chuckle at my own cleverness.

The sky was now completely orange, but the festival was still going strong. In fact, festivals in the city tended to take on a whole new life at night. So while there were certainly many that were beginning to leave the city center to return home for the evening, there were just as many pouring in to replace them.

Children laughed and chased each other through the streets, while adults chatted ecstatically with one another. And it wasn't just people on the move: casks of alcohol, bags of potatoes and theater props were just a few of the other goods I watched cross my path, as merchants got ready for the second wind of business.

I was still wet, so as the sun continued to set, I found myself shivering and dancing in place to keep warm.

Where were they? The guards would definitely be taking Fleur through here, right?

I grew more anxious with each passing moment, but luckily I didn't have to wait much longer. Donned in armor and carrying ornate shields, the guards were hard to miss as they entered the junction with a dolorous Fleur between them.

Perfect!

I hopped down from the crate, and began making my way towards them. I felt like a thief the way I was sneakily passing through the crowd. If possible, I wanted to get Fleur's attention before putting my plan in action, but she was looking down at her feet, and in a sad daze.

I tried standing in her peripherals and waving my hands—as I feared, she wouldn't look in my direction. Not to mention, there were too many other people around. Though she was ignoring them, many were clamoring for her attention, or congratulating her. Others just stopped to whisper and watch in confusion as the guards forcibly escorted her through the city.

Well, if she wasn't going to look up from her feet...

I picked up a small rock off the road, and tossed it in front of her path. That did catch her attention! She listlessly looked up to see where the rock came from and our eyes met. I gave her a thumbs up and her face broke into a huge smile!

"Isabel!"

"Shhhh!" I said with a finger to my lips.

Fleur nodded, and composed herself.

"I can walk myself, thanks!" She snapped at the guards, trying to tug her arms free.

The guards exchanged unsure looks with one another, but decided to release their grips on her. "Just stay close, Princess."

"Hmph." She replied haughtily.

Now was my chance! Again, my plan was really simple...

"Princess Fleur!" I shouted at the top of my lungs. "Congratulations!!"

"Hey!" I caught the guards by surprise, who immediately stepped in front of her defensively.

"Congrats! Congrats Princess!" I continued to shout, lifting my hands to prompt others to join in.

I was being rather obnoxious, so if people weren't already looking at Fleur, they were now. Foot traffic in the intersection slowed to a halt as more and more people stopped to join in, and everyone's exclamations began having a snowball effect.

I think I have enough attention now.

I quickly moved in on Fleur. "I'm so happy for you! Can I shake your hand?"

"Congrats princess!"

"I want to shake her hand, too!"

"Princess Fleur, congratulations!"

"Let me shake your hand!"

As I had hoped, others began swarming to Fleur alongside me. The guards were able to keep us back at first, but as the crowd grew in size, it became harder and harder to control. Soon, they were overwhelmed by the people shouting and clamoring for a chance to congratulate Fleur. After all, it wasn't every day you got to mingle with royalty.

"Get back!" One of the guards shouted, using his shield as a barrier.

"Order! Cease this at once!" The other one was also fending people off with his shield.

"Fleur!" I shouted, extending my hand.

"Isabel!" She reached for me, and we clasped hands.

"You!" One of the guards growled, reaching for me. She grasped my shoulder tightly.

Ow! What a grip!

But Fleur was quick to play along.

"Thank you so much everyone!" She shouted, as loud as she could. "I'm so moved, my guards here will now select three of you to attend the wedding as my guests!"

At this, pandemonium broke loose! Suddenly, the crowd wasn't rushing Fleur, but the guards instead.

"Pick me!"

"Choose me, please!"

"Pick me! I love the princess!"

We now had a full-blown frenzied mob on our hands! The guard was forced to release her grip on me, as people pushed against each other and pushed against her. The other guard was also being bombarded, and unable to move.

"Keep this on!" I told Fleur, taking my hat and roughly placing it on her head. Hopefully it would help her escape notice amidst the chaos.

She pulled the brim down over her face and kept her head down as I struggled to pull her through the mess. The crowd was being rather rough on each other, so we weren't able to escape without some bumps. I was nearly knocked off my feet twice, and Fleur accidentally got shoulder checked, but soon we were free of the horde.

"Princess!" One of the guards shouted.

"She's getting away!" That's when the other guard began blowing on a whistle to call for reinforcements.

"Shoot! We gotta go!"

More guards were quick to arrive. It was no secret that the streets were more heavily patrolled at night, and that was more true during a festival. And we were running straight towards three of them!

"It's the princess!"

"Gah! This way!" I quickly turned on my heels and took off to my right, almost yanking Fleur's arm out of its socket in the process.

"Ow!"

"Sorry!"

"Stop right there!"

Two more guards! Are you serious?

We weaved through several different stalls, drawing the ire of their respective merchants, but a lively group of dancers in the middle of the street blocked us from going any further.

Shoot. Now what?

"Isabel, through here!" Fleur pulled me into a small tavern, right off the street.

It was extremely noisy inside, the patrons extra rambunctious due to the particularly strong ale they were consuming. No doubt it came from special casks, only opened during festive occasions such as these.

Half-dried spills coated the floor, sticking to my shoes with every step and filling my nostrils with the scent of stale beer. In my hurry, I narrowly avoided a waitress with a tray full of drinks, or so I thought. A single mug of ale from that tray shattered everywhere on the beer-soaked floor after I grazed it with my shoulder.

"Hey!"

"Sorry!"

But there was no time to stay and help clean up the mess. At that moment, the two latest guards who had been pursuing us entered the tavern and spotted us immediately.

"Isabel!" Fleur panicked.

"I know!"

We boldly went past the bar and into the kitchen, where cooks were busy preparing food for the drunken mass inside the tavern: Salted bread, roasted pheasant and honey-glazed calydonian boar were just a few of the dazzling dishes to catch my eye. Had I not been so full from all the festival food, the enticing smell would've been enough to make me drool.

"Hey!" You can't be back here!" One of the cooks angrily shouted at us, after we nearly knocked into him.

He was a dwarf, and because he fell below my chest, I didn't see him as we scrambled in. He was carrying a tray of freshly-cooked pheasants, but quickly set it down on the nearby counter to regain his balance.

"We're leaving!" Fleur assured him, as we continued to run.

"Pardon us!" I added.

The kitchen had quite the colorful cast, with humans, dwarves and orcs working side-by-side. This wasn't an unusual sight in Aramore, but it was still a bit funny to see a dwarf scolding the orc, towering over him, for burning garlic.

Another orc chopping meat watched in bewilderment as we flew by. He raised a hand to stop us, but instead just shook his head.

The backdoor—used mainly for trash removal and deliveries—was straight ahead, and we hastily pushed our way through. The cool air that met us following the heat of the kitchen was a big relief, despite our wet clothes.

"Isabel... I don't think... I can run... for much longer." Fleur panted.

I was getting pretty tired myself. And after a full day of walking around and dancing, my feet were killing me.

"Hang in there..." I replied, looking for our next move. I spotted a stone bridge to the left. I didn't realize, but the tavern was right next to the river that cut through the city. Maybe if we could cross it...

"This way!"

The bridge was paved with cobblestone, and arched over the river. Torches on either side cast the stones in a yellow glow. But we didn't even get halfway across when guards appeared at the other side.

We came to an immediate halt and spun around on our heels to run back, but the guards who had been chasing us were now there too. There was nowhere left to run!

"I… I demand you move aside!" Fleur shouted, stepping forward and asserting herself.

The guards didn't heed her commands, instead continuing their advance forward.

"… Worth a shot…" She muttered under her breath, retreating back towards me.

I dug my heels into the pavement. *Think. Think! Wasn't there anything I could do?*

At that moment, Fleur sighed and let go of my hand. "Enough, Isabel."

"What? But…"

"It's okay, really. You've done enough." Fleur whispered. "I can't have you running away from the guards like a criminal, just for my sake."

She held out my hat to return it to me.

I clenched my fists. "No."

"No? Isabel— "

"I promised I'd get you to the riverbank, didn't I?"

"Forget about that now."

The guards all stepped onto the bridge, and slowly began closing in.

"Look to your right, Fleur."

"To my right? But there's nothing…" Fleur did as I said, and gasped. "You don't mean…"

"The castle is downstream, right? That's where we'll find your riverbank."

The river roared beneath us like a wild animal, but I knew for a fact it had been at least two weeks since it last rained. It wasn't moving nearly as swiftly as usual. We could do it.

"You're crazy…" Fleur muttered in disbelief.

I grabbed her hand again, and in a teasing tone said, "What, afraid of getting your clothes wet?"

I ran for the edge of the bridge.

"Isabel!"

"STOP!" The guards were quickly closing in.

"JUMP!"

***

As I laid there on the riverbank struggling to catch my breath, I couldn't help but appreciate how stunning the sky was. Luna was full and its silver moonlight made for a bright night, drawing my eye first. Its neighbor Oceana was still hard to miss, casting a blue glow from off in the distance. That moon was only half full, but still magnificent even among the endless sea of dancing lights.

I wondered, were there more stars twinkling at me from above than grains of sand supporting me from below?

Fleur laid next to me, both of us too tired to move or speak. It made me realize, she had been right earlier. This riverbank *was* quiet. I mean, sure, the frogs and crickets were singing together, and the flowing river accompanied them pleasantly. But it was still a special kind of quiet.

Fleur broke the silence. It started as a soft chuckle, but the princess was laughing louder with each breath. I was confused, but it was infectious. Wet, cold and tired I began to laugh too, and soon we were doubled over bellowing in unison—our own song drowning out the crickets, frogs and the river.

"Haha… ow… haha! W-What is… wrong with you?!" Fleur wheezed.

I could only continue to laugh. That was, hands down, the craziest thing I had ever done.

"Does... does this make me your knight in shining armor?" I joked, as the laughter died down.

"What?" She chortled, wiping her eyes.

"I saved a princess, like right out of a fairy tale!"

"No, you're definitely a criminal!" She retorted, eliciting a couple more laughs from each of us.

"But... thank you..." She whispered bashfully.

We laid there in silence for several more moments, just looking up at the stars, before Fleur spoke up again.

"You know... Reynard and I found this place together as kids. We fell asleep on the riverbank just like this. When we were finally found, we got in *so* much trouble."

I smiled to myself. Fleur had quite the attitude, but when she spoke about Reynard, her tone changed. It was softer. It was clear she really loved him.

"And... this is where he asked me to be his wife, too."

I bolted straight up. "That's the most romantic thing I've ever heard!"

"Shut up!" Fleur sizzled.

"Oh, that reminds me!" I reached into my ruined messenger bag, and withdrew something from the wet mess inside. "I got you this."

Fleur sat up with a curious expression on her face, and gingerly accepted my gift in her hands. "Isabel! This is..."

Now in her possession was a simple, silver pendant, set with a tapered, mahogany stone. It was the Aramorite necklace.

"Idiot! How did you pay for this?"

"Well, he said it was one of his more affordable pieces." I chuckled.

The truth was, I didn't have nearly enough money on me at the time, but that's one of the benefits of being an apprentice to a renowned witch. I opened a line of credit and asked him to send the bill to the apothecary.

Besides, I had the money saved away at the shop!

"You didn't have to get me this crummy stone…" She muttered with embarrassment.

"If it's crummy, then give it back!"

"I-I didn't say I didn't want it!"

I chuckled to myself. "That's a stone common to this region, right? I just thought if you're ever feeling homesick in Marza, it might help to have a little piece of home right there with you."

"Isabel… I… "

Before she could say anything else, the sand beneath me suddenly gave way! I yelped in surprise.

Panic set in as my mind raced to try and figure out what was happening. My arms flailed above my head as I sunk further down into the ground, and I began shouting.

"Isabel!" Fleur jumped to her feet and grasped one of my hands to try and pull me up, but it was no use.

I was swiftly sucked in, as if the ground below me was swallowing me whole! When I was buried below the chest, it just as suddenly stopped. As if it were…

Magic. Crap.

"Now I've got you," Out from the darkness stepped my teacher, her Arcanus glowing and pointed at me. "Isabel."

Typically, you could describe my teacher's expression as carefree. Other times, it even seemed mysterious. But in that moment? She looked about the angriest I had ever seen her.

"M-Master Wis!" I exclaimed, trying to wriggle free of the sand. No chance, she had me totally trapped!

"Princess Fleur. Now this silly game can come to an end." Master Wis wasn't alone. Ambroys, the chief minister, stepped out from behind her and he looked just as furious. "It's far beyond the time to go home."

His two guards from the apothecary were with him.

"H-How did you find us?" I stammered, still struggling to free myself.

"Can you imagine my surprise and embarrassment? After being summoned before King Eilsorin himself, my locator ritual was unable to find his missing daughter. And then we hear the princess was spotted running around with a young witch, with red eyes and peach-colored hair."

I gulped. Even scarier than Master Wis' face was how calm she sounded right now! I was in serious trouble...

"I went back to the apothecary, and when I noticed the Bracelet of Cloaking was missing, I put two and two together. So I just changed the target of my ritual... to you."

"W-Wow... that's my teacher for you!" I chuckled nervously. "Y-You're so wise, and—"

"Enough!" She interrupted. "Isabel, how could you? You impeded my work, threatened the apothecary's reputation, made a mess in the city, ran from guards..."

I winced with each charge she laid against me with the lash of her tongue. Before I could even begin to apologize, Fleur spoke up.

"Please Madame Wis! None of that is Isabel's fault. It's mine."

"Princess, enough of your foolishness!" Ambroys interjected. "She needs to be held accountable!"

"No, it's true. I broke into the apothecary, threatened Isabel with a weapon, and forced her to fashion me a disguise that would also protect me from your magic. She's been my hostage the entire day."

"Fleur!" I tried to protest, but she silenced me with a look.

"Princess... surely you jest." Ambroys replied.

"It's the truth." She said resolutely. "Punish me if you must, but you will not touch Isabel. That's an order."

"Princess, please. There's no need for such nonsense. The King's Guard has told me all about what happened in the city."

"Are you questioning the official account of King Eilsorin's daughter?"

Ambroys grumbled, but faltered against Fleur's authority.

"But you're right, Ambroys. It's time to go home." She admitted. "I wasn't ready to leave. Now, thanks to Isabel, I am."

Fleur smiled softly at me, and I giggled in embarrassment.

Master Wis didn't say anything at first, but after several moments of silence, sighed deeply. She lifted her hand, muttered an incantation to herself, and I began to rise out from the sand.

What a relief!

"My foolish apprentice. What am I going to do with you?"

I scratched my head, and chuckled nervously.

There's no way Master Wis bought Fleur's story one bit. But I wasn't waist deep in sand anymore, so... I can only guess Fleur's words had some kind of impact on her, or at least granted me mercy for the time being.

Fleur helped me to my feet, and cleared her throat while looking away bashfully. "Isabel, I'll only say this one more time. But thank you so much… For everything."

"I didn't really do much…"

"That's not true! Thanks to you, I really did see more of Aramore today than I ever expected to. Seriously." She laughed, gesturing at the river.

"And this little piece of home? Now, no matter where I am, Aramore will always be close to my heart." As Fleur spoke, she put the pendant around her neck. It dangled at her chest gracefully, as if it truly belonged there. I smiled.

"It suits you."

"This piece of rubbish? I've seen prettier." She smirked. We laughed together one last time.

"Princess Fleur, let's be off." Ambroys declared. "We have a lot of preparation for the procession tomorrow, and not a lot of time left."

"Right. Well, Isabel… Goodbye."

"Are you crying?" I teased.

"Shut up! Ugh, I'm leaving." Fleur shook her head, and joined Ambroys. "Oh, and you better be at my wedding!"

A royal wedding?? My face was probably brighter than the stars at that moment!

"Princess!" Ambroys objected.

"It's the least I can do for holding her hostage." Fleur insisted. "Hear that Isabel? If you miss it, I'll never forgive you!"

I stepped forward, and joined my teacher on the grass.

"You can count on me!" I happily replied. *If Master Wis ever let's me leave the apothecary again, that is…*

A Potion for Adults

"Alright, carefully add the crushed barley now."

I did as my master instructed, but coughed as steam from the cauldron billowed into my face.

"And flowers of the humulus lupulus…" Master Wis continued.

Easy enough, so far.

"Oak chips."

Done.

"Miracle Berries."

Cloud loved miracle berries, so I was sure to "accidentally" drop one as I dumped them into the cauldron. My snow white cat, who was watching from nearby, immediately pounced on the fallen fruit. Master Wis raised an eyebrow at me in disapproval, but her smile was twisted in wry amusement.

"Isabel…"

"Hehehe…"

"Now then... For some flavor, let's add a pinch of fairy dust. Just a pinch!"

In potion brewing, it could be disastrous to add too much or too little of any one ingredient. So I was careful to heed my master's directions.

I gingerly sprinkled a small amount into the potion, which caused an immediate reaction. The brew began hissing and turned a bright blue! A sweet smell filled the air.

"And finally, we'll add... common bread yeast."

"So we're letting this potion ferment?"

"Very good, Isabel!"

"But you still haven't even told me what it is we're brewing!"

"That's because it's a secret." She winked, holding a finger to her lips.

"Ugh..."

That was six weeks ago. Now we found ourselves before the cauldron again. The mixture inside had darkened considerably, and was now a very deep blue.

"Alright Isabel, let's see how you did!" Master Wis grabbed a ladle and scooped some to her mouth.

"Is that safe?!"

"Mmmm!! Excellent work, Isabel" She clapped, before pouring some more into a small chalice. "This is delicious!!"

"Wait a minute..." I growled. "Is this just a drink??"

"Of course not, Isabel!" Master Wis chuckled. "It's an elixir! Of... inebriation?"

So alcohol. It was alcohol.

"Master Wis!!" I protested.

"You're so cute when you're pouting!" She ruffled my hair, and I swatted her hand away.

"Well, if it's tasty…" I grumbled, going for the ladle. But now it was Master Wis' turn to swat *my* hand away.

"Sorry dear, this is a potion for adults *only*."

"But I made it!!"

Master Wis only laughed as she retreated upstairs, chalice of alcohol in hand.

She had left me alone in the laboratory with Cloud. I looked at the cauldron, and then my cat with a mischievous smile. I peeked up the stairs, and called for my teacher.

"Master Wis?"

No response.

I waited a few more moments, and then hurried back over to the cauldron. I filled the ladle and lifted it to my lips, opening my mouth eagerly.

"Bleh!!"

Gross! So gross! Why is it so bitter??

Maybe it was a potion for adults after all…

What We Pass on to Others

A steady shower was falling, treating the windows to the apothecary like a canvas for some abstract painting. A gentle wind danced alongside, disturbing the window shutters ever so slightly.

Tap. Tap. Tap.

The pattering rain was almost hypnotic, one of those gentle showers that left you feeling drowsy and lethargic.

"Isabel?"

"Hm?"

"It's your turn."

"Oh! Sorry…" I muttered.

Master Wis and I were sitting across from each other in the common area of our home, which was just upstairs above the apothecary. Cloud was with us too, sleeping peacefully at my feet.

It was a cozy little den, with warm-colored, comfy furniture and lots of soft pillows. It smelled of incense, and multicolored tapestries hung from the ceiling. The room was well lit by a collection of enchanted crystals scattered throughout the living space and affixed to the walls. It was a bit cramped—we were surrounded by cluttered shelves that housed an impressive collection of old, magical texts and intriguing artifacts.

We were both wrapped in blankets and dressed for bed. So while an oversized, pointed hat usually helped me hide my unruly hair, tonight it was held back with a simple, black headband.

I had finished all my studying and chores for the evening, so my teacher and I were wrapping up the night with some chamomile tea and a fun little game.

The game was called Eledance. It was a board game where you used tiles enchanted with runes in combination to trigger certain elemental reactions. The goal was to strategically use these reactions to capture your opponent's tiles, and control the most territory.

I had never beaten Master Wis. Not even once.

I hastily pushed a wind tile forward without paying much attention. And it was a fatal mistake.

"Isabel." My teacher tisked. "You shouldn't have ignored my earth tile."

"Wait, what?"

Master Wis leaned forward and waved her right hand. A ring on her finger began to glow, and her earth tile slid forward all on its own. It stopped next to one of her water tiles and their runes began to resonate.

"Oh no! A mudslide?!"

I watched in dismay as the runes on four of my tiles in front of hers faded, indicating they had been successfully captured.

"Pretty sneaky, right?" She grinned.

"And using your Arcanus to move the tile?" I grumbled. "How cocky…"

But really, I may have just been a little jealous. It was so cool!

Master Wis taught me the artifacts replaced the traditional wand or stave at the turn of the century. Sure, there were still some practicing witches that clung to those antiquated mediums, but for the most part wands were just used ceremoniously these days.

Really, it didn't make sense to use wands. At the end of the day, they were just another tool that could be used to channel magic, like runes or ritual circles. But they took up one of your free hands, were fragile and hard to store on your person.

An Arcanus on the other hand was discreet, always accessible and much more durable. It channeled magic using runes engraved into a special metal, with a crystal as the focus. Typically, the crystal was something like Dragon Glass or Panther's Eye, but it could be anything as long as it was magically potent enough.

I couldn't wait to get my own Arcanus! But I wasn't really sure when that would actually happen. An apprentice could only receive one when his or her teacher thought they were ready. And because I was only 14, I still had nearly four years before I could even take the test to certify as a witch. In other words, I was going to be an apprentice for a while. So really, who knew?

"So, what next? You don't have many moves left." Master Wis smirked.

I glared at my teacher. *I don't need you to tell me that!*

It was painfully clear. And as my chances of winning waned, so did my interest in the game. Instead, I once again found myself getting mesmerized by the rhythmic rainfall.

"There." I yawned, sliding one of my fire tiles forward with my left hand.

"Tired?" Master Wis asked. "Want to go to bed and cuddle instead?" Like an older sister or overbearing mother, she could be annoyingly affectionate at times.

"Stop!" I groaned. "I'll sleep in my own bed, thanks."

Why is she so embarrassing?!

Still, I *was* pretty tired. It had been a particularly busy day at the apothecary, and of course, the hot tea and steady rainfall certainly weren't doing me any favors.

As I waited for Master Wis to counter my move on the board, I ended up dozing off. I was startled awake by loud banging. Someone was pounding on our front door, and it sounded urgent!

"Who could that be at this hour?!" Master Wis stood up from the coffee table and tightened her bed jacket across her torso.

I stood up too, annoying the restful Cloud in the process, and apprehensively followed Master Wis down the stairs. The candles weren't lit and the luminescent crystals weren't activated either. So we were met by total darkness. Master Wis fixed that with a wave of her Arcanus, illuminating all the crystals at once.

Our archaic laboratory of rough cut stone and timeworn pine was immediately filled with lots of soft light, but it did little to soothe my unease. And as we entered the store, another series of loud raps cut through the silence of the rainfall and reverberated off the walls.

"One moment, please!" Master Wis called to our unexpected guest.

She hurriedly made her way to the door, with me still at her heels, and fiddled with the locks for a couple moments before getting it open. She looked outside the partially open door and gasped in surprise.

"Goodness!"

I had to peek under Master Wis' arm to get a good look, but a young boy was standing at the doorstep, supporting a very elderly man over his shoulders. The boy looked to be just a couple years younger than me, and was clearly struggling with the weight. Both were drenched—the boy from sweat, the man from rain.

"Please Madame Witch! You have to help my grandpa!" The boy pleaded. "He's dying!"

Indeed, the older gentleman looked like he was barely conscious. Both his skin and eyes had an unnatural, yellow tint to them.

49

And though his breathing was labored, he still had the energy to sneer and scold the child.

"Shut... up. For the... last time... I'm not yer... grandpa! Argh!" The old man cried out, and clutched his stomach in pain.

Without asking any questions, Master Wis threw open the door and quickly ushered them inside.

"Isabel? Help me, please." She replaced the child under the old man's arm and directed me to his other side.

To be honest, I was pretty frazzled. Everything was happening so suddenly! But Master Wis was as calm as could be, so I just obediently followed her instructions.

Together, we carried the old man upstairs, and after getting him out of his wet clothes, gently laid him down in our only spare bedroom. It was a meager dwelling, with just a single bed, a chestnut dresser and a small armchair in the corner. A simple nightstand accommodated a candle beside the bed, which Master Wis promptly lit with a snap of her fingers. A window over the bed gave a small glimpse of the rainstorm.

The boy had tearfully followed us upstairs and Cloud was cautiously watching the commotion from out in the hall.

"I'm... gonna be... sick..." The old man muttered.

"Isabel, go get a bucket!"

"Is he going to be okay?" The boy cried.

The old man really wasn't looking good. Now in the light, the yellow in his eyes and skin were even more apparent. His eyes were sunken, and his entire body was shaking. It was hard to tell what was sweat, and what was just rain from outside. Even his thick, white beard seemed wiry and devoid of vitality. I had never seen anyone in such a state before. A lump formed in my throat.

"Gah!" He rolled to his side.

"Isabel!"

"S-Sorry!" I came back to my senses, and scrambled out of the room. I returned as quickly as I could with a bucket, but it was too late. He had already made a mess on the floor.

"Oh no! I'm sorry! Master Wis, oh no… I'm so sorry!" I panicked, biting my thumb.

The little boy was crying, and I felt the urge to cry too. I didn't even know why. My chin began trembling and my feet nervously danced in place.

"Hey, Isabel?" Master Wis reached out and gently touched my hand. "It's okay. Alright? You're okay. Just take a deep breath."

Fighting back tears, I nodded my head. I inhaled sharply, but it was shaky and shallow. So I tried again, filling my lungs with as much air as possible. Then, I slowly exhaled, trying to keep my breath as steady and even as possible. I did this a couple more times, improving with each attempt.

"Better?" Master Wis asked.

I did feel a lot better. I no longer felt like crying, and could think more clearly. It was like the world came back into focus.

"Yes ma'am."

"Good, now listen carefully. I'm going to need you to bring me some towels, both a basin *and* jug filled with water, a bottle of echinacea syrup and a couple vials of our wormwood tincture."

"Okay!"

Cloud watched as I ran back and forth, bringing all the items my teacher requested. In that time, Master Wis had already cleaned up the mess, and dried off the young boy—both using magic, I presumed. It was as if he had never stepped outside at all!

I was lugging in the final item—the basin of water, which was so heavy I had to stop twice on my way up the stairs just to catch my breath—when I found Master Wis comforting the boy. He had messy, black hair and brown eyes. Like all boys his age, he seemed a bit mousy, and he wore loose-fitting clothes that seemed worn with age, like they were hand-me-downs.

"What's your name, boy?" She spoke gently.

"J-Jonah..."

"We're going to do everything we can for your grandfather, okay Jonah?"

"I'm... not his grandfather!" The old man stubbornly insisted, before coughing.

Jonah seemed hurt by the declaration and bit his lip.

"Please. Sir..." Master Wis turned to the old man.

"No, he needs to know. Before I—"

"You need to rest. Now." She spoke firmly, but wasn't unkind.

Master Wis stood up and placed her hand on Jonah's shoulder. She pointed at the armchair, and gestured for him to sit down.

"Isabel, come with me. I need to grab some Dwale Elixir."

If I remembered correctly, the potion was a strong hypnotic and could also be used as an anesthetic.

"Don't worry, I can get it! I know where it is."

"I appreciate it, but let's go together."

"Huh? Okay..."

Master Wis told Jonah we would be right back, and I followed her out of the room and downstairs into the laboratory. She didn't have to peruse her collection long before she found the elixir she was looking for. She pulled it from the shelf with a quiet "Aha," and placed it into my hands.

"Time is of the essence here, so listen carefully Isabel. I have to go now."

"What? Now? B-But why?! And where are you going?!" I was panicking again.

"The gentleman up there, he's dying. His liver is failing him. And by the looks of him, he doesn't have long."

Master Wis wasn't a doctor, but as an apothecary and a witch she had an expert understanding of disease, the body and health. If she said it, it had to be true.

"He's... dying?"

Master Wis gave me a sympathetic look. "I might be able to save him, but I'll need a powerful restoration potion. And I'll need a very rare ingredient to brew it: a caladrius mushroom."

At that moment, Master Wis flicked her wrist and conjured her broomstick in her hand. "I know where I *might* be able to find one, and if I'm both lucky and quick, I can be back before the witching hour with it."

"But..." I started to protest.

"I need *you* to stay here and keep him comfortable. If he complains of more stomach pain, give him more wormwood tincture. If he has trouble sleeping, the dwale." As she spoke, she was already heading for the door. Her voice was calm and matter-of-fact. "Mix the syrup in his water to fight the fever. And he'll need lots of fluids, so have him drink often. Replacing the rag on his forehead regularly will help keep his temperature down too, and hopefully make him feel more at ease."

My eyes spun as my teacher rattled off her instructions, and as I frantically followed from behind, I began to unravel. Master Wis exuded confidence and seemed to always know exactly what to do at any given time without hesitation.

Me? I was just an apprentice! He was *dying*. It was too much responsibility! How could she possibly put someone else's life in my hands?!

"Master!" I tried calling after her one more time.

"Isabel. You're not breathing."

She turned to look at me and my chin quivered.

"Hey, it's going to be okay. You can handle this." She squeezed my shoulder reassuringly.

"How can you be so sure?" I squeaked.

"Because you're *my* apprentice, of course." She winked.

Master Wis clapped her hands together twice and her pajamas transformed into robes and a rain cloak. A wide-brimmed, pointed hat also appeared on her head, bearing her signature amber-colored bow.

As she opened the door, she straddled her broom, and right there from the doorstep, took off into the sky with an amazing burst of speed. I watched as she flew away, until she was completely swallowed by the rain and dark clouds looming above.

"Meow." Cloud appeared at my feet, rubbing himself against my leg.

"You're right. I can't let her down." I whispered, clenching a fist to my chest.

***

Why did I want to become a witch? Because I believe magic existed to help people, it was as simple as that. For that reason, I was thankful to be working with my master at an apothecary. I reminded myself of this as I re-entered the room upstairs, gently closing the door behind me.

Jonah was sitting on the edge of the armchair, rocking back and forth and watching his grandfather in worry. For the moment, the old man seemed to be at ease. His eyes were closed and he was breathing with ease. Perhaps it was the wormwood tincture, but the slightest bit of color seemed to be returning to his skin.

As I walked in, the boy looked at me, though he seemed visibly confused by the absence of Master Wis.

"Where's the Madame?"

"She'll be returning shortly," I assured him. I tried to sound confident, so as to not panic him. "She's off to get an ingredient she needs for the potion that'll help your grandfather."

"I see…" He replied. "I heard Wisteria Amberfinch is an extraordinary witch."

"She is." I knelt down by the bedside, and dipped a washcloth into the basin of water. I wrung it out, and went to replace the towel on the old man's forehead, but unexpectedly, he slapped my hand away.

He was awake? What was his problem?! I was just trying to be helpful!

"Leave me… alone." He turned his head away from me. "You look like… someone… I hate."

I flinched at the unsettling comment. *What did he mean?*

"Grandpa…"

"Enough you!" He started to sit up, but was once again taken by a fit of coughing.

I hesitated for a moment, but I couldn't let myself be intimidated. Master Wis left me in charge as the caretaker.

"Well, I've never met you before. My name is Isabel." As I introduced myself, I clutched the washcloth in my hand and tried again.

This time he didn't have the energy to fight me, and I was able to successfully trade out the washcloth on his forehead. "What's your name?"

"Feh." He huffed.

"Your name is Feh?" I asked innocently, knowing fully well it wasn't.

He just glared at me in response.

"It's Guille." The boy spoke up for him. "Guillemot Cormier."

I gave Jonah my thanks with a soft smile.

"I don't know who I look like exactly, Mr. Cormier. But it's nice to meet you anyway."

It may have been my imagination, but though he still wasn't making eye contact with me and remained silent, it looked like his facial expression softened a little.

My only job was to make sure Guille remained comfortable. And to my relief, it was a much easier job than I was expecting. Besides occasionally replacing the washcloth on his forehead and making sure he drank plenty of the syrup water, I only needed to medicate him once with the wormwood. The most difficult part was staying awake.

Time passed strangely in that small room and I had no reliable way to track it, but my body knew it was way past my usual bedtime. As my eyelids grew heavy, I looked enviously at Jonah, who had managed to fall asleep in the armchair. Because it was a chilly night and because I thought some activity would help keep me awake, I went and got him a blanket.

I was tired of kneeling on the floor, so I also got myself a chair. I sat down beside Guille and lightly pressed my hand against his cheek to check his temperature. He was warm, but the syrup seemed to be helping, though his clammy skin felt at odds with my own.

Cloud somehow made his way to the foot of the bed without me noticing. And before I could stop him, he jumped up on the bed and began nestling between Guille's legs.

"Cloud!" I hissed, standing up. "Get off!"

I went to remove him, but Guille spoke up and stopped me.

"Leave him." He whispered sharply, though his eyes were closed. "He's warm."

"I'm sorry, did my cat wake you?"

"I've... been dozing... on and off."

"I see..." I muttered, settling back into my chair. Cloud continued making himself comfortable.

"Do you need anything?"

Guille didn't reply, but after several moments of silence, did say something strange. "I think I prefer cats. They can't hurt you... like humans can."

"I'm not so sure. Cloud has scratched me loads of times!" I even flashed a semi-fresh cut on the back of my hand as I said this.

"That's... not the kind of pain... I'm talking about."

I wasn't sure how to reply to his remark, so we sat in silence for a few more moments before he turned his head towards me and opened his eyes.

"Isn't it sad? That all we can do as humans... is push our pain onto others?"

Suddenly, Guille was very talkative. And that made me nervous. "Are you feeling okay?"

"Forget it." He sighed. "You're just a kid. You... wouldn't understand."

I huffed at his condescension. "I might be young, but even I know humans are capable of more than that."

"Feh. Would you... like to hear a story then?" There was bitterness in his voice.

"I'd *like* you to get some rest."

"Shut up." He growled. "I'm dying. At least... hear me out."

"Master Wis will definitely save you!" I argued.

"I don't care... either way."

"How can you say that?!"

Silence filled the room again. But then Guille took a deep breath and began his story.

"I wasn't much older than you are now, when I first fell in love. I was from a small village, in a kingdom not too far from here. I can't even bring myself to say her name, but... I imagined nothing but spending the rest of my life with her."

"Is this..."

"Yes. With eyes like apples."

I shifted uncomfortably in my seat.

"But then my kingdom went to war, and being the young and stupid boy I was, I thought that was my ticket to glory and honor. But... becoming a murderer doesn't bring you glory. And there's nothing honorable about surviving while your comrades are being butchered."

"I... can't imagine..."

"No, you can't." He crudely replied. "There's nothing more primal than fighting for your life on the battlefield. We were animals. I didn't charge forward with my sword because I was brave. I charged forward because I was scared to death, willing to do whatever it took to survive."

I opened my mouth to say something, but I couldn't find any words. Was there anything more awful than war?

"In a short two years, the war was finally brought to our kingdom's doorsteps. The writing was on the wall and it was only a matter of time before the enemy took the castle. So you know what I did?"

Guille looked me directly in the eyes as he spoke. "I ran. Back to my village with my tail tucked between my legs like a beaten dog.

And before I even got home, our king was dead and new colors flew above the castle."

A heavy lump formed in my throat and dropped down into the pit of my stomach.

"Call me whatever you want, but after so many days of fighting, I had forgotten what I was even fighting for. I missed my bed, and I missed *her*. She was waiting for me, or so I thought."

"You mean…"

"That's right. If running away like a coward in the face of defeat didn't sting enough, I came home to find her pregnant with another man's child. She had forgotten all about me."

"But is it right to hate her for that? I mean, maybe she thought you had died…"

"Of course it's not!" He cried out, almost too vigorously. His face contorted with pain and I reached out towards him in concern, but he continued anyway, so I pulled my hand back.

"She wasn't my wife. There were no promises between us. But I came to hate her anyway. And whether it was to make her jealous, self-loathing or out of spite… I married her younger sister, Margaret."

"But you didn't love her?" I asked.

"No." He replied. "And I treated her poorly. I did nothing but drink, and we did nothing but argue. Still, we had a child together. And to escape rising taxes, we moved here. When I looked at that child, it made me want to be a better person. I thought this could be my chance to be a new man."

For a moment, Guille sounded hopeful and I smiled softly. My own father told me something similar once and it made me think of him.

"For a time, things were good. I thought things were getting better." Guille then paused dramatically. When he continued, bitterness had returned to his voice. "Then one night, just before our daughter's eighth birthday, Margaret just up and vanished. She disappeared in the middle of the night, without so much as a word."

My gentle reminiscing was brought to a sudden halt by the sad, unexpected turn in his tale. At that moment, I could feel the pain in his voice. Again, I found myself unable to say anything.

"I had no one to blame but myself. Nonetheless... I now found myself all alone with a small child. And I could've come up with any number of excuses, but at the end of the day, I was scared. I was hurt. To try and numb that pain, I fell back into my old habits of excessive drinking..."

I bit my lip, as the yellow of his skin stood out to me even more—a side effect of his failing liver.

"Don't look at me like that." He jeered. "I know what's killing me. I don't need your pity, nor do I deserve it..."

"I- I'm sorry..." I whispered, looking away from him.

"My daughter, Emilia, was a beautiful girl. But she looked too much like her mother. I found myself avoiding her and not giving her the attention she needed. A divide grew between us, and as she got older, I wasn't even sure how to speak with her anymore. I loved her, but... what was I supposed to say?"

"*Couldn't you have told her that?*" I wanted to say, but I couldn't summon the courage.

"Then, one night... I did something unforgivable. We were arguing about something, money I think. I had been drinking and wasn't right in the head. I- I... struck her."

I inhaled sharply and gripped the edge of my chair. As Guille stared up at the ceiling and began to cry, I felt tears forming in my own eyes. He spoke about hating others, but it was clear by the look on his face that there was no one he hated more than himself.

"From that day, I never drank another drop of alcohol. But the damage was already done. We never really spoke again. It wasn't long before she was old enough to make her own decisions, then she was gone. She ended up rushing into a marriage just to leave our home."

I wiped my tears, but continued listening. I wasn't sure I wanted to, but I did so anyway.

"They had a child too. Somewhere along the way, I had become a grandfather without even knowing it. That is, until I received a letter three years ago," Guille paused and collected himself. It was getting harder for him to speak.

"Apparently, the man I pushed her into the arms of was even meaner than me. According to the letter, the terrible abuse had become too much for poor Emilia, and she turned a knife on him before turning it on herself."

Only the rain coming down could be heard, scuttling against the window and bouncing off the side of the house. In the silence, I felt sick to my stomach.

"How awful…" I cried, as tears flowed freely down my cheeks. Guille had begun crying again, too.

"Of all the lives I've taken, Emilia's life weighs on me the hardest."

"B-But that's not fair! You didn't—"

"Yes I did. Yes I did." He coughed, and after a long, uncomfortable pause, he composed himself. "And so when the magistrate asked me if I would accept their child into my home as my own, I couldn't refuse. That child was my blood, and my responsibility."

"So Jonah…"

"No. Emilia had a daughter."

I was surprised by his response. "What?"

"Her name was Adela. But before I could gain custody of Adela, she became very ill. It was a virulent disease and it took her quickly."

My heart ached for Guille, but I was also confused. As I once again wiped tears from my face, I looked at the boy in the armchair and asked, "Then who is he?"

"I was heartbroken after the loss of my granddaughter. The priest who ran the orphanage where she was being temporarily housed took pity on me and incessantly checked in on me. He came by every day, like clockwork. It was rather annoying, really."

I couldn't help but chuckle at his wry candor as I dried my tears.

"Then not long after Adela passed, the priest came to me. He told me that soon he would be coming into the care of a young boy, whose parents seemingly passed away due to the same disease that took my granddaughter. He asked me if I'd care for him instead."

"And you said yes?"

"I did."

I was silent for a moment, then a thought occurred to me. "See? So humans are capable of more than just hurting one another!"

"What? Stop babbling nonsense! Weren't you listening?" Guille growled.

"It's not nonsense." I argued.

"For my entire life, all I've been able to do is shoulder others with my pain. Then they went off and passed that pain forward to someone else. It's just one vicious, unending cycle…"

"Look, if you don't want me to pity you, then fine, I won't." I replied flatly. "You're certainly responsible for all the decisions you've made. But you're responsible for *all* of them."

Guille was clearly confused as to what I was getting at.

"Mr. Cormier, why did you accept Jonah into your home?"

"What?"

"You didn't have to. He's not family. And you had nothing to do with his circumstances. But you accepted him anyway, didn't you?"

"Y-Yeah…"

"Then why?"

"I don't know!" He growled defensively.

"I think you do."

Guille sneered and looked away from me. "I suppose… I suppose I was looking for a second chance. I couldn't do right by Emilia, and I never got the chance with Adela. So maybe with Jonah…"

"I think agreeing to look after him was rather selfless of you. And just like that, I think your cycle of pain has been broken." I looked over at Jonah again, who was sleeping on the armchair so peacefully, with streaks of tears dried onto his cheeks.

"Whether he believes you're his actual grandfather or not… Jonah is worried sick about you. He helped get you all the way here in this storm, and hasn't left your side all night. He even came here because he knew of Master Wis' reputation. He really loves you."

"Feh."

"Humans don't just push their pain onto others. They push their love onto others, too. And maybe when he wakes up, you can tell Jonah you love him too."

Guille chuckled in spite of himself. "Don't talk… like you know everything, kid."

He rolled his head to his side away from me, but I could still hear him mutter, "Maybe… maybe when he wakes up… I will."

I smiled brightly and got out of my chair before pouring him a cup of water. It was also time to replace the washcloth on his forehead.

"I think I'm ready to sleep now."

"Oh, okay. I have some elixir if you can't manage on your own."

"I can... manage."

Guille fixed his head, and after helping him drink some syrup water, I quietly and gently traded out the washcloths. His breathing seemed haggard again, but he looked comfortable. I thought Master Wis should be getting back soon and I looked out the rain-covered window, half-expecting to see her zipping by on her broom.

"Thank you... Isabel." Guille's voice once again broke through the tranquil atmosphere.

"No, please. I haven't done anything special." I chuckled bashfully.

"Can I... say one more thing?"

"Of course."

"I think your eyes... are really pretty."

***

The door to the bedroom burst open and Master Wis stood in the entryway, out of breath and wet from head to toe. Her hat was askew, and a bright, white potion was glowing in her hand.

"Isabel, I have it!" She practically shouted. "How is..."

I wonder what went through her mind, the moment she set her eyes on the scene before her?

There I was, sobbing in the middle of the room, collapsed on my knees and wailing as I clutched tightly onto Jonah. The tears wouldn't stop, no matter how brave I tried to be for the boy. His cries mixed with mine in a terrible symphony, as he wept into my shoulder. His arms hung loosely at his side.

Guille didn't make it.

That must have been painfully clear to her. His corpse was covered by a loose-fitting sheet, which I had placed over him out of respect. The chair which I had been sitting on previously was knocked over on its side. I don't even remember how it fell. Everything happened so fast. Cloud was curled up next to us, trying to offer us comfort, but I don't think I was really even aware of his presence.

So many emotions were running through my head. I barely knew Guille, yet I grieved for him anyway. He lived a tragic life, but he was turning a corner, wasn't he? And what about Jonah? Would he just return to the orphanage now, after losing someone he truly cherished? It was all so unfair...

To make matters worse, I felt like I had failed somehow.

"Isabel..." Master Wis whispered.

I tearfully looked at my teacher, and without even thinking, tore myself away from Jonah. I lunged at her and buried my head into her chest. I clung to her robes with one hand and pounded on her with the other.

"Why weren't you faster? Why didn't you make it?! How could you let this happen?!?"

Master Wis didn't say anything, but held me by the back of the head. She was drenched, but her grip was tender and warm.

I continued to pound on her, but soon my arm grew tired and fell limp. "I-I'm sorry... I'm sorry... that's not fair... I know it's not..."

"Shhhh..." She cooed, still holding me firmly.

"I just... I just thought everything was going to be okay." I whimpered. "What did I do wrong? Why couldn't we save him?"

"Isabel, listen." She took my head and raised my chin up with her thumb so we were looking at each other. Her gaze was serious, but gentle. "This isn't your fault, okay? No one is to blame here. Medicine, even magic, has its limits."

"B-But... we're witches... aren't we?"

65

"That doesn't mean we can save everyone. You did everything you could for him, didn't you?"

After some contemplation, I solemnly nodded my head.

"Then you gave him the greatest gift anyone could be given at the end of their life."

I stared at her in confusion, tears still pouring down my cheeks.

"You gave him love."

I re-buried my face into her robes and continued to bawl. As my cries drowned out the sound of rain, the storm outside was quickly forgotten.

The Royal Wedding

Phwwwwwwt... BANG!

A shower of lights exploded in the burnt sky with a loud pop, taking the dazzling form of an elephant. The crowd oohed and ahhed as the elephant pranced around, pyrotechnic flowers appearing at its feet with each step. The elephant then raised its trunk and trumpeted it, and with the loud cry, a new, colorful animal emerged: a magpie the size of a large eagle, with brilliant blue plumage, a twin tail and a two-pronged crest of feathers, eliciting a roar of applause from the audience as the elephant faded away into the fevered sun dimming in the backdrop.

The witch underneath the spectacle had her palm outstretched above her head and sent up another blast of magic. I'd like to say that witch was me, but...

"Wow!!" I squealed in delight. I was in the audience, just as enraptured as everyone else, as the firework exploded and swirled into the form of a large, red fox!

Well, almost everyone.

Master Wis stood next to me, halfheartedly clapping with a disinterested look on her face. She herself was quite an accomplished and talented mage, so perhaps she just didn't get the appeal of something so frivolous and flashy? But I thought it was terrific!

The fox and magpie began dancing together for a short time, and then the bird gracefully landed on the fox's tail. The two shimmering animals looked at each other, bringing their faces together, and when the beak and snout touched, there was a scintillating explosion as an array of vibrant fireworks filled the evening sky.

When the breathtaking finale of lights finally came to a stop, the embers cascaded down in the single shape of a heart, before fizzling away into nothingness.

The cheers of the audience were just as deafening as the fireworks themselves. I hollered at the top of my lungs and smashed the palms of my hands together. I looked at Master Wis and was surprised to find that even she had a small smile on her face.

The witch at the front of the aisle took a bow, before retreating back towards the outdoor dais, where a staggering number of truly important people were also seated.

Master Wis and I were at the royal wedding of Prince Reynard Whitforth II of Marza, and Princess Fleur von Eilsorin of Aramore.

I had never once been in such a setting, yet now I found myself seated before two pairs of kings, two pairs of queens, and all of their children and retainers—not to mention the nobles and aristocrats from across the region.

I was just a girl from a humble fruit orchard, and among so many people of status, I felt completely out of place! I felt like an imposter! Quite frankly, it was pretty intimidating.

Even the clothes I wore felt strange and alien. I wore a sleeveless, red satin dress that matched my eyes. My shoulders were covered by a long-sleeved cardigan, pink in color like champagne. And while an elegant hairband did it's best to conquer the unsightly cowlick that was always sticking up from my head, I'm sorry to say that it still failed, despite the formal occasion.

Oh, and for the first time in my life, I was wearing makeup! *Who was I??*

My teacher, on the other hand, seemed effortlessly refined and composed as always. She was wearing a violet ball gown, with a low neckline and a wide skirt that flared like a mermaid tail. It accentuated her fine figure, and was silky and luxurious. She was almost unrecognizable without her glasses, which she left back at the inn thanks to an ocular spell. Her lavender hair was twisted behind her head with several intricate braids.

By the way, it was Master Wis I had to thank for my new wardrobe. I'd like to say I felt bad that she spent so much money on me, but...

I think she enjoyed dressing me up like some kind of doll. She wouldn't leave me alone, pinching my cheeks and going on about how cute I looked. She practically smothered me with affection – it was mortifying!

In other words? I'd like to think that the debt was more than paid...

Even now, I *still* caught her gushing over me from time to time! *Why was she so embarrassing?!*

We were all seated outside in the courtyard of the Marza castle, a beautifully manicured quadrangle with an ancient oak at its center. The dais arced around it, draped with lavish, golden curtains that glittered from the limbs.

An altar was situated at the base of the majestic tree, which faced all of the wedding guests. We were divided in two groups, separated by a wide aisle and seated in rows of long, wooden benches. Everything was aurically decorated, reminiscent of the streets of Aramore during last weekend's festival.

Marigolds lined the aisle and primrose petals flooded the dais. Not only that, but the benches were cloaked with sun-kissed fabric. As the sun continued to set, fireflies were released into the courtyard, so even the air was filled with golden light. Everything was so pretty, it was like I was in a fairy tale!

Despite the beauty in front of me, I think I was most excited about the beauty *behind* me. At the back of the courtyard, a large table was stacked and filled with plates of tasty looking desserts and delicious smelling pastries!

And one confection—quite literally—towered above the rest. I had never seen anything like it before. A series of colorful, puffy pastries were layered on top of each other in the shape of a large cone, held together with drizzles of chocolate and caramel. It seemed to take the place of a cake and looked absolutely mouthwatering!

"What is that?" I quietly asked my teacher, getting her attention and pointing towards it. I was practically drooling.

"That's a croquembouche." She replied with a whisper. "Each of those pastries is filled with cream, and—"

Her explanation was interrupted by boisterous fanfare, as a band of trumpets stepped forward off the courtyard wall and began playing. Everyone in the audience stood up, and I was quick to follow suit. No time to think about food, it was starting!

From behind us, a procession of Marza royalty made their way up the aisle. You could tell by their regalia, which was emerald green and bore the crest of a fox.

A priest led the group and knights in full armor escorted them from behind. In the center, a solitary individual walked, with everyone else intentionally and carefully keeping an even spacing from him. It had to be Prince Reynard!

He was more finely dressed than anyone in the procession, and a small, golden crown rested on his head. A pair of fox ears sticking up from his dirty blonde hair caught the eye first. I thought they may have been ornamental, but then I noticed the matching tail swishing at his backside.

He was a Hybrid?

The fireflies danced off of his lush jacket, and their light glistened in his crystal blue eyes like it was the surface of a pond. A ceremonial sword was at his hip and he carried himself like I would expect any member of a royal family. His face was gentle and clean shaven.

Wow! He's so handsome! Go Fleur!

When he reached the dais, he knelt before the King and Queen of Aramore, and greeted his own parents the same way, though they stood and gave him a hug after. They seemed to be speaking with him jovially, his mother wiping tears from her eyes.

Awww!

Like Reynard, the King and Queen of Marza appeared to be fox Hybrids.

Aramore was primarily a human settlement. Though it was only across the river from its neighbor (sometimes nicknamed the Twin City), Marza was a land of mostly animal-human hybrids. An ancient and mystical forest positioned near the kingdom's capital was thought to be responsible for this special race of people after centuries of evolution.

Or so I learned recently, through my studies.

After he finished paying respects at the dais, Prince Reynard moved to the altar where the priest was waiting for him. The knights ceremoniously stood on either side of the dais, and in perfect symmetry, drew their blades and clanged them against their shields. This put an immediate end to the fanfare, and the trumpeters returned against the wall.

A moment passed, then the beautiful melody of a violin filled the air. At first, I didn't know where it was coming from, but as everyone turned and faced the aisle…

Fleur!

I gently gasped, and my breath caught in my chest.

Our princess was absolutely stunning! She was cloaked in a sumptuous, golden yellow dress that flowed behind her like a river. It sparkled and glittered in the firefly light, dazzling my eyes. And while the dress seemed to be made of satin or silk, a mesh material covered her arms and upper torso, save for a diamond-shaped cutout at her chest. I couldn't see her face, because it was covered by a delicate veil that also came down to her waist behind her.

I couldn't help but snicker to myself. Her face must have looked like a tomato underneath that thin fabric! I knew how much she hated this kind of attention, so she was probably really embarrassed with so many eyes on her.

As she advanced, the marigolds at the edge of the aisle burst, sending a shower of flower petals up into the air with each row she cleared. And the violinist, a dryad with bark-like skin and ivy hair, followed behind her with their mesmerizing instrument.

When Fleur passed our row of seats, a flash of mahogany from around her neck caught my eye. The sight made me smile softly. I tried to wave to her, but my teacher smacked my hand down and gave me a stern look.

How am I supposed to know what's improper?!

The King of Aramore stood from his seat and left the dais to meet her in the aisle. He slightly lifted her veil and kissed both her cheeks, before linking her arm and escorting her the rest of the way to the altar.

As she approached, you could see the joy in Reynard's face. In fact, he looked like he was on the verge of tears. Reynard bowed to her father once more and the king helped Fleur up to the altar before returning to his seat. He squeezed Reynard by the shoulder as he departed.

The bride and groom faced one another and Reynard lifted the veil over her head. For the first time, we could all see Fleur's face. And as I had guessed, she was blushing furiously. She had trouble making prolonged eye contact with Reynard, though her timid gaze always settled back on him. Still, it was clear she was really happy, and though she tried to remain poised, a smile managed to break through. Despite her flushed cheeks, she looked absolutely beautiful.

Her summery, sky blue hair was braided like a crown and tucked behind her ears. Her lips were a deep red, like wine, and green eyeshadow accentuated her emerald eyes.

"Wow…" Reynard smiled, squeezing Fleur's hands.

Fleur muttered something that I couldn't hear, but if I had to guess, it was a bashful, "*Shut up!*"

The priest then cleared his throat and addressed the courtyard, "My Lords and Ladies, we are called here this evening to bear witness to one of life's most sacred treasures: love. This union not only solidifies the precious bond Prince Reynard and Princess Fleur share, but will also ensure continued prosperity between the people of Aramore and the people of Marza. Please join me in celebrating this beautiful moment."

The priest paused, then everyone in the audience clapped zealously. Master Wis smiled down at me, and I smiled back.

"Marriage is the most hallowed of promises." The priest continued. "It's a promise that must be made with honor, reverence and respect. It's a promise you're making to each other, and to your kingdoms. From this day forward, that promise means you are *one*. This is immutable and uncompromising. From joy to sorrow, from trial to trial, you share it all."

Reynard winked at Fleur, who in response gently nudged him in the chin with her head. At this, I wasn't the only one left chuckling.

"With that said, Prince Reynard, if you'd please: underneath the Astral Gods, and with our two nations as witness... your vows."

"Fleur, do you remember what I said to you at the river... when I asked you to be my wife?" Reynard began.

Fleur scratched a cheek and meekly nodded her head.

"When I think about that moment, and this moment now... it reminds me of when we were kids, laying together on the riverbank with nothing but our entire lives ahead of us." Reynard continued. "And nothing has changed. Because we still have nothing but our entire lives ahead of us... only now it's together."

Reynard is so well spoken! It was like a scene out of one of my romance novels. I couldn't take how cute they were!

Reynard gently squeezed Fleur's hands. "As kids, whether we were exploring Aramore Castle, or playing pretend right here in this

73

courtyard… pranking our siblings or running away from Ambroys to escape trouble… with you, every day felt like an adventure. And I promise, we will continue to have nothing but adventures together for the rest of our lives."

Fleur liked to try and act tough, but she was actually more sensitive than most. As Reynard finished his vows, she had a difficult time keeping it together. Tears formed in her eyes, which she tried to hide by faking a gentle cough into her elbow. But she wasn't fooling anyone.

"And Princess Fleur, underneath the Astral Gods, and with our two nations as witness… *your* vows."

"How am I supposed to follow that?!" She snapped, perhaps half-seriously, but everyone from the priest himself to the barons sitting in the back of the courtyard were amused. Master Wis and I were no exception.

"Look… Reynard…" She started nervously. "You love me, don't you?"

"Weren't you listening?" He quipped. There were more laughs.

I can see they're meant for each other!

"Then… I promise not to do anything that would mess that up, okay? I wouldn't just leave my home for anyone, you know? And… I'll hit you later for making me say this out loud, but… I also promise to stay by your side forever! Because… because… that's always where I've wanted to be!"

This time, I was the one moved to tears. To profess her love in front of family and strangers alike must have been really difficult for her. She spoke with courage and from the heart. It was really such a beautiful moment! Though you could practically see the steam coming from her ears.

I placed a hand on my cheek as I gushed over the two of them. Could this be any sweeter?

"You're so cute." Master Wis teased, bumping me playfully. "I can't wait for your wedding, one day!"

"As if!" I growled, snapping out of my stupor.

"And who will be presenting the helixes, for the bride and groom?" The priest called out.

"I have the helixes!" A young man sitting to the right of Marza's king stood up and made the declaration. He was clearly older than Reynard, but much younger than the king. Given the resemblance and his fox ears, I'd guess this person was Reynard's older brother. He descended the dais and approached the altar, while withdrawing a small jewelry box from inside his jacket.

He handed the box to Reynard and placed his knuckles endearingly on Reynard's cheek with a closed fist. After he returned to his seat on the dais, Reynard presented the jewelry to the priest.

Helixes were a pair of earrings that were worn on, well, the helix of the ear. And it was customary in marriage for partners to each wear one of a matching set. The man typically wore the earring on his right ear, while the woman typically wore the earring on her left.

The priest muttered a small prayer to himself, blessing the jewelry. "If you would each hold out your hand."

Fleur and Reynard did as instructed, and he placed an earring in each of their outstretched palms. From this distance, I couldn't get a good look at the jewelry, but I did notice what may have been a sparkle of green and a silver-colored metal. The design and style of helix earrings tended to vary, especially among those with wealth, but typically the jewelry wasn't especially flashy. My parents, for example, wore simple and tiny, rose gold hoops.

Fleur turned her head to the right and cocked it so Reynard would have better access to her ear. He moved gently and deliberately and clasped the accessory in her left helix without any issue.

Next, it was Fleur's turn. The jewelry fumbled around clumsily as she struggled to clasp it on his ear. Granted, she was also dealing with a completely different anatomy…

"Ouch!" Reynard cried out, sucking air through his teeth.

"I'm so sorry!" Fleur gasped.

"Kidding!" He snickered.

"Jerk!" Fleur scoffed, playfully punching him in the arm after getting the earring in place.

Once again, the audience was left chuckling at the couple's candid chemistry. And once the exchange was finished, everyone once again cheered for the bride and groom.

"And with the commemoration of this union complete, may I introduce to my Lords and Ladies… Prince Reynard and Princess Fleur Whitforth of Marza! By the blessings of the Astral Gods, may their love continue to prosper! Prince Reynard?"

At his cue, Reynard grabbed Fleur from behind her waist and pulled her close.

"Last chance to change your mind." He smirked.

"Shut up already!"

With that, Reynard pressed his snout to her beak. Let's just say their personal fireworks were far more magical than the real ones.

Now then, about that croquembouche…

The Thorny Truth

With a loud clatter, the broom fell to the ground in front of me for the dozenth time.

"Why isn't this working?!" I groaned in frustration, slumping down on a nearby stool in defeat. I tugged the pointed black hat off my head and ran a hand through my hair. It always got quite warm under my cap, and my hair was slightly damp with sweat. The cool, fresh air was a welcome relief.

Cloud gently rubbed against my ankles. His sky blue eyes met my apple red ones, and he meowed at me in sympathy.

"Ugh, whatever…" I sighed, carelessly tossing the empty potion vial over my left shoulder and into the sink. Well, that's where I *intended* for it to go. I winced as I heard it shatter against the ground instead. Cloud jumped into the air and bolted off in surprise.

"Oops… hehe…"

Good thing I'm already sweeping the floor.

Well, technically I hadn't started sweeping *yet.* I was testing out an Animate Object potion on the broom so it would sweep the floor itself, but the concoction proved to be a little outside my expertise. What should've just been a ten-minute chore ended up wasting an entire morning.

Master Wis was away on business again and I was left to tending to the apothecary. Though, I guess I was *always* tending to the apothecary, even when she was here. Sometimes I felt more like a shopkeeper than a student.

"Time to get back to work." I let out a melancholic sigh as I put my hat back on my head. Before I could get to cleaning, I was stopped by the cool breeze that wafted into the apothecary. It carried with it the scent of fresh baked bread from a nearby bakery. It was a gorgeous day out in the capitol, so I had left the shop's door open.

I was just thinking about running down the road and grabbing a loaf of that delicious smelling bread, when at that moment, a customer stepped into the shop. She looked to be about my age, with rich umber skin and braided, black hair that came down over her shoulders like floppy bunny ears. She wore modest clothing stained with what looked like flour, and as she entered, she was looking over her shoulder as if she was trying to make sure no one saw her come into the store.

"Hello. Welcome to Wis' Apothecary!" I greeted brightly.

"Um, hello..." She meekly responded.

"My name is Isabel. Can I help you find anything?" I asked, setting the broom down once again.

Am I ever going to finish sweeping this floor?

"I was wondering... um, do you carry any... love potions?" Her face turned bright red as she sputtered out her request.

"Love potions?!"

I'll be honest, her ask was a bit unexpected. The girl was clearly nervous or perhaps a bit shy, but she was also pretty cute. Did she really need something like that?

"Eep!" She buried her face in her hands. "Sorry, I should leave!"

"No, wait! Sorry, I wasn't being judgmental!" I frantically waved my hands in front of my face.

Master Wis also always said it was important to handle customers and their requests delicately, as trust and discretion were very important at an apothecary.

The girl's face was still flushed as she slowly dropped her hands from her face, but she didn't move to leave the store.

"Let me get you one!" I basically shouted before she could change her mind.

Ugh, I'm so awkward.

I scurried back behind the counter and clicked my tongue as I searched the shelves for the potion. It's distinct golden color quickly caught my eye, given to it by the use of oil from a pink rose. See, roses aren't just a universal symbol for love, but a powerful aphrodisiac.

Of course, it wasn't *just* rose oil. Swan feathers dissolved in lemon juice, a crushed four leaf clover... and was it powdered eggshell from a freshly hatched chick? We just studied the topic recently, but I'd have to look it up later...

I retrieved the potion and gave the girl a thumbs up as I brought it up to the counter. To be honest, I was really curious who she was trying to give the potion to, but it would've been inappropriate to pry... right?

"I'm surprised a cute girl such as yourself even needs a love potion! He must be a really lucky guy..."

What? I wasn't asking directly!

"No, no, no!" She quickly shook her head in denial. "Um... He'd... never notice someone like me..."

"What do you mean?"

"I'm just the daughter of a baker... And he's one of the youngest knights in the kingdom! He's a prodigy, *and* really handsome." Suddenly, the girl's face lit up as she spoke with a renewed vigor, her hands coming together near her face. "He buys bread from our bakery almost daily! He's super polite, is really tall and has a gorgeous smile!"

"I-I see..." I was slightly taken aback by her sudden change in demeanor. "Well, he'll for sure notice you now!"

The girl smiled softly, but then paused. "Say Isabel... have you... um, ever been in love?"

"W-What?" I chuckled nervously. "Of course, like... loads of times!"

Actually, this was a lie. I hadn't even held a boy's hand before.

Cloud jumped up onto the table and meowed at me in disapproval.

Shhhh!!

"That makes sense. You're really pretty. And a witch, too? You must be really talented!"

"Oh, please!" I laughed bashfully waving my hand, though secretly I enjoyed the praise. "I'm just an apprentice though. I can't even get that *stupid broom* to clean the floor!"

I directed a frustrated growl at the broom leaning against the counter, and to both my surprise and the customer's, it sprang to life— just like that!—and began sweeping the floor.

"Ahhh!!" I shrieked in delight. I grabbed the girl's hands in excitement and began jumping up and down. "I did it! I did it!"

The girl wasn't sure how to handle my reaction and pulled away with a nervous laugh. "Good for you, Isabel."

She clearly didn't understand why I was so excited. But I had been working on it *all* morning!

"Ugh, I'm so dumb though... Guess all I was missing this whole time was the verbal component..." I smacked my hand on my forehead.

Some forms of magic required a spoken command or incantation to work—potions were no exception.

"Anyway, let's get you checked out." I coughed, regaining my composure. My hat had started to fall off my head and I straightened it back to its proper position.

"Still, I wonder…" The girl held the potion in her hand and stared at it indecisively.

"Hm?"

"Nevermind me!" She quickly dismissed herself with a small laugh.

It was a rather expensive potion, but the girl had no problem pulling the required amount from her coin purse. She declined a box and we exchanged the money for the potion.

"Thanks Isabel! I'm Heidi. My family's bakery is just around the corner, so um, if you're ever hungry, feel free to stop in! We've got the freshest bread in the city!"

My stomach growled at the offer alone.

"I just might take you up on that!" No doubt, it was the bread from her bakery that taunted me every day. "Please be sure to visit Wis' Apothecary again!"

Heidi thanked me, gave Cloud a soft scratch behind the ears and stopped at the door to wave goodbye. She then peeked around the doorway before discreetly scurrying off to her bakery.

"*She was a really nice customer.*" I thought to myself as I watched her disappear. "*I hope things work out for her!*"

"Now then, about you…" I watched the broom in wonder as it continued to work. It even had made its way to the broken vial and was sweeping all the debris into a neat pile.

I opened the nearby spell book I had been referencing, so I could learn more about the required verbal component of the potion. And sure enough, upon a second reading, the Animate Object Draught entry indeed discussed how *"the bewitched object won't act unless under specific direction."*

Ugh...

Master Wis often scolded me for not paying close enough attention to what I was studying. So while I certainly was going to brag about my accomplishment... *maybe* I would leave this tiny detail out.

With the floor swept, there wasn't much left for me to do. So the afternoon passed by with me reading through grimoires at the counter with Cloud napping on my lap. It was a slow business day—besides an elderly man coming in for a tonic to soothe his upset stomach, nothing much else of note happened.

That is, until a very handsome young man walked in laughing with a friend. His smile was just as charming as his laugh, and his teeth practically shined from inside his mouth. His almond-colored hair was messy, but in a dreamy kind of way, and his eyes were the deepest shade of blue I had ever seen. He was tall and had an athletic build.

I also couldn't help but notice that he was wearing a breastplate with a cuisse and greaves, and a sword was affixed to his hip.

Could this be...?

"Welcome to Wis' Apocethary... I mean, apothecary!"

Kill me.

"My name is Isabel, can I help you find anything?"

Despite my frayed nerves, I found myself standing a little taller as I greeted him—paying almost no attention to the completely ordinary boy who entered the shop with him. Or at least, he seemed completely ordinary in comparison.

"Good afternoon." He replied, looking me directly in the eyes and flashing a radiant smile. I felt my face flush and I had to grip the counter to keep my balance as I literally swooned.

What was with this charisma?! It should be illegal, absolutely illegal!

82

As he approached the counter, I found myself speechless. We stared at each other awkwardly for a moment, before he put his arms on the counter and leaned forward. Suddenly, he was just inches away from me. My nose picked up on the deep and rich scent of sandalwood and my heart began racing.

"Yes?" I squeaked.

"Listen…" He lowered his voice, as if he was getting ready to tell me a secret. "I'm looking for a little pick-me-up. I'm competing in a jousting tournament in just a couple of days and could really use… an edge."

"So… like a performance enhancer? Isn't that…"

"Our little secret? Yes it is." He winked at me, causing my heart to skip a beat.

"Let me see what… what we, uh… have!" I stammered, quickly pulling away from the counter to put some distance between us. I turned from him and took a deep breath.

Wow.

I collected myself and began looking at what we had out on the shelves. This knight's request was pretty unethical, but not illegal. Master Wis certainly wouldn't have turned him away, so I wouldn't either. He *was* a paying customer, after all.

Now, let's see… a Potion of Strength? Or perhaps an Elixir of Vitality? I decided the latter was probably more appropriate, but it didn't look like we had any available. Unsurprisingly, we went through a lot of it here. For that reason, I had actually brewed plenty of the elixir myself, and it wasn't a particularly difficult solution.

"I'm sorry, nothing looks readily available." I turned back towards him, but tried not to look directly into his glowing gaze. "But if you don't mind giving me a few minutes, I would be happy to go in the back and whip something up."

"Please, take your time. We're in no rush." He flashed an alluring smile and casually reached out to pet Cloud, who was napping on the counter nearby.

"Ow!" He yelped, as Cloud swiped at him before hissing and scurrying off.

"Cloud!!" I scolded, running quickly back over to the knight. "I'm so sorry! Are you okay? He's usually never aggressive towards customers like that…"

He looked annoyed for a moment, but quickly relaxed and smiled again. "Don't worry about it at all! Just a tiny scratch."

"Are you sure? I can grab something for it."

I mean, we were standing in the middle of an apothecary.

"Please don't trouble yourself! It didn't even draw blood." Though he hid his hand behind his back as he said that.

"Okay… Sorry again! I'll get started on that potion right away!"

I hurried into the back, where Cloud was bathing himself near the cauldrons. I glared at him and chased him off with my hands.

"Bad kitty! How could you? You're lucky he was so nice about it."

Cloud just growled at me, before hiding behind a nearby bookshelf.

Brat…

I grabbed a small cauldron, gathered the necessary ingredients, and immediately got to work. As I was grinding some ginseng in a pestle mortar, I overheard the knight and his friend talking.

I had left the door to the back slightly open, and it was a small apothecary. I wasn't *trying* to eavesdrop.

"Are you okay, Sir Matthew?" I heard the knight's companion ask.

"Yeah, I'm fine." He growled and clicked his tongue. "I hate cats. What stupid animals."

He was no longer talking in his soothing, hypnotic tone.

"The witch, she's pretty cute though, right?"

"Are you kidding? You'd need dozens of missing posters to find her chest!"

Hey!! I accidentally snapped the dried bone marrow I had just picked up for the potion.

"You're too picky, Sir Matthew! What about the baker's daughter then? She seems to really like you."

"Gross. That peasant? 'Um, um, um, um!'" He mocked, in an insulting inflection.

Wow, Sir Matthew was actually a huge jerk!

"I'd be much more interested in Lady Marissa. And if I can win the jousting tournament this weekend... well... let's just say *there's* a chest you don't need any missing posters for."

Gross. Gross. He was so gross!! I looked back apologetically at Cloud, who I could only imagine was thinking to himself, *'See? Told you so.'*

I finished the potion as quickly as I could, grumbling to myself as I did so. Who cares about big breasts, anyway?! Master Wis was always complaining about back pain!

When I returned to the front with the elixir, I wore a fake and pained smile and practically shoved the vial into his hands.

"Here you go! Is there anything else?" I just wanted him out of my store.

"Thank you so much, beautiful. Have a great day." He flashed another one of his dazzling smiles as he dropped a pile of coins onto the table, but the spell was broken. I could no longer be charmed by such a man...

85

"Mm-hm." I collected the money and gave him a hollow wave as he left the store.

Once he was completely out of sight, and I was sure he was out of earshot, I pulled my hat down over my eyes and shrieked while stomping my feet. What was I going to do?!

Poor Heidi! She was such a nice girl, and he totally didn't deserve her. I shouldn't get involved, right? Master Wis did always say business was business. It wasn't *my* problem.

I lifted my hat and saw Cloud sitting on the counter in front of me. He was looking at me flatly. We stared at each other for a moment, before I groaned in defeat.

"Okay! Fine, fine. You're right!"

I grabbed the keys to the shop and rushed out the door, locking it behind me.

***

I found Heidi's bakery quite literally found right around the corner, a quaint little shop, with a heavy wooden door and two small windows on either side. Like our own apothecary, it rose to a second story with even more windows. Heidi and her family likely lived above their shop, too.

I still wasn't exactly sure what I was going to tell her, but I took a deep breath and stepped into the shop. A bell jingled above me as I opened the door. It was especially warm inside due to the heat the stone ovens put off all day, but it was cozy and welcoming. The smell of bread overwhelmed the senses, though it was late in the afternoon and there wasn't much stock of bread or pastries left. I immediately spotted Heidi tending to the counter.

"Good aftern... oh, Isabel! Here for some bread already?" She seemed surprised and a bit anxious.

"Hey Heidi, listen…" I hurriedly approached the counter. I was nervous, still at a loss for words. Then, I noticed an older woman with braids — her mother, most likely — cleaning the ovens nearby. She smiled at me and I returned a small wave.

"Can we talk somewhere… in private?" I whispered. I looked over at her mother and smiled. *Nothing to see here!*

"Um… sure." Heidi seemed confused. "Mama, um, I'm stepping out for a minute. Girl stuff."

Heidi undid her apron and laid it over the counter, before taking me out the side door of the bakery. We entered a small alleyway, which was a small bubble of tranquility, surrounded on each side by the torrent of commerce and activity of Aramore's busy streets.

"So, here's the thing… I wanted to talk to you about that love potion."

"Yes! I've already mixed it into some jelly. I'll slather it onto his bread if he comes in and orders tomorrow! Great idea, right?"

"Well, that's just it… I don't think you should try to charm Sir Matthew at all…"

"Eh?" Heidi's face turned bright red. "How d-did you know it was him?!?"

"Oh! Uh, wasn't it… obvious?" I lied, scratching my cheek with a finger.

I didn't want to hurt her feelings by telling her what Sir Matthew said, so I thought it best to not mention he came into the apothecary.

"It was?" She asked anxiously, pulling down on her braids.

Maybe I wasn't actually doing her any favors…

"But, um… why do you think I shouldn't use the potion?" She nearly whispered.

For a moment, I considered telling her the potion was defective. But that lie could hurt the apothecary and my master's reputation.

"I… just don't think he's right for you… is all."

"How would you know?"

"Call it a... witch's intuition?"

"But I've gotta try! And it's a *love* potion, isn't it?!"

"I just think it's a bad idea."

"But why?!?"

I was getting frustrated. *Maybe I should just tell her the truth?*

"Look, having 'dreamy blue eyes' doesn't make you a nice guy!" I snapped.

"Um... I never told you anything... about his eyes..."

Uh-oh.

"Y-You didn't?" I chuckled nervously.

"Isabel... do you, um, *know* Sir Matthew?"

"Well, no... I wouldn't exactly say I *know* him..."

"Oh. I get it..."

"Ah, thank goodness!" I raised my hands.

"You like him, too! You're jealous!"

"What? No! That's not it at all!"

This had quickly turned into a mess...

"I'm sorry Isabel." Heidi took a deep breath and puffed out her chest. "They say all is fair in love and war! So I... won't back down!"

Why did she sound so oddly confident all of a sudden?!

"No, Heidi! Listen..."

There's no way she would have believed anything I had to say now, right? I struggled to find the right words.

"Goodbye Isabel."

Before I could say anything else, Heidi went back inside and roughly closed the door behind her. The alley no longer felt tranquil, but dark and cold.

I let out a deep sigh. Now what? Maybe it wasn't my business, but I really didn't want Heidi getting mixed up with such a two-faced jerk! I mean, wouldn't she be hurt if she knew what he was really like?

I thought to myself for a moment, when suddenly I had an idea! I knew *how* and *when* she planned on charming Sir Matthew. And if I knew that much, maybe there was still something I could do after all!

So I ran back to the apothecary as quickly as I could, excited to set my plan into motion.

***

I gave the cauldron a couple more stirs until I was satisfied by the consistency, then turned the heat down.

It looked ready to me! *Now for the taste test...*

I scooped out a little of the contents with a spoon and put it in my mouth.

"Delicious!"

Sweet, and just a little tangy!

Back at home, I wasn't a very good cook. But brewing potion after potion really helps a girl learn to follow a recipe. And homemade jelly was no Animate Object Draught!

Cloud rubbed himself against my legs and yowled loudly.

"Yes, you can have some." I crouched down and let him lick the spoon.

Now that I had some jelly of my own, it was just a simple matter of swapping it with the jelly Heidi spiked with love potion. Well, I say *simple*, but…

I sighed to myself as I looked at the huge mess I had made. Sugar and discarded fruit stems littered the laboratory, like a bomb had gone off. Maybe buying some jelly from the market would've been easier, but I thought this would be more fun. And honestly, I didn't regret it. It actually *was* kind of fun—*not to mention tasty!*

The jelly still needed some time to set before I could jar it, so I reluctantly cleaned up my mess in the meantime. Master Wis was set to return tomorrow, and since the shop was in my care, I wanted it to be absolutely spotless!

"Broom! I need some sweeping in here!" I smirked.

***

There were all kinds of different magic in this world. There weren't just potions, but the creation of wards and charms, and the enchantment of items. And that just scratched the surface of what magic was capable of. And while we specialized in potions and medicines at Wis' Apothecary, we wouldn't be proper witches if we couldn't do it all.

That's why I was able to sneak into Heidi's family bakery unseen and undetected the next morning, a Locket of Invisibility hanging delicately from my neck. Master Wis *technically* didn't like me using her enchanted items without permission, but I couldn't very well ask while she was out of town, could I?

The sun had barely climbed into the sky and already the bakery was bustling with activity as people clamored in for their daily needs. Heidi and her mother were both up at the counter, caring for the customers and filling their orders, while her father was in the back with the ovens.

I stayed close to the wall as I made my way back towards the counter. Just because I couldn't be seen didn't mean I couldn't be touched, so I wanted to be careful not to bump into anyone.

Someone passed dangerously close to me after being given their bread, and I held my breath as I froze in place.

"Thanks so much! Be sure to see us again!"

Now where did they keep the jelly?

"Hi, could I get some toast with strawberry jam?" The next customer who approached the counter asked.

"Certainly! Coming right up!"

Lucky!

I watched as Heidi turned around and reached down into a white chest — an ice chest. It exhaled an icy breath as it was opened, and Heidi smiled as she was blasted with the cool air. Ice chests used a simple frost enchantment to keep its contents cold and they were common to most homes and businesses.

She returned with a jar of jelly and began slathering a piece of toast with it. Now was my chance!

I made my way to the ice chest, when I heard a familiar voice.

"Good morning!" It was a pleasant and charming greeting. I looked towards the door and saw Sir Matthew had entered.

"S-Sir Matthew! Um, h-hello! Thanks for s-seeing us again!" Heidi was so flustered she accidentally flung some jelly across the counter, which hit the man who had just ordered the toast. He looked very annoyed.

"Oh!! I'm, um, so sorry! Here, um, let me clean that up!"

Oh, Heidi…

Well, I didn't have time to pay that any mind. While everyone's attention was occupied, I opened the ice chest and quickly scanned its contents.

Inside, there were eggs, bottles of milk and an assortment of jellies. But which was the charmed jelly? There were about half a dozen, all of different colors. There was only one that looked unused and it happened to be auric in color, like the love potion. That had to be the one, right?

I had figured this might be the case, so I made my own jelly with apricots to try and mimic that color. I withdrew it from my satchel and quickly made the swap, before turning to make my way to the exit. But my eyes remained on the ice chest for a moment too long. By the time I properly looked to see where I was going, it was almost too late! I was heading towards a direct collision with Heidi's father, who was carrying a sheet of freshly baked bread!

I spun out of the way and threw myself up against the wall. But in my haste, I knocked into a nearby hanging shelf! A small sack of flour that was sitting on the shelf was shaken loose, then fell to the ground.

No!

There was nothing I could do. It exploded on impact near my feet, sending up a plume of flour. No doubt I was exposed in the cloud, but I ran. I ran as quickly as I could! I barreled out the side door and sprinted down the alley, hanging a quick right onto the main road.

I coughed profusely as the dry taste of flour settled in my mouth. I had left my hat at home for this stealth mission, so it was even in my hair and behind my ears! Now covered in the powder, there was no more use for the locket. So I took it off and rested on a nearby bench with my eye on the front of the bakery.

Did anyone see me?! Goodness, I hope not…

But I suppose that was wishful thinking.

"Isabel!"

"Ahh!" turned to see Heidi standing behind the bench, her arms crossed and her fingers tapping in agitation.

"Heidi! How's it going?" I tried to ask coolly.

"What were you doing hiding in the bakery?!"

"What are you talking about?" I chuckled, but it wasn't very convincing. I was still covered in flour.

"You made a really big mess!"

"I'm sorry…"

"You weren't after this, were you?" Heidi withdrew a small jar of jelly from the breast pocket of her apron. Sure enough it was golden in color, but the container was no bigger than the palm of her hand.

"Wait, *that's* where you were keeping the charmed jelly?"

"So you were! How could you?!"

But then…

I looked back at the bakery, as Sir Matthew exited. He held a piece of toast coated with golden jelly in his hand. He raised it to his mouth to take a bite.

"No!"

Without even thinking, I made a mad dash for him.

"Isabel, stop!"

I closed the distance between us as quickly my legs would let me. And when I was within striking distance, I raised my hand and slapped the piece of toast out of his hand.

"Don't eat that!" I shouted.

It fell to the ground, but a bite was already missing.

Uh-oh.

"What the—?!"

At first, he seemed incensed, like a fit of anger was coming. But then he looked up at me and his expression softened.

"Wow..." He muttered. "You... I don't know how I didn't realize yesterday, but you are the most beautiful girl I have ever seen."

Double uh-oh.

"Please, tell me your name." He got down on one knee and grabbed my hand. People in the street began noticing the commotion, and I felt my face turning hot by their stares.

"Isabel..." Heidi had caught up beside us, tears forming in her eyes. "I... I... I hate you!!"

She spun around on her heels and ran off, her face buried in her hands.

"No, Heidi! Wait!"

But Sir Matthew gripped my hand tightly. "So your name is Isabel? It's a gorgeous name, fit for a gorgeous girl."

"Let go!" I growled, ripping my hand from out of his grasp. "Heidi!"

I tried to chase after her, but Sir Matthew was quick to stay on my heels. "Forget that peasant, my love! You have me now!"

Gross.

"No, I don't!!"

In the crowded streets, I had already lost sight of Heidi. Now, I had a much bigger problem on my hands. Even in his heavy armor, the athletic knight had no trouble keeping up with me.

"Excuse me! Pardon me!" I tried to use my smaller size as an advantage and quickly squeeze through the opposing traffic. But what I had in dexterity, he had in strength.

"Move! Out of the way! Coming through!"

He was so infatuated with me, he wasn't even feigning politeness anymore. He was forcing his way through the crowd, pushing and tossing aside anyone in his path.

I quickly cut right off the street and ran into the first shop I saw: a small fashion boutique. Because it was a permanent shop and not some stall at the market, the clothing and accessories here were bright in color and of expensive quality. The place smelled of a gentle perfume, and display tables showed off a wide variety of fine goods. On either side, racks of elegant coats and dresses lined the walls.

A small workshop was located near the back, with pieces of cloth and fabric scattered everywhere. A portly tailor working at the spinning wheel stopped his work, and while he smiled at me politely, I couldn't help but notice him eyeing the state of my clothes apprehensively.

"Good morning Madam Witch. Can I... help you with something?"

I was so out of breath, I didn't even bother correcting him. I looked over my shoulder to see if I was still being followed, before addressing the shopkeeper.

"Umm... I'm in need of some new clothes." I gestured at my flour-stained wardrobe and laughed it off with a gentle chuckle.

"Ah. I see." He replied wryly. "Yes, of course."

I snatched up the first thing within my grasp, though there was no way I could afford anything here. "Can I try this on?"

I held up a bright green tunic dress, which felt like it was made of silk. It was softer than Cloud! I glanced at the price tag.

Maybe one day...

"Certainly. Use that door there." He pointed me to a small room off to the side, and I quickly ducked inside of it.

Now if Sir Matthew came in looking for me, he'd think I wasn't here. Pretty clever, I thought, though I couldn't stay here forever. Otherwise the shopkeeper would get suspicious.

The dressing room was more of a closet, but there was a stool and a mirror. I sat down to catch my breath, and was grateful for the small respite. I imagined trying on the dress and the time that would take. Then I waited several more moments, just to be safe. I opened the door, peeking out into the store.

A luxury boutique like this had a certain serenity about it. It wasn't just still, but quiet too. The clothes were all organized and folded neatly, and the lacquered wood floors didn't even have a speck of dust. And it looked like I was still their only customer.

Phew.

"Ah, there she is. How did you like it?"

"Uh…" I began to reply to the tailor, but once I stepped out from the other side of the door, I found myself at a loss for words. Standing next to the portly man was Sir Matthew, as if the two were pleasantly chatting just moments before.

"You would look exquisite in that, my love. Did you like it? Should I buy it? Kind Sir, I would like to buy it!"

"No!!" I tossed the dress back onto the display table and dashed out of the store.

Actually, *should* I have let him buy that for me? *No…* I quickly dismissed the unscrupulous thought.

I cut across the street, running into the nearby park. For such a populated city, Aramore actually had quite a bit of green space. Besides trees and a small pond, there was also a small stage. And it was there that a theater troupe was performing for a small audience.

"Wait! Just give me a chance!" Sir Matthew remained close behind, and in the open field was gaining on me quickly.

"You're a pig! Leave me alone!"

You'd think a man with a sword chasing a young girl through the city would attract more attention, but perhaps everyone in this city was too caught up in their own busy worlds. *Unbelievable.*

I really wished I could just perform proper magic already! Then I could turn him into a toad, or turn invisible…

Wait! I didn't need to perform magic to turn invisible. The enchanted locket was still in my pocket!

I tossed off my cloak, which still held a majority of the flour, and I threw it in Sir Matthew's direction. The wind caught it and obstructed his vision momentarily. In that moment, I made a dash for the nearby audience. Once I was blended in with the crowd, I threw the locket around my neck, then poof!

"Isabel? Isabel?" Sir Matthew shouted, looking into the crowd.

"Shhh!" Someone growled.

"Can't you see there's a performance going on?" Another snapped.

"Isabel?" Sir Matthew ignored them and began pushing his way through the crowd, further disturbing the audience.

Meanwhile, I quickly and quietly moved to make my exit. I needed to double back to pick up my cloak, too.

As if Sir Matthew's outlandish behavior couldn't get any worse, he jumped up onto the stage and snatched a guitar out of one of the actor's hands!

What is he doing?

"Isabel, dearest Isabel!" He strummed the guitar and began to sing. "The fairest mademoiselle in this citadel!"

Oh no...

At first, the actors were trying to politely push him off the stage and dismiss him as part of the act. But when it was clear he wasn't going anywhere, the troupe began getting more aggressive. Jeers followed from the audience.

"You fill me with desire, so please return to me so we can light this fi—"

At that moment, one of the actors tackled him. And as he tried to resist, others began getting involved.

"Isabel! Isabel!" He continued to shout, as the audience helped drag him off the stage and restrain him.

How embarrassing...

***

Needless to say, this was bad. This was very bad.

Having managed to give Sir Matthew the slip, I was back at the apothecary. I needed to figure out what I had done, *and* how to fix it! I furiously flipped through grimoire after grimoire until I found the Philter of Love entry in a particularly dusty tome. In fact, I was so frantic I didn't even hear the door to the apothecary open.

"Isabel! I'm back, and with presents! Come give me a hug!"

My eyes widened and I looked up in horror.

Oh no! What was *she* doing back so early??

"Master Wis!" I stammered. "W-Welcome back. I thought you weren't going to be here until later this evening?"

Wait, did she just ask for a hug?

Master Wis eyed me suspiciously.

"Isabel... what are you up to?" With a flick of her wrist, she made her broom vanish as she approached the counter.

"What makes you think I'm up to anything?" I looked away, as I chuckled nervously.

"Isabel."

I sighed, looking down at my feet as I nervously tapped at the floor. "So don't be mad, but..."

I hurriedly explained the situation, in what was a long-winded run-on sentence. Master Wis listened calmly without interrupting, and when I finished, she reserved any immediate comment. I looked up at her apprehensively.

Was she mad? She was totally mad…

"I'm disappointed, Isabel."

Oh no! That's so much worse!

I pulled my hat down over my eyes in shame. "I'm so sorry…"

"Didn't we just study the Philter of Love? Look here." She pointed at the entry in the grimoire I had already flipped open.

My eyes scanned over the text. "Ah! I knew it was powdered eggshells from a freshly hatched chick!"

Master Wis let out a soft sigh and tapped impatiently at a block of text a little further down.

"This philter is also nicknamed Cupid's Draught due to the imprint charm placed on the user upon consumption. The user will immediately become infatuated with the first person to meet their gaze."

I slapped my palm to my forehead. How could I forget something so important?

"Once again, it's a case of—"

"Not paying close enough attention to my studies, I know…" I grumbled.

"Furthermore, you interfered with a customer's private business."

I winced as her tone turned sharp.

"And… as much I'd like to teach you a lesson… I've seen your heart. It's too kind, and I know without a doubt there will be many other opportunities to dole out punishment."

… Thank… you? Wait, wait! Huh??

Suddenly, Master Wis' tone softened, as did her eyes.

"Instead, I'd like to teach you something that will be far more important to you as a witch, *and* as a socially-conscious young lady."

"Okay?"

I wasn't sure where this was going...

"Everything in this life—even something as beautiful as a rose—can be painful. Everything. And the truth is no exception. Just because something can be painful doesn't mean we shouldn't give it to others. We just have to handle it carefully, so we don't get pricked by its thorns."

I thought hard about what she said for a moment, before slowly nodding my head in understanding. "So... in other words, I shouldn't have lied to Heidi to spare her feelings."

"Precisely. There's nothing wrong with you wanting to help Heidi, but you should've been honest with her from the beginning. And then maybe you could have avoided this entire mess."

I considered what Master Wis was saying thoughtfully, and knew she was right.

"Yeah, Heidi deserved the truth. Hearing what Sir Matthew said about her might have hurt her feelings, but at least she could have decided for herself whether or not it was still a good idea to give him the love potion."

Master Wis nodded as I spoke.

"Instead, I interfered and may have hurt her more..."

Cloud leaped up onto the counter and consoled me by rubbing himself against my arm. I smiled softly, scratching him behind the ears.

"I knew you were more than just a cute face." Master Wis teased, while pinching my right cheek.

"Hey!" I growled, pulling away.

"Now then, don't just stand there! Don't you have something to do?"

Ignoring the fresh red mark on my cheek, a big smile broke out across my face. I nodded resolutely. The sun was starting to set, so I grabbed my cloak and my hat and bolted to the door.

"Oh, and Isabel?" Master Wis called when I was at the door. "Breaking the spell is rather quite easy. All you have to say is…"

***

"*Your little arrow has gone astray, so Cupid, Cupid go away!*"

I hadn't even rounded the corner on my way to the bakery, when I could hear the incantation being chanted loudly.

That sounded like…!

I quickly peeked around the corner and saw Heidi standing in front of Sir Matthew, not far from her family's bakery.

So it *was* her! Heidi must have really done her research…

The sun had dipped below many of the kingdom's steeply pitched hip roofs, dyeing everything in a warm orange. Most of the area stores were closed or closing, so there weren't as many people out and about anymore. This meant it was much more quiet than usual, an oddly calm end-of-day lull overtaking the city.

All this together created quite the dramatic scene, with Heidi staring intently at Sir Matthew.

"Wha— what's going on?" Sir Matthew, who had been bewitched just moments before, was coming back to his senses.

"I… I'm sorry… you were under the spell of a love potion. And, um… it was my fault…"

"What are you talking about?!?"

"Giving you the love potion, um, that was wrong. B-But, um… the truth is… um…"

Heidi coughed and cleared her throat.

"The truth is, Sir Matthew, I like you. I like you a lot! I just wanted you to notice me, so please accept my feelings!" She looked him directly in the eyes and leaned forward passionately.

I was stunned! Heidi really put herself out there!

But...

"Heh... hehehe... hahahaha!!" Sir Matthew broke out in laughter. Heidi seemed startled.

"I'm sorry, let me get this straight." His laughter began to die down. "So, you bewitch me? And now you have the gall to stand in front of me and tell me you like me? You, some poor peasant girl? Are you mad? How pathetic!"

"Hey!!" I appeared suddenly, throwing myself between Sir Matthew and Heidi.

"Isabel!" Heidi gasped, choking back tears.

"Where do you get off talking to people like that?" I aggressively began stabbing my index finger into his breastplate.

You!" Sir Matthew was clearly startled by my sudden appearance, and he stumbled backwards. He actually looked a bit embarrassed.

"I don't care if you *are* some hot-shot knight! That doesn't give you the right to be a jerk!"

"Hey, watch it!"

"No, you watch it!" I snapped back. "Pathetic? Heidi has more courage and character than you ever will! And at least *she* can admit she doesn't need a potion to win!"

Okay, so blabbing about your customer's private requests in public was a big apothecary no-no, but I couldn't help it! I was livid!

Sir Matthew's eyes widened, but he quickly regained his composure. "I have no idea what you're talking about."

He huffed and spun around on his heels in an angry retreat. "Stay away from me! Both of you!"

I stuck my tongue out at him as he stomped off.

"Isabel!"

I turned around to find Heidi throwing herself at me, which sent my hat flying. She wrapped her arms around me and began crying. I returned in kind and did my best to console her as my hat settled to the ground.

"I'm sorry, Heidi. I should've told you the truth from the beginning. Sir Matthew is a big jerk. You deserve someone way better."

"What you said... that was really nice..." She hiccuped.

I grinned happily. "I think I could learn a lot from you, Heidi."

Heidi chuckled as she pulled herself away from me, wiping her eyes. "I'm sorry I accused you of being jealous, and said I hated you. You were just trying to protect my feelings..."

"But I lied! That was wrong..."

"Honestly, you did me a favor. I think I've decided I don't want to have to resort to tricks to make someone like me. I want that special person to like me for me!"

"Yeah!" I smiled.

"Friends?" She asked, extending her palm.

"Friends!" I happily agreed, ignoring her outstretched hand and instead going in for another big hug.

***

The next day, I was straightening things up around the apothecary when I noticed the small gift bag Master Wis had placed on the counter the day before.

Whenever Master Wis went away on business, she always returned with something for me. It was a sweet gesture, and I made sure to appreciate it. There was only one problem…

Master Wis was notoriously bad at giving gifts!

Most of the time, she seemed absolutely clueless about the kinds of things I liked. Who gives a teenage girl wool socks and enchanted, talking dolls? (That gift was just plain creepy!)

But every once in a great while, she struck gold! One of my most prized possessions was actually a gift from her, the latest in a series of romance novels from one of my favorite writers—signed by the author himself! She just happened to be at the right place at the right time.

So it was with that cautious optimism that I approached the gift. As I began rustling through the bag, Cloud jumped up on the counter to get a closer look himself. Inside was a little box, with a pretty bow on the lid.

It was probably pointless to get my hopes up…

I opened the box and gasped in delight! It was a small collection of cute and delicious looking pastries! Dark in color, they had to be chocolate. My favorite!

I happily opened my mouth and took a big bite. Immediately, an earthy smell assaulted my nostrils.

"What is this?" I spat, as I let the desert fall from my mouth in disgust. It littered the floor my broom had worked so hard to clean that morning.

It was a bad gift again! I wanted to cry...

"Oh! Do you like your present?" At that moment, Master Wis entered from the laboratory with a cheerful look on her face.

"Why do these pastries taste like dirt?" I gagged, as I forced more of the treat to slough off my tongue.

"That's because dirt is the main ingredient!" She happily responded, as if it was the most obvious thing in the world. She helped herself to one of the deserts and hummed blissfully to herself as she ate. "They're goblin cookies! I'm told they're a delicacy in the Under Realms."

I gagged again as I watched her eat. "I'm not an Underling! Cloud wouldn't even eat this! I don't know how you can!" As if to prove my point, my cat quickly backed away as I shoved my half-eaten cookie in his face.

"So you don't like the gift then?" Master Wis sounded hurt and appeared crestfallen.

Shoot. I went too far…

"No! It's not that…" I was thinking of what to say next, when suddenly I thought of Heidi. And honesty.

"Actually Master Wis…" I sighed. But at that moment, I was saved by the startling sound of our shop's door being thrown open.

We both looked in surprise to see Sir Matthew storming into the store. His hair was a mess, but not in a dreamy kind of way. His face was covered in dirt and sweat, and his breastplate had a crack in it. He looked absolutely furious about something!

"You!" He shouted, pointing his finger at me.

"Me?" I tried to feign innocence. But I had a feeling I knew why he was here…

"The potion you sold me didn't work at all! It was a dud! I lost in the first match! Thoroughly!"

"Really?" I stifled a laugh and averted my eyes as he approached the counter.

"Isabel, what's going on?" Master Wis asked.

"That's what I'd like to know!"

It looked like I had missed something *again*. I think a giant's tooth? *Silly me, I should really pay more attention.* Without it, the potion was nothing more than a strong cup of coffee.

But I think anyone would have "forgotten" too, given the circumstances.

I'd like to say I did it for Heidi, but... that wouldn't exactly be true. And hey, I'm just trying to be more honest.

"Well? Say something! Aren't you supposed to be a witch?" He continued angrily.

"Actually, I'm just an apprentice." I replied smartly, with a twinkle in my eye and a sly wink to my cat.

Letters to the Apothecary #1

Dear Isabel,

It's ben a while! How are you and Madam Wis doing? I hope everything is going well at the apothokary. And of course, I hope Cloud is doing well too! (Give him a skratch behind the ears for me.)

I wanted to thank you both again for coming to my grandpa's funerul, and everything you did for us. He had a hard life, but I'd like to think in the end he found peace. And I know your efforts helped him rest easy. Maybe that's all we can really ask for when it's our time.

Sorry, a kid probly shouldn't be talking about sad stuf like that, huh?

I wanted to let you both no I'm finally settled with his family in Briar's Glen. Well, my family! We may not have ben blood, but he will always be my grandpa, and his family mine.

Anyway, it was quite the jernee! I've never been outside of Aramore before, but its peacefull and really pretty. I think I'm going to like it here!

Aktually, it's my grandpa's hometown. I thought he didn't get along with his family, but Preest Martin told me my grandpa left him with speshul instructions in the event of his death. Those plans can't have been easy for him to make, given what a pridefull and stuburn old man he was.

I'm living with my great-aunt and her family. We all live together in a single house, so it's a little like being back at the orfanage. But I think I prefer being around lots of family! It's cozy, and evryone is really nice to me. There are also some other kids in the village about my age, so I've even made frends!

About my great-aunt, I think you'll get a kick out of this - she has eyes the color of aples, just like you! Can you belief it?? Because you both look alike, I think about you and Madam Wis often. Even tho the reezon was sad, I'm really glad we met. Your both wonderfull people.

I no that you'll become a grate witch one day, so keep studying hard! By the way, is it true that once you beekum a witch you get your very own flying broom? If that's the case, you better come visit! In the meentime, I hope you don't mind if I send a letter every now and then.

Your Frend,

Jonah

Pinky Promise

It was hot. Inescapably hot.

Even with the windows and front door to the apothecary open, there wasn't enough breeze to keep us cool.

Cloud, who usually liked to hang out on *top* of the counter to be close to me, was choosing to spend his time with the darkness *underneath* it instead. But I doubt it made much of a difference.

We recently had rain, so the humid heat was clinging to my skin like wet parchment. I could taste the moisture hanging in the air with every breath I took. My hair clung to my forehead, as sweat ran down my brow so ferociously that it stung my cardinal eyes.

To make matters worse, we were especially busy that afternoon!

The only bright side was this meant Master Wis was behind the counter with me to help with the increased traffic. Usually she left the store in my hands while she made medicine or conducted experiments, so it was a rare treat to be able to work alongside her. And I think the customers enjoyed seeing her up front too.

After all, Wis' Apothecary had been a staple in Aramore for more than 15 years. Master Wis opened the store at the young age of 22, which is impressive enough. But she's also one of the youngest witches in modern history! Apparently she was so talented as a teenager that the Mages Guild let her test to certify as a witch two years early at just 16. Usually, apprentices had to wait until they were 18. I was incredibly fortunate to have her as my teacher!

With that in mind, I mustered the energy to feign a cheerful greeting as another customer entered the store, "Welcome to Wis' Apothecary!"

How many is that now?!

"How can we help you?" Master Wis asked pleasantly from my side.

"Well, I'm not sure." The customer responded, as she approached the counter.

This guest was a middle-aged woman with dark brown skin and eyes the color of chestnuts. Her curly, black hair was held back behind her head in a simple bun and she was dressed in ordinary clothes. She wore a disconcerted look on her face.

"Do you have anything to protect against... vampires?"

Not this again!!

This was why we were so busy — everyone was in a panic! There had been a number of recent attacks across the city, with the victims showing up at infirmaries anemic and with puncture wounds on their necks. But the most unsettling part? When they woke up, they didn't remember anything! A chill ran down my spine at just the thought...

I was fortunate to live in a tolerant kingdom—people of all races and sizes walked into the apothecary. There aren't many I wouldn't meet with a smile. But ghosts and ghouls? No thanks! Monsters freaked me out, okay?

"We have some Repel Undead talismans, as well as a salve I've concocted with garlic and holy water. Just apply it to the neck." Master Wis explained, pointing to a stack of the ointments nearby on the counter.

I couldn't help but sigh. Those ointments were currently being sold at three times their normal price. Given the circumstances, wasn't that a bit... shrewd?

With a possible monster on the loose, I felt we should have actually been selling them for *less*. They could really help people! But instead, it was as if Master Wis was just profiting off a panic.

How shameless!

"I'll take four!!" The woman quickly replied. "And a talisman!"

Gah... The outrageous price certainly wasn't fazing the customers.

"Perfect! Thank you so much for your business!" Master Wis said cheerfully. "Isabel here will take care of the rest."

I took the woman's coin and returned her some change along with her goods. "Thank you. Come see us again!"

"Thank you so much!" But as she left the counter, she hesitated and turned back towards my teacher.

"Say, Madame Wis. I hear the Guild is offering a sizable reward for the capture of the one responsible for these attacks. And the King's Guard is paying for information. Couldn't *you* do something about the vampire?"

Master Wis just laughed softly. "Maybe once upon a time. But that's not the work for me anymore. I'm just a humble apothecary."

Once upon a time? What did that mean?

"I see." Our guest smiled weakly and made her way towards the door. "You both stay safe out there."

"You too." I responded, as Master Wis and I waved her out the door.

Once the door closed behind her, I immediately sought to satiate my curiosity. "Master Wis, have you hunted a vampire before?!"

"Mmm… once or twice." She answered cryptically.

"So you really could deal with it!!"

"Perhaps. But I'm sure quite capable Hunters are already here in the city searching. While the reward *would* be nice, *this* is my only concern." She replied, gesturing to the store. "Maybe I'd do something if the vampire walked in through the front door."

"But you have no problem price gouging customers?" I asked sheepishly, picking up one of the ointments from the stack on the counter.

"Price gouging?"

"Those ointments were only five gold pieces last week! Aren't you taking advantage of your customers a little bit?"

"That's a nasty way of putting it." My teacher frowned. "Isabel, you won't make it far as an apothecary with that mindset. We're making more ointment, so we need more ingredients. That, of course, costs more money. And that also requires more of our time, which is valuable too."

"Well…" I started to argue. But I wasn't expecting such a logical explanation.

"Besides…" Her eyes twinkled with mirth. "Having you around isn't exactly cheap."

"Hey!" I scoffed.

My teacher just laughed, but then clasped her hands together. "Oh! Speaking of salves, I think I have something that will help us with this heat!"

She quickly retreated back into the laboratory, returning moments later with a similar concoction. She handed it to me with a smile.

"What's this?" I asked, setting the garlic ointment down so I could receive it. But as I turned around to face the counter and open up the container, I made a really unfortunate mistake!

"'R'awrrr!!"

My cat bolted out from under my feet and fled into the laboratory.

"Ah! Cloud!!" I threw the ointment down, running after him. "I'm so sorry!"

I had accidentally stepped on my precious companion's tail!

He jumped up on top of a bookshelf to put distance between us and looked down at me with eyes narrowed in betrayal and anger.

"Cloud…" I tried to reach out and touch him, but he hissed and swatted my left hand away with his paw.

"Let me apologize! Let me love you!" I pouted. But he just continued to look at me with scornful, blue eyes.

I sighed and returned to a bemused Master Wis at the counter. "Is everything okay?"

"I'm sure he'll be back under this counter in no time!" I chuckled away my guilt, thinking of just how temperamental my cat could be. "Now about this ointment…"

I opened the jar, my nostrils immediately assailed by a pungent and unpleasant stench. "Yuck!"

"The smell is strong, but trust me! Just apply a little to the back of your neck."

"Okay…" Apprehensively, I scooped a bit onto my fingers and slathered it over my neck's nape.

"Uhh… what am I supposed to be feeling?" I asked, after several moments passed of no reaction.

"What do you mean?" Master Wis asked incredulously, snatching the container from my hand. She read the label and rolled her eyes. "No silly!"

She set the jar down firmly and picked up the other one that had been sitting right next to it, before jamming it into my face.

"This one!"

No wonder it smelled so… garlicky! I had accidentally mixed up the two salves, following the cat fiasco.

Oops… Hehe…

I opened up the small container and looked inside. This one was a light blue gel that, oddly enough, smelled just like a cold winter's day. But as my nose neared it, I noticed it didn't just *smell* cold, it *was* cold!!

"I call it Liquid Ice. It's a popular item with farmers who work in the fields all day." Master Wis explained.

Dipping my fingers into the salve was like dipping them into an ice bath! As I spread the medicine across my neck, it felt like Father Winter himself had whispered something chilling to me with an icy breath. In this summer weather, it was an immediate relief.

"Ahhh!" I sighed blissfully. "Master, this is incredible!"

"Right?" She smirked, taking it for herself before setting it down on the counter. "It uses aloe vera, snow berries, Lausks Breath leaves and icicles from a barbegazi."

Not only did the magical salve cool down my body temperature, it also gave my system a refreshing shock! Like getting a jolt from a cold bath, I was suddenly filled with energy and ready to take on the rest of the day!

And so, re-invigorated, the rest of the day ended up passing pretty quickly. Before I knew it, the sun had set and we were saying farewell to our last customer of the evening.

"Good job today, Isabel!" Master Wis praised, as she locked the door behind them.

"I'm beat!" I cried out, slumping onto the nearby stool.

"Well, don't get too comfortable just yet. I still have a delivery I need you to make."

"Tonight?" I asked, in surprise. "But, it's almost curfew!"

"So? Mrs. Edinger needs her medicine. She's not in a good enough condition to come and get it herself."

"I know, but…" I glanced nervously at the Repel Undead talismans we had for sale.

It was a subconscious and quick movement, but didn't go unnoticed by Master Wis. "Oh. I get it."

"W-What?"

"You're afraid you'll bump into the vampire!" She teased.

"Of course not!" I quickly rebutted, though my face betrayed me by turning the same shade as my eyes.

"Come here, Master Wis will protect you from the Big Bad Blood-Sucker!" She spoke to me as if she were talking to a baby, with her arms outstretched wide.

"Stay away from me!" I snapped, grabbing one of the talismans and thrusting it out towards her as if *she* were the monster. Though at times, she really was…

"You're absolutely adorable!" Master Wis was laughing so hard, she was clutching her sides. "But seriously, you'll be okay. There haven't been any attacks in this part of the city, and Mrs. Edinger's is right around the corner. Be sure to take one of those talismans, just in case."

I muttered under my breath.

"What?"

"I asked, why can't you go? Aren't you the powerful witch?"

"Because powerful witches don't make deliveries, their apprentices do!" She retorted, with a smirk. "Besides, I wouldn't make a very good vampire if I happened to get bitten…"

"Master Wis!"

***

"Thank you so much, sweetheart!" Mrs. Edinger smiled warmly, accepting her medication from me at her door some time later.

She was a kind and lovely old woman, who leaned on a cane and wore many layers of clothes — even in the summer. Her eyes always looked almost closed behind heavy wrinkles, but I got the impression that she could see just fine. She was a longtime customer of the apothecary, so I had come to know her well.

"You're welcome, Mrs. Edinger! Master Wis sends her regards."

"I would invite you in for some tea and cake, but you probably shouldn't be out too late these days…" She frowned.

I resisted the temptation — her baked goods were to die for — and smiled politely. "Yes, I better be getting back. Take care!"

"Goodnight."

Once she shut the door, I found myself alone out on the empty streets of Aramore. I shivered and briskly began the walk back home.

The heat still stubbornly clung to the air, despite the sun retreating below the horizon. And since it was past curfew, there wasn't anyone else out and about that I could see — though surely in a city this big there were still some out on urgent business, or apprentices returning home for the evening after a long day's work. It's possible the recent rumors had everyone getting home in a hurry, however.

It was eerily silent. Though many of the streets were paved and well-lit by torches, without the crowds and clacking of horse hooves, the city felt empty, and that made for a lonely walk. A walk so quiet I soon became very conscious of how quiet it actually was.

My footsteps. The flickering torches. The restless, unrelenting cacophony of crickets. Otherwise, the night was completely still.

And maybe because it was so silent, I soon began sensing *other* things. An unpleasant sensation began creeping over me, that I was being watched. I looked over my shoulder nervously, but found that I was still quite alone out on the road.

"Probably just my imagination." I told myself, before swallowing my discomfort.

"Meow!!""

"Wah!" I yelped in surprise as a cat suddenly appeared in my peripherals. It ran past me with a hiss, before quickly disappearing into the darkness.

Was that cat running from something? No, I'm being ridiculous.

I laughed to myself to calm my nerves. Though my heart was pounding in my chest from the sudden scare. I couldn't help but look over my shoulder once more.

I was getting pretty close to the apothecary but still couldn't shake the nerve-wracking sensation that something was... off. I quickened my pace, not even really aware that I had done so. The sooner that I could get home, the better.

I turned onto a different road, but saw something move in my peripherals. It was only for a moment and then it was gone, but something told me it absolutely wasn't my imagination this time. My instincts were screaming at me to run!

I took off in a dead sprint, now just minutes from the apothecary. An alley came up on my right that I knew I could cut through to get back more quickly. So my body moved on its own reflexively.

"Wait! Ah!" I groaned, forced to a stop by a dead end.

It was the *next* alley! I was so freaked out, I wasn't even thinking straight. But as I tried to calm down…

… a pair of footsteps slowly came to a stop behind me.

Fear seized at my chest, as my heart began racing madly. Every muscle in my body tensed, rooting me right where I stood. A cold sweat ran down my forehead, catching on the bridge of my nose before coming to a stop at the tip.

I would run. I would just turn around and run as fast as I could!

I mustered every ounce of courage in my body, then slowly turned around to face my creepy pursuer. But…

It wasn't a madman or monster I found myself in front of. No, standing there before me was just a small, innocent-looking little girl. She looked to be only about ten years of age.

Phew!

The wave of relief that washed over my body was indescribable. I could finally breathe again!

"What are you doing out here by yourself so late at night?" I asked sweetly. "Are you lost?"

Her hair was peculiar in color, a dark gray that appeared silver in the moonlight. She wore a black, lacey dress of fine material. Was she some nobleman's daughter or something? Her bangs covered her eyes, but she was biting her bottom lip, distraught. She tugged on my sleeve.

"What's your name?" I got down on my knees to speak with her at her level, but in that moment, I knew I had made a grave mistake. Crimson in color and shining maliciously, her eyes were unmistakably those of a monster!

I let out a sharp gasp and tried to pull away, but her grip on my sleeve was too tight. How did this little girl possess so much strength? I opened my mouth to scream, but she quickly readjusted her grip and pulled me into her. She moved like a blur, and the next thing I knew she was going for my neck!

I closed my eyes... It was over!

But...

"Ackk!!" The vampire hissed, releasing her grip on me and jumping backwards with inhuman speed. "Why do you smell so funny?"

She put her arm up to her nose and began coughing profusely.

I reflexively rubbed my neck, just glad she didn't sink her fangs into it! But why? Then I remembered... the garlic salve I accidentally applied!

"You're a funny one!" She giggled, just like any other small child would. But the laugh had my hair standing on end.

Still, I wasn't going to just sit here and become dinner! As quickly as my body would let me, I scrambled to my feet and attempted to run right past her. I took huge leaps, bounding forward like a deer.

If I could just get near the apothecary...

But the vampire was so fast, my eyes couldn't even follow her movements! Giant bat wings burst out from her back in a spray of shadows, and she leaped up off the ground before slamming me into the nearby wall. She remained airborne, with one of her hands on my throat, the other pinning my right arm to the wall.

"Gah!" I choked.

"I'm not through playing just yet!" She giggled. "But... what should Becca do? Hmmm..."

She was psychotic!!

My dominant hand was still free, so as she hummed to herself, I slowly reached down into my left pocket, fumbling around for the talisman.

"I can't bite you, which means I can't use my blood magic to make you forget... So, I guess I'll just have to kill you." She spoke so innocently and matter-of-factly, she might as well have been talking about the weather. "Oh well!"

"Get... off!!" I choked, grabbing a hold of the talisman in my pocket and thrusting it into her face.

Often talismans were shaped like religious symbols or other simple geometric patterns that were easy to craft, but they could be anything as long as they were imbued with the right kind of magic. This particular talisman was shaped like a cross and used holy magic to repel the undead. And luckily for me, it was extremely effective.

The vampire who called herself Becca began smoking as her skin and clothes started to catch fire.

"No!" She shrieked, dropping me and retreating backwards once more. "You meanie!"

Once she was a safe distance from the magic, the flames extinguished themselves and her body began to miraculously mend itself. It was like no damage had been done at all. But that didn't mean I was out of danger yet!

I shakily stood to my feet, keeping the talisman thrust out towards her. "Stay back!"

At first, Becca just growled at me, watching me warily. Then something completely unexpected happened.

"It's not fair! It's not fair!" She cried. "Becca just wants to eat! Becca is *so* hungry!"

Was this vampire really having a juvenile meltdown right now?

"Hey, hey..." I began.

"Wahhhh!!!"

"Hey!" I got her attention and her wails stopped. "Look, I can understand being hungry. But you can't just go around attacking people, you know!"

"Becca... can't?" She asked, tilting her head.

"Of course not! We're not food!"

Becca seemed genuinely confused. "But of course you are! It's no different than *you* slaughtering a cow or pig to eat, is it?"

I stiffened. "But that's..."

"Cows feed on grass, humans feed on the cows, and vampires feed on the humans. Isn't that what you humans call survival of the fittest?" She spoke without even a hint of maliciousness. To her, it truly seemed just as natural as breathing. "Besides, you humans *kill* the cows. I just want to drink a little blood."

"You just tried to *kill me*!"

"Well, that's true." She admitted with a laugh. "Becca didn't *want* things to turn out this way. But people learning about Becca is no good either. Becca can't run yet. There's something here Becca has to do."

"Something... you have to do? What?"

"Becca has no idea!" She readily responded, with a giggle.

... Huh?

"It was as if something... drew Becca here. But Becca hasn't figured out what yet..."

"But if you figure it out, you'll leave Aramore?"

"Probably."

I sighed to myself.

"And if I promised you a steady supply of food, would you promise not to hurt anyone in the meantime?"

"You mean it?" She asked with glee.

I couldn't believe I was doing this... maybe it was the tantrum? I was scared to death just moments ago, but now it was kind of hard to see her as a frightening monster...

Am I crazy?

"But you've got to promise!"

"Becca *pinky* promises!"

***

"Okay, be very quiet." I told Becca in a hushed voice, as I opened the door to the apothecary. "Follow me."

Earlier that afternoon, Master Wis joked that she might do something about the vampire if it walked in through her front door. And ironically, that's exactly what was happening now. We would have to be careful.

I wasn't sure how Master Wis would respond to a vampire as a guest, but I couldn't imagine she'd respond very kindly. Even though I had taken pity on Becca, the fact was... she had attacked people. At best, Master Wis might insist we turn her in to the authorities. At worst, well...

So, for now, it was important Becca remained a secret. At least until I could get her to leave the city.

But Becca didn't follow me past the door. As I went into the store, she remained outside.

"What are you waiting for? Come on!"

"I can't! You've got to invite Becca in!"

I had read that as undead, vampires had to be invited inside places of the living, but, that was in a fictional romance novel about a vampire! I didn't actually expect it to be true.

"Huh. Okay, you can come inside."

Becca gave me a childish, fanged smile and stepped into the building.

"Okay, *now* follow me."

I led her through the dark shop, which Master Wis had finished closing, and into the laboratory. I lit a few of the wall sconces and the large room was soon filled with a soft, orange glow. Shadows danced across the walls, as the candle flames flickered lazily.

Cloud must have been waiting for me nearby, and he meowed at me in greeting as he rubbed up against my legs.

"Kitty!" Becca dropped down to her knees in excitement and reached out for my companion.

But Cloud sensed something was *off* about Becca. My typically friendly cat let out a distressed cry and retreated quickly up the stairs.

"Awww…" Becca pouted.

"I'm sure he'll come around!" I reassured her.

"Isabel? Is that you?" My teacher called from upstairs.

"Be right there!" I replied.

In our laboratory, we had a rather large enchanted Ice Chest that we used to store potion ingredients that would otherwise expire if left at room temperature. Blood was one such ingredient. We had all kinds of vials of blood: pig, sheep, unicorn and even dragon. And of course, we had plenty of human blood.

I assure you, that blood wasn't obtained by any nefarious means! Master Wis had an arrangement with several of the morticians in the city, paying for blood collected from fresh cadavers. If a ritual or spell called for blood any fresher than that, she'd use her own.

It's kind of a chilling thought, but as a witch, that's a price you have to be willing to pay I suppose…

I opened the Ice Chest and withdrew a vial of human blood for Becca.

"Isabel?" Master Wis called again.

"Here, take this." I said handing Becca the bottle. "I'll be right back... Coming!"

I hurried upstairs and found Master Wis reading and drinking tea in the den — a favorite pastime. It was a cozy, albeit cluttered, little space next to the kitchen, with lots of comfortable furniture and shelves full of old books and other oddities. A pleasant smelling incense was burning, the glowing crystals casting a mystical light.

"Welcome back." She greeted me affectionately from her favorite armchair. "How did the delivery go? You took a bit longer than expected."

"Oh, did I?" I laughed nervously. "It went fine! Mrs. Edinger looks well."

"I'm glad to hear it." She replied, flipping a page in her book.

"I'm surprised you're still up!"

"You are?" She asked, with slight bewilderment. "It's not even 10 o'clock."

To double check, she glanced at the magic dial hanging on the wall, which didn't need sunlight to accurately track the time of day.

"I suppose you're right." I admitted with a weak chuckle.

Master Wis eyed me suspiciously, but didn't say anything else on the subject. "Want to play a game of Eledance before bed?"

"Actually, it's been a long day. I think I'm going to turn in a bit early."

"Really? Too bad." She frowned. "At least come sit with me for a little bit."

"I can't fit in the armchair with you!"

"Of course you can! Just sit on my lap." She quipped with a childish and playful tone.

"I'm way too old for that!" I retorted.

Why did she enjoy embarrassing me?

At that moment, our banter was interrupted by the sound of glass shattering downstairs.

"What was that??" Master Wis immediately began to sit up from her chair.

"Uh, I'll check!" I quickly replied, putting my hand out to reassure her. "Cloud probably just knocked something over."

"But didn't Cloud just run through here a moment ago?"

"He's such a spaz!" I forced a laugh, before running downstairs.

What's that vampire child getting into?

"Becca!" I exclaimed, as the horrific sight met my eyes. "What did you do?"

The ground was littered with several empty vials of blood, one of which had shattered into hundreds of little pieces. Becca stood at the center of the mess, with blood dribbling down from her chin and onto her dress.

Honestly, with her eyes glowing in the dim light, the sight would've been frightening if I wasn't so furious.

"Oops." She giggled innocently.

"Oops? Look at the mess you made! And how much blood did you drink?"

Master Wis was going to notice for sure…

"Becca was hungry!" She huffed.

"You drank way too much!" I got down on my knees and began picking up the empty vials. "I'm going to get in so much trouble!"

"I'm sorry..." She muttered, wiping her chin on her sleeve.

"Just... don't take any more blood that I don't give you, okay?"

"Fine..." She grumbled.

"Is everything okay down there?" Master Wis shouted.

"Yes!" I called back. "Looks like Cloud knocked some glassware over. I'm cleaning it up!"

I hastily rinsed out the vials and put them away so Master Wis wouldn't notice. I then swept up the glittering debris, before rearranging the Ice Chest to disguise the missing stock best I could. All while Becca watched, swinging her feet listlessly from a nearby table.

"You could've helped..." I growled.

Becca just tilted her head in response, looking at me blankly.

"Forget it." I groaned. "Where are you staying?"

"There's an abandoned building not far from here, with a comfortable crawl space."

"Okay, if I open a window, would you be able to sneak out?"

"Um... actually, if it would be okay... could Becca stay with you tonight?" She asked timidly.

"Huh? Why?"

"Please!" Becca begged, batting her hellish eyes. Somehow, it was still pretty endearing.

If I was going to be helping her, it wasn't a bad idea. But... having her stay here under Master Wis' nose would be tricky and dangerous. Plus...

"You're not planning to attack us once we're asleep, are you?"

"Becca promised, didn't she?" She sulked.

I hesitated. It was a promise, but… I reflexively brushed my hand against the talisman in my pocket to make sure it was still there. After a moment of debate, I ultimately gave in. She just looked too pitiful.

"Okay, sorry. But still, my teacher is right up these stairs." I scratched my chin as I thought aloud. "I don't know how I'd get you past her…"

"Just leave that to Becca!" She replied happily, hopping off the table. "Where's your room?"

"Uh, upstairs. It's in the hallway past the den. Last door on the right."

"Watch this!"

Shadows quickly enveloped Becca's body, and I watched in awe as her body seemingly dissolved away into a cloud of fine, dark mist. It was only when this cloud began moving up the stairs that I realized Becca hadn't disappeared. She had just taken on a more nebulous form.

"Woah!"

I hastily followed, anxiously looking on from the top of the stairwell as the mist drifted past Master Wis unnoticed. My teacher was enamored in her reading, and this cloud was as quiet as any other.

Master Wis did look up as I entered the room, but Becca was well past her at that point and easily disappeared without a trace underneath my door.

It was like magic!! I wondered if I could find a similar spell in one of the grimoires? That would be handy.

"Get it all cleaned up? Master Wis asked.

"Yes ma'am. Sorry…"

"No need for apologies. Cloud's just a cat. It's what they do." She lightly chuckled.

"Okay, well I'm off to bed now."

"Alright then." Master Wis sounded a little disappointed. "Goodnight."

"Goodnight." I replied, before disappearing into my room.

Inside, a reconstituted Becca was sprawled out on my bed, with her head hanging off its foot. She was looking at me from upside down, with a proud smirk on her face. "Pretty cool, huh?"

She was occupying Cloud's usual spot, who was instead hiding from her in the closet. He was poking his head out warily.

"I'm not going to lie, I'm impressed!" I admitted, as I touched the enchanted crystal beside my bed to illuminate it. "I didn't think you'd be able to get past my teacher so easily."

"Hehehe!" She giggled, rolling over onto her stomach.

"So how long have you been a vampire?" I asked, sitting down on the bed next to her.

"Hmmm… at least 150 years?"

"That long?!" She wasn't a child at all!

"Yeah, but Becca was just a thrall until pretty recently."

"A thrall? What's that?"

"It means I could only do what my Papa said I could do."

"By Papa, do you mean the vampire that turned you?"

"Yep! But he was a meanie. He just made Becca stay in Papa's castle all day every day. Becca was never allowed to go anywhere, or do anything fun."

"What changed?"

She flashed me a fanged grin. "Becca drank his blood! Now she's free to wander and do as she pleases."

Is that how it worked? Scary...

"And so you came to Aramore? But you don't know why?"

"Right."

"Hmmm... maybe it has something to do with your previous life!" I suggested.

"Maybe, but... Becca doesn't really remember anything from her time alive."

"Nothing at all?"

"It's mostly just flashes. Maybe because Becca died at such a young age?" She hummed. "I know I was called Becca and I think I lived on a farm? Becca remembers an old man's smile, and a tree with petals like snow."

An old man's smile could have belonged to anyone, but...

"Petals like snow, huh? I wonder if..."

Before I could finish my thought, Becca looked at me with a panicked expression on her face. "She's coming!"

I looked at her in confusion. At first I didn't know who she was talking about, but moments later I heard the footsteps myself!

Shoot!!

I quickly tapped the illuminated crystal again to reverse the enchantment, then turned to tell Becca to hide. But she was already gone.

As the door handle turned, I threw myself under my sheets and pretended to be asleep.

"Isabel?" Master Wis whispered, peeking into the room.

I didn't reply, but let myself breathe heavily.

"Hm... I could've sworn..." She muttered something to herself, before closing the door and walking away.

Phew...

"That was close, huh?"

I opened my eyes and found Becca looking down at me. I had to cover my mouth to stifle a yelp, as her sudden reappearance startled me half to death.

"D-Don't do that!" I snapped, as my racing heart began to calm down.

"What?"

"Nevermind." I said dismissively, as I crawled out of bed. "Let's talk more in the morning."

I hastily changed into my nightgown and combed my hair. It really had been a long day—I was ready for bed for real. I went to the closet and tried to coax Cloud out from within. When he refused to leave, I settled for a kiss on his forehead before tucking myself back in bed.

I felt a bit guilty, but the talisman came with me, clenched tightly in my hand and hidden beneath the sheets.

"Wait, you're not going to sleep are you?" Becca asked incredulously.

"Yes. I'm tired!"

"Who is Becca supposed to talk to then? Becca is a creature of the *night!*"

***

The next morning, I made breakfast for Master Wis as usual; a simple meal of eggs and toast. But at the table, I had trouble staying alert. The back of my eyelids felt like they were being weighed down with lead, and I barely touched my food as I was too busy resisting the urge to fall asleep right then and there.

"Isabel!" Master Wis snapped, bringing me back from my daze.

"Hm? Did you say something?"

"I asked if the tea was ready yet?"

"Mmmm…"

"Didn't you go to bed early last night? Why do you look so tired?"

It was entirely Becca's fault! Fortunately, the talisman was never necessary. But I didn't get much sleep because my nocturnal roommate wouldn't stop with the questions. "Where are you from?" "Why do you want to be a witch?" "How old is Cloud?" And whenever I asked her to stop, she was only quiet for a few minutes before resuming her interrogation!

Of course, I couldn't explain that to Master Wis.

"Are you not feeling well? Perhaps you're coming down with something." She stood up and placed her hand on my forehead. "You don't feel warm…"

Suddenly she roughly tilted my head to each side, then brushed my hair out of the way to inspect my neck.

"Ow. Stop it! What's the problem?" I growled, pulling away from her.

"Oh, nothing." She assured me quickly, before returning to her chair. "The tea?"

"Ugh…" I stood up and trudged over to the stove, where the tea was steeping in a copper kettle.

Not sure why I had to do this when she was already standing up… *Whatever.*

I returned to the table with the kettle and filled her cup with the hot liquid, though my hands were shaky, spilling a little in my drowsiness.

"Sorry..." I muttered, wiping up the mess with a nearby towel. I then poured myself some, hoping the properties of the green tea would perk me up a little.

"You know, I thought I heard you talking to someone last night." Master Wis remarked.

"Really?" I replied, feigning ignorance.

"That wouldn't have anything to do with why you're so tired, would it?"

"Of course not! Who would I even talk to? My cat?"

"You do talk to your cat, though."

Well, that was true...

I quickly moved to change the subject. "Hey, do you think I could take the day to help a friend with something?"

"Help a friend? Who?" She asked curiously.

"Her name's Becca." There was no need to lie about that part. "She's new to the city, and I thought I could show her around."

"Oh? I haven't heard you mention her before."

"Well, like I said, she's new to the city."

"How did you meet this person?"

"Well, I recently bumped into her while running errands."
"I see..." She took a long sip of her tea. "I could probably manage the store, but what about your studies? And your other chores?"

"I'll make that all up this weekend, I promise."

"Okay, fine. But on one condition."

"Yes?"

"You bring Becca by later. I'd love to meet her!" Master Wis beamed, clapping her hands together.

"Uh…" I knew that was a very bad idea, but I was sure I could figure a way out of the deal later, so I agreed. "Yeah, okay. I'll see if she wants to."

"Great!"

After breakfast, I cleared off the table and returned to my room. Typically my curtains were drawn open because I enjoyed waking up with the morning light, but that wasn't the case now — I had to protect Becca. Instead, the heavy fabric bravely held the sun at bay, only allowing a dim light to trickle in.

I opened the door to my closet, where I found Becca sleeping peacefully. With her porcelain skin and gentle features, she looked like a doll. Mind you, she seemed a little cramped. Inside, there wasn't a lot of space – even for a child.

She had told me she actually prefers it that way, something about confined spaces limiting the sensory overload she has to deal with all the time.

But given how tired I was, something about how restful she looked ticked me off. "Hey, wake up!"

"Nmmm… Just a little longer…"

What a brat!

"Come on, there's a tree with white petals I want to check out."

"Really?" Immediately, she perked up and sat forward. "Where?"

133

***

It was another warm day in Aramore. Luckily, most of the humidity had subsided, but there also wasn't any cloud coverage. The sunlight reflecting off the store windows was blinding, heating the cobblestone streets.

Becca protected herself with a parasol every bit as gothic and frilly as her dress, and cast a shadow over her so large that it threatened to swallow her whole. As an extra measure of protection, she wore a hooded cloak that she was ready to throw up over her head at any time. She also wore gloves, ensuring every inch of her blanched skin was covered.

Despite being a vampire walking among the living in broad daylight, she walked proudly and hummed happily to herself. That in conjunction with her fine clothes made me feel like her humble servant, as I followed closely behind.

And I wasn't the only one who might've thought she belonged to some aristocratic family. A flowing river didn't stop and notice every unusual rock that laid in its bed, and the busy streets of Aramore were largely the same. That didn't mean she would be ignored by everyone – Becca was going to attract attention.

Along with each odd look she'd get would be whispers, some curious of the spectacle, others wondering who this small girl was, dressed head to toe in black during a heat wave.

"We're almost there, Becca." I announced, after I had us turn left onto another main road.

As I wiped my forehead with the sleeve of my dress, I looked at Becca's parasol enviously. My witch's hat with its large brim paled in comparison and did little to keep me cool. Growing up on an orchard, I knew better than most the value of shade on a dry, hot day like this.

"Is that it over there?" Becca asked, pointing to the gigantic tree that loomed in the not-so-far distance.

It towered over its domain, a small pocket of green space wedged between two shaggy, brick buildings. Its territory was very clearly marked with a rather ordinary wooden fence. The tree was unmistakable by the hundreds of white blooms that extended from its limbs and reached for the sun.

"That's it!" I replied.

Becca took off running towards the tree, moving faster than anyone might expect of a small child, her parasol bobbing in and out of sight within the crowd. It was more attention we didn't need.

Wasn't the gothic clothing already a bit suspicious? It would be bad if onlookers started asking too many questions. Luckily, I'm not sure anyone really noticed.

When I caught up to her, I found her leaning on the fence, looking a bit haggard and out of breath.

"Are you okay?"

"Yes, don't worry... Becca... just gets a little tired... running in the sun." She panted.

"You shouldn't push yourself like that then!" She was ten times older than me, but was still ruled by childish impulses.

"Hehe... Look!" She pointed up. "It's snowing!"

Delicate petals dropped with every gentle quiver of the tree's limbs like listless snowfall. The grass was partially buried by the fallen flowers directly under the tree, giving the illusion of early winter. The tree trunk was thick, with smooth, ashen bark.

I didn't know what the tree was called, but Becca made me think of it immediately when she described the petals. It wasn't far from the apothecary and I passed it often while I was out on deliveries or running errands. Its beauty always caught my attention.

"So? Does it look familiar?" I asked.

"Hmmm..." Becca opened the gate to the fence and entered past the boundary.

I followed her in, and she began investigating around the tree. So did I, immediately noticing something I never could have from the street.

The grass wasn't the only thing coated in a dusting of flowers. About a dozen grave markers were dusted in petals, looking cold on this hot day. The tombstones were all of different shapes and sizes, and some were more worn down by time than others. But they all had something in common: an identical coat of arms.

It was a simple shield, adorned with a decorative wreath and topped with a crown of antlers. The visage of a deer could be seen in the top right.

"Becca, do you think your family could be buried here or something?"

She scratched her head, but didn't answer. Her face was contemplative, a strange look for her. She continued to look around, inspecting the grave markers. Soon after, something caught her eye.

"Hey, Becca found something!" The vampire exclaimed. "Flowers!"

I looked towards Becca, who was standing in front of one of the newer looking tombstones. At its base was a colorful offering of flowers.

"Let me see."

I approached to get a closer look and knelt beside the floral tribute. They were slightly wilted, maybe there for just a day or two. Most of the flowers were still recognizable to me, as someone who studied botany as a part of her trade.

"Hey, there are some pegasus lilies in here!" I remarked, admiring the strange flower.

The perennial was recognizable by the two or three petals that grew longer than the others, which flapped in the wind like wings of the mythical horse. It was particularly toxic if ingested raw, but could also be used in medicines to make scars disappear or treat issues with reproductive health.

I missed Master Wis in the moment. She would have been proud I remembered this.

"So?" Becca asked, disinterested.

"*So...* this is a really rare flower! They're very hard to grow and can only bloom under very specific conditions." I explained. "If we can find the florist responsible, maybe they can tell us about the family that owns this graveyard. They must be important, or rich!"

"Oh! Good idea, Bel-Bel!"

"Bel-Bel?" I rebuffed. "My name is Isabel!"

Becca just giggled in response.

We spent the rest of the morning visiting area flower shops. I hoped we'd get lucky and find the flowers at a florist near the graveyard, but that would have been too convenient. As I feared, the rare flower was hard to find.

After checking the fifth or sixth shop it was hard to not feel discouraged. Finding the seller in a city as big as Aramore in one day was a next to impossible task!

"Cheer up, Bel-Bel!"

"Hm?" I asked, lost in thought.

"You look sad."

"I'm not sad," I replied. "I'm just a little frustrated, I suppose."

"But... isn't this fun?"

"Fun?!"

"It's like a treasure hunt! We're on an adventure!"

I smiled softly and let out a small chuckle. We didn't have any other leads, but Becca was staying pretty positive — despite ignoring her sleep cycle and dealing with the threat of sun. If she could deal with it, so could I. After all, I had promised I would help and if it kept her from attacking anyone else, this search was a small price to pay.

With renewed vigor, we approached the next store. It was a fairly typical florist's shop, with a window filled with vibrant floral arrangements. Though it stood out from the others we had already visited with its upstairs balcony, covered with blooming ivy.

I opened the door to the quaint but fragrant store, which jostled a bell hanging above. Its delicate chime interrupted the otherwise warm and quiet atmosphere.

Before we entered I asked, "Hello? May we come in?"

Having to ask that question so many times was a bit annoying, but Becca wouldn't have been able to enter any of the stores if I didn't.

"I can't sell you anything if you stay out there." The shopkeeper, a portly woman tending to some hydrangeas, joked. "Please come in. How can I help you?"

I replied with a hollow laugh. It was a kinder response than some though. Many of the storekeepers just looked at me strangely for asking such a question when the store was clearly open.

We stepped into the store, the wooden floorboards creaking with age. Immediately, my nose was pleasantly greeted by the scent of topsoil and the wide array of flowers like gardenias and peonies. Well, pleasant for me...

I glanced over towards Becca, and to my mild amusement, she was plugging her nose like she had done at the other stores. Garlic was particularly effective, but it seemed a vampire's sharp senses were easily overwhelmed by other powerful aromatic. I actually felt a little bad for her...

Worried her reaction might offend the shopkeeper, I stepped in front of Becca to partially block her from view.

"Um, we're looking for pegasus lillies. Do you have any?" I asked.

"My, you have expensive taste!" The shopkeeper chortled. "Unfortunately, I do not. But won't any lily do? I have plenty in white."

"No, I'm afraid it *has* to be pegasus lilies." I frowned. "I'm sorry to have wasted your time." I turned to leave. Yet another disappointment...

"Well, I don't like to make a habit of doing this, but since you young girls are so cute... if it *has* to be pegasus lily, I think I know where you might find some."

"Really?" I immediately perked up.

The shopkeeper went on to tell us about a florist across the river, who specialized in rare flowers. She was even nice enough to give us directions.

"Thank you so much!" I said one more time, as we opened the door to leave.

"Thank you, kind lady!" Becca added cheerfully, before stepping out onto the street.

"Hey! Becca, watch—"

Smack!

Becca stepped out right in front of a large man, and the two collided. Given their difference in size, Becca was the only one knocked over. Thanks to her quick reflexes, she was able to catch herself before completely hitting the ground, but her parasol went flying from her hand and onto the ground.

Oh no!

Becca hissed in pain, exposed to sun, then threw the hood of her cloak over her head before the light could do any more damage. It happened so quickly, I couldn't really tell, but it looked like her skin may have begun to blister.

"Oh no! I'm so sorry!" The man gasped. "Are you okay?"

He was a giant of a man, standing over six and a half feet tall with broad shoulders. He had strong features, a sharp jawline and a muscular neck. His chin was grizzled, and he wore a pair of glasses. Behind them were a pair of eyes as black as the night sky. His hair was a dark mahogany and was tied back in a short ponytail.

Strangely enough, he was dressed just like Becca. Not in fashion – his clothes were old and worn – but in color. From his felt hat, to the fingerless gloves on his hands and the boots on his feet, he wore black – just like his eyes. A heavy trench coat two sizes too big disguised any accurate estimate of his figure, and it draped down to his ankles.

He quickly grabbed Becca's parasol and helped her to her feet before returning it to her. Becca didn't say anything, but put the parasol back over her shoulder. She gripped it tightly and shuffled behind me.

"Is she…?"

"I'm sure she's fine!" I quickly replied. "Don't worry. It's just… she has a skin condition. She can't handle sunlight well."

"I… see…" He muttered, adjusting his hat. He was quiet for a few moments, before breaking into a big, embarrassed smile. "Well again, I'm very sorry! I really should pay better attention to where I'm going."

"No, if anyone is at fault, it's us!" I chuckled nervously, waving my hand at him.

"Well, take care." He took his hat off and placed it on his chest, before dipping his head at us in farewell. Once he walked past, I looked back at him over my shoulder and noticed he was doing the same. Embarrassed, I quickly returned my gaze forward.

"Becca, are you okay?"

"Becca doesn't like that man." She muttered sourly.

"But he was so nice!"

"He smelled like *death*."

"Huh?" I looked over my shoulder one more time, but he was gone. He had already disappeared into the crowd.

***

In the time that it took to get to our next destination, Becca's face was already healed of its burns. I still couldn't believe how fast she could heal!

The brick shop that now stood before us was quite impressive. And as the lady promised, it was impossible to miss.

It seemed almost every inch of the building was covered with flora. Blue Ivy crawled across the walls and colorful flowers dangled from the roof like decorative lights. Daffodils, tulips and dragon scale zinnias lined the windows, while azaleas of different shades squeezed themselves through holes in the brick. The door itself looked like it belonged in the forest, partially coated with a soft moss.

I turned the knob and, like always, poked my head in to ask if it was okay to enter.

"Hurry and come in! You're letting the moist air out!" Came the shopkeeper's voice from somewhere deep within the shop.

We entered as instructed and I was delighted to find the place even more enchanting on the inside. From the ordinary like cosmos, to the tropical like hibiscus and even the fantastical like the sphinxian fly trap — this shop had it all! There were many species I recognized, but many more I did not.

Tendrils and root systems freely crawled across the floor while bright blue water sprites zoomed above like fireflies, tending to the plants and laughing to each other in fae. Besides the windows which allowed sunlight to feed the nearby plants, artificial light was created through the use of strategically placed sun crystals. I watched as one grew dark and another across the store lit up, which I recognized to be a simple timing spell used to ensure the plants were getting the perfect amount of exposure. The air inside was warm and muggy, like stepping into a rainforest.

"Hello?" I called out, but no one responded. Instead, one of the sprites flew several quick laps around my head, before darting off into a back room.

"I guess we're supposed to follow?"

"This place is funny!" Becca giggled, through a pinched nose.

We went after the sprite, but Becca was stopped in her tracks as we approached the back room. "Woah! Becca can't go in there!"

"Why not?" But as I continued towards the doorway, I soon found out.

A strong stench was coming from the back room, so pungent my eyes began to water! It even made me doublethink entering, but I pushed ahead.

"You stay here then, Becca." And to think for a moment, I was actually a bit envious of her advanced senses...

"Hello?" I asked timidly, entering the room.

Inside, an elderly man was kneeling down at a large planter box. He was wearing goggles and thick leather gloves that went to his elbows. He also had on an apron smeared with dirt, and I couldn't help but notice the pointed hat on his head. The crown was wrapped in dried thorns.

"What?!" The shopkeeper barked grumpily. He wasn't even looking up. His hands were buried in the dirt, as if he were digging for something. And if the flies buzzing around were any indication, I think the dirt was the source of the foul stench...

"Um, I was told you sell pegasus lilies."

The shopkeeper sighed in exasperation and looked up at me warily. "What do you need with such an unusual flower?"

"Well..." Before I could explain, he interrupted me.

"Hey, that ribbon! You're Wis Amberfinch's apprentice, aren't you?"

"You know of me?" I was taken aback.

"Of course! It's nauseating the way she dotes on you all the time." He scoffed, pulling his arms from the ground.

That sounded like Master Wis alright...

In one of the florist's hands was a small plant, with a black, bulbous root and milk white flowers.

"Hey, is that moly?" I asked, stepping forward.

"She taught you well. Yes, it's an herb meant—"

" —to lift charms that affect the mind!" I finished.

"Good."

"Um, how do you know my teacher?"

"Where do you think she gets *her* moly from?"

"Oh wow! So you help supply the apothecary!"

Master Wis foraged, grew or collected many of her own ingredients, but she couldn't get everything she needed on her own. Luckily she could rely on both the Merchant's Guild and Mage's Guild, where members were quick to support each other with supplies.

"Yep, I'm a witch too. Completely different coven, of course. But... your teacher and I go way back."

"I'm Isabel Pirige. It's nice to meet you."

"Salen." He stood up and peeled his glove off before extending a hand towards me.

I hesitated, but didn't want to be rude. So I shook his hand, even though I was worried about the smell...

"So what do you need the lilies for? Did she send you here on an errand?"

"Erm, no. Actually…"

I explained to him how I came to find his shop, and that I was looking to help a friend identify the crest we found in the familial burial plot.

"Well, you're in luck. Not only do I sell the flowers you're looking for, but I also happened to place those particular flowers there myself."

"Huh?"

"My partner is buried there."

"Oh. I'm sorry for your loss."

"Don't be. That grave settled years ago. But the Dirkin family died with him."

"Really?" That didn't bode well for our investigation…

"My friend… we think she might be related to the Dirkin family somehow. We were wondering—"

"Impossible." His curt answer strangled my question. "The Dirkin family never once produced a female heir."

"Not ever?" I repeated.

"Not once. Which is why his family was… quite upset with *us*." Salen admitted. "He may not even have been buried there if it weren't for the fact that he outlived everyone."

"I'm sorry to hear that…"

How sad.

"Needless to say, I don't know where your little friend came from…" He started, leaning over to peek at her curiously through the doorway. "… but she didn't come from the Dirkin line."

My face fell. Did we hit a dead end?

"No!" Becca pouted, stamping her foot on the ground.

"Becca!" I spoke sharply, before a tantrum ensued. I could tell by the look on her face that she had reached her breaking point. The fun and games were over.

"I'm sorry I couldn't be of more help…" Salen continued to look at Becca cautiously. "But perhaps since you're here, you'd be able to help your teacher?"

"Hm? Uh, sure. How?"

"Follow me." He replied, removing his other glove and leading us from the back room to the front counter. Becca grumpily trudged along beside me.

"I just harvested some adder's tongue, and Wis wanted to make sure she got some. It's already paid for, so why don't you be a good apprentice and save her the trip?"

"I'd be happy to!" I smiled.

Salen went to pick up a bunch of the adder's tongue from behind the counter, but withdrew his hand quickly with a hiss, "Ouch!"

"What happened?!"

"Damn thorns got me good." He muttered. "Did you useless sprites leave the firethorn up here again?! Keep my pick-ups separate, dammit!"

In an obvious admission of guilt, the fairies all quickly disappeared into the back room to escape Salen's ire. He held up his thumb to inspect it, and I watched as a streak of blood ran down the side of his hand.

"Are you okay?"

"I'm fine." He growled. "Part of the job."

Becca stepped forward, her gaze transfixed by the crimson staining his hand. I quickly grabbed her by the shoulder and pulled her backwards.

"Is… *she* okay?" Salen narrowed his eyes.

"She's fine. *Right*, Becca?"

Becca didn't reply, but instead continued to stare intently at the blood.

"Becca." I grabbed her hand and squeezed it tightly.

"Huh? Oh. Yes, Becca is okay!" An innocent smile returned to her face, but only for a moment.

Salen didn't reply, but his gaze lingered on Becca.

"Well, we better get going." I chuckled nervously, hanging on to her hand. "I'll be sure Master Wis gets the adder's tongue… and give her your regards."

After thanking him for the information and the fern, and saying some quick goodbyes, we stewed in defeat across the street on the curb. It seemed like the "treasure hunt" was over, which was a crushing blow to morale. Suddenly the toll of walking around the city all day had caught up to me. I was tired, my feet ached, and…

"What happened back there?" I asked Becca.

"Sorry Bel-Bel, I almost lost it. But… Becca's hungry!" My vampire companion whined.

"Me too." I replied with a sigh. "But thank you for controlling yourself."

"Well, Becca promised…" She muttered. "But so did you! Why am I here?"

"Hey, it's not my fault!" I snapped back, equally as frustrated. "Can't you remember anything else?"

"No…"

We both sighed and sat quietly together for a moment. We watched as a few kids played with a leather ball in the street.

"That must be nice…" Becca whispered, longingly.

I looked at her in surprise. "Vampires are interested in that kind of thing?"

"It looks fun, doesn't it?"

"Then why don't you ask them if you can play too?"

Becca just pointed at the sun while she watched them, with a vacant expression on her face. It was late in the afternoon, but still plenty bright.

"Oh, right…"

At that moment, one of the kids threw the leather ball, but no one managed to catch it. It went right over their heads and landed right at Becca's feet. She picked it up and stared at it in her hand.

"Sorry about that!" A cute, little girl panted as she ran over to us.

She had eyes like sea foam, and her dirty blonde hair was held up in pigtails that bounced as she ran. She approached us and reached her hand out for the ball.

Becca hesitated—for a moment, it looked like she wasn't going to return it to her. Then, she did.

"Hey, do you want to play with us?" The girl asked spiritedly, after thanking her for the ball.

Becca just shook her head.

"Awww. Maybe next time? I live just over there!" The girl said, pointing to a nearby shop. A sign outside advertised a sale of fresh meat. "We play out here all the time!"

And with that, she beamed at us before running back to rejoin her friends.

Becca wasn't smiling. It dawned on me then that she may not have played with anyone in 140 years!

Sure, she was a vampire, but… that didn't mean she was a bad person! She was just lonely. I think she wanted to belong somewhere. And to me, that seemed really human.

"Hey…" I spoke up. "After we figure out why you're here, would you want to play some time? After the sun goes down, of course."

My words seemed to immediately lift Becca out of the doldrums. She looked at me with a big, fanged smile and sparkling eyes. "Really, Bel-Bel? You mean it?"

"I pinky promise!"

***

After a deep inhale through my nose, I let out such a heavy sigh that it threatened to fill the entire kitchen with its weight. I was troubled, and bored – flipping through page after page of *The Botanist's Encyclopedia* I had splayed out across the breakfast table. To its left, I was absently picking at my morning bowl of fresh fruit, but I wasn't really in the mood to eat any of it.

The night had come and gone, but despite our brainstorming, Becca and I were no closer to figuring out what to do next than we were the afternoon before sitting on the street curb. So I was scanning through the thick text, desperately searching for any clue about trees native to Aramore with white flowers.

Did she live right next to such a tree? Did she turn undead by such a tree? Did she come from a wealthy family with such a tree as their sigil? Or maybe she grew up on an orchard, like me?

Even worse, the other clue—an old man's smile—was even more vague and useless. There wasn't enough to go on, and I was driving myself crazy grasping at straws!

Cloud was sitting in an empty chair next to me, looking at me with sympathetic eyes. Master Wis, on the other hand, kept shooting me the occasional dirty look from across the breakfast table.

As if I didn't notice!

"What?" I asked shortly, after catching her doing it yet again.

"Nothing." She replied haughtily, before biting into a piece of toast.

"What?!"

She swallowed, then wiped her lips with a napkin. "Nothing." She reaffirmed.

It didn't seem like *nothing*. What was her problem? She had been like that since I came home with the adder's tongue the evening prior. I didn't even get a thank you!

I rolled my eyes and returned to my book. She was certainly acting childish...

"What are you doing, anyway?" She asked, in a tone that made her sound disinterested.

"I'm looking for trees that bloom white flowers."

"Why?"

I looked up from the book. Should I just explain everything to her? She might be able to help, but I was also still worried how she would react to Becca being a vampire...

I decided to split the difference and try to get her help while omitting the whole vampire business.

"Hey Master Wis, are there a lot of trees like that around Aramore?"

"Not too many. There are Eastern Crape Myrtles, like the big one found here in the city. And growing up on an orchard, you should be familiar with Aramorian Pears." She paused and thought for a moment. "Oh! And there's my personal favorite, Lausks Breath! Though, actually... forget that last one. You're looking for flowers, right?"

"Lausks Breath? Why does that sound familiar?" I asked, flipping to the entry out of curiosity.

149

"You don't remember? It's one of the ingredients in my Liquid Ice salve."

"Ah!!" I remembered now! I found the entry and scanned it as we talked. "And it doesn't flower?"

"Nope. Instead of losing its leaves in autumn like most trees, this magical plant freezes itself instead. The leaves turn as white as snow and don't thaw until the spring." She explained. "There's a big grove of them just south of the city walls, right next to the river."

"No way?!" I stood up out of my chair so quickly, I nearly knocked it over, startling Cloud who ran off at the sudden movement.

Was I looking at this all wrong from the start? Becca had said, "*petals* like *snow*." I had assumed she meant the petals fell like snow, like the Dirkin tree. But was she talking more literally, and didn't even realize it herself?

"Master Wis! Can I have a little more time off??" I asked hurriedly.

"No." She replied simply, with a smile.

"No??" I honestly didn't expect her to refuse. "Please? Just through the afternoon!"

"No." She repeated firmly.

"But…"

"Yesterday we had a deal, did we not?"

"Huh?"

"I said you could go, but you'd have to introduce me to your vampire friend later."

"That's why you're mad?"

I was so tired and defeated yesterday, I completely forg—

Wait.

The color drained from my face. I must have looked as pale as Becca! Yet Master Wis kept smiling at me, all-knowingly.

"Did... Did you just say vampire?"

"Isabel."

I sighed and sunk down into my seat. It was time to come clean. Not only was the deception exhausting... it was wrong. I was a poor excuse for an apprentice. She was my teacher and deserved the truth.

"... How long have you known?"

"Did you really think I wouldn't figure it out? The missing blood, your unusual sleep schedule... I had my suspicions. And then when Salen told me he was pretty sure you were running around with a vampire, they were all but confirmed."

"So you talked to Salen, huh?" I chuckled in embarrassment. *Of course he figured it out too...*

"Becca, you can hear me, right? You can come out now."

Moments later, a shadowy vapor blew into the kitchen before settling beside me. The mist came together to form a solid shadow, and Becca appeared. If Master Wis was surprised, her face didn't betray her. Becca stood behind me, bashfully looking down at her feet while grinding the toe of one of her shoes into the ground.

"Master Wis, this is my *friend* Becca. Becca, this is my teacher Wisteria Amberfinch."

"Hello..." Becca muttered.

I then proceeded to tell Master Wis everything. I recounted being attacked by Becca, and the promises we made to each other. I came clean about the stolen blood and the search across the city that really led me to Salen's shop. And when I finished the short tale, I hung my head with bated breath — anxiously awaiting my teacher's judgement.

"Thank you. For finally being honest with me." Master Wis said after several moments of silence. "And Becca, it's nice to meet you."

The small vampire and I looked at each other in relief.

"You're not mad?" I asked.

"Of course I'm mad." She replied.

Yikes. Not out of trouble yet...

"More than anything, I'm hurt that you felt you couldn't come to me with all of this sooner. Aren't I your teacher? Aren't I someone you can trust?"

"I know, I'm really sorry." I bit my lip in shame. "To learn you've killed vampires... I was worried for Becca. But I should have had more faith in you. You *are* my teacher, and... I'm really thankful for that."

Master Wis smiled softly. "Well, you've shown me some trust. So I suppose it's my turn."

She stood up, and from her robes withdrew a simple, hooded cowl. She reached across the table and handed it to Becca. "It's going to be another sunny day. You may need this if you're going to be out with my apprentice."

"You mean...?"

"Yes. You can go check out the grove today. The hood is enchante, and will protect Becca from the sunlight."

Wow!

"Thank you Master Wis!"

"Yay!" Becca cheered. "Yes, thanks Wissy!"

"Don't be so informal with her!" I snapped. "It's Madame Wis to you!"

Becca protested, then we began to bicker. Master Wis just returned to her seat and laughed. But our argument was interrupted by Cloud, who returned to the kitchen to investigate the commotion. He casually strolled over to Becca and rubbed himself against her ankles.

"Ah!" Becca squealed in delight, forgetting the argument and scooping him up in her arms. "Kitty!!"

I couldn't help but smile, rubbing Cloud behind the ears. "See? I told you he'd come around!"

***

Making our way to the grove wasn't a terribly difficult task. It was only a couple of miles away, and once we got out of the city, the scenery made for a pleasant walk. The problem with being *in* the city is all the people, and dealing with the congestion of goods and people at the gates. Whether it was farmers arguing with the guards about taxes on their way in, or merchants arguing with guards about taxes on the way out, everyone was always in a foul mood and in a rush.

We passed caravans of traders and market stalls set up along the main highway. Soon, we were in farmland, and I waved at the men hard at work in the wheat fields. Some of them waved back.

Becca and I chatted pleasantly all the while, mainly about Master Wis. My teacher had gained another fan. Like yesterday, Becca's signature parasol was hanging over her shoulder, protecting her from the sun. She preferred it to the cowl, though the new enchanted fabric now replaced her old hood.

As we neared the river, I knew we were at the right place. Trees dotted the lush landscape, dancing along with the gentle, summer breeze. Thickets of them stood together, like little families. And though their leaves weren't white, I could recognize them as Lausks Breath due to the leaves I had seen in the encyclopedia: palmate in shape, like a green star.

I bet it was a sight to behold come winter! Maybe Master Wis could come together?

I don't think Becca was nearly as impressed.

"There's nothing out here... how is this supposed to help Becca?" She sulked.

"Let's just look around. Maybe we'll find something!"

I sounded optimistic, but to be completely honest, I still had no idea what we were looking for. I mean, what evidence of Becca's past life could even survive 150 years? Or what if she was drawn to Aramore for a reason completely unrelated to when she was alive?

"Does any of this look familiar?" I asked, as we inspected the trees. "Can you remember anything else?"

After several quiet moments of searching, her shoulders fell.

"No..." Becca sighed.

"I'm not seeing anything unusual..."

It was too bad she wasn't a Dirkin. The tombstone was the perfect clue: obvious to spot, a clear identifier and timeless. There certainly wasn't anything like that here, only leafy towers reaching towards the sky.

Though, now that I think about it, trees are pretty timeless too, huh?

I approached a rather large tree and looked up in admiration. The charcoal trunk was so thick, I wouldn't have been able to even hug it. Each of its heavy limbs seemed like they could sprout trees of their own. Sunlight somehow managed to cascade down through its thousands of leaves and gently tickled my face.

"This tree must be even older than you, Becca." I noted out loud, running my hand across the rough bark as I circled the tree. "Hey..."

The palm of my hand scraped against something odd. On the other side of the tree, I found that the bark was disturbed. Looking closer it was carved away!

"There's... a man's face here!"

154

"Huh? What are you talking about?" Becca hurried over to my side to see for herself.

The carving was a likeness of one, etched deep. The bark had strategically been shaved away with a knife, to form a nose, eyes, a mouth and even a beard. It was a magnificent piece of art, with even wrinkles around the eyes and at the corners of his smiling mouth!

Wow!!

"Hehe...hehe...hehehe…" Becca began to giggle.

"Right? Isn't it—" But when I looked down at Becca, tears were flowing from the corners of her crimson eyes, rolling off her chin and falling to the ground below. Yet, she continued to laugh.

"Becca, are you okay?"

"It's Mr. Tree!" She dropped on her back, reaching up at the tree like she was grasping for something. "Yep. This is where Becca died."

I was stunned. Oh... of course! Petals like snow, *and* an old man's smile. Those were Becca's exact words!

"Really? Becca, that's great!" I cheered. "Well, not great that you died, but— "

Suddenly, Becca bolted upright and jumped to her feet. She got into a defensive position, like an animal out in the wild. Even her face turned feral.

"... Becca, what's wrong?"

"Oh well. There goes my ambush." A man's voice cut through the quiet grove.

The stranger stepped out from behind a tree and into view. He was dressed in a heavy trench coat and had a crossbow pointed towards Becca. It was the man in black!

Becca growled and dug her heels into the earth beneath her feet.

"Wait!" I shouted, jumping protectively in front of Becca and holding out my arms. "Why are you aiming a weapon at my friend?"

"Isn't it obvious? She's a monster. And I kill monsters."
"Becca isn't a monster!"

"Bel-Bel…"

"You poor thing," The Hunter said. "She has you enthralled, doesn't she?"

"No, you're wrong!" I showed him both sides of my neck to prove I wasn't injured.

Then, he began laughing. "Ridiculous! You're actually defending this monster? Why?! Because she looks like a child? I assure you, she's *not*."

"I told you: she's not a monster. She's my friend."

"Do yourself a favor; step out of the way. *She* might be able to dodge a crossbow bolt from this distance. But you can't."

I gulped, but I refused to budge. "I'm not moving!"

"Very well."

Fwoosh!

"Bel-Bel!"

"Argh!" I shouted, as I found myself roughly shoved out of the way and into a nearby tree. "Owww…"

I slid to the ground and clutched my hat, which had fallen off. My shoulder ached from the impact. But it was better than the alternative…

The bolt that would've gone straight through my chest was now buried deep within Mr. Tree's forehead!

"You hurt Mr. Tree!" Becca roared. But I noticed she was out of breath... The sun! Dodging the bolt and saving me must have taken a lot out of her.

"You're lucky." The hunter remarked, reloading his crossbow. But to both Becca and my surprise, instead of firing again, he dropped it. Instead he withdrew a large, silver sword from within his coat. "After all, how many people get to die in the same place twice?"

With that, he charged in with his blade at the ready! Becca collapsed her parasol and used it to parry his first strike. Clearly, it was no normal accessory...

Now, other than the foliage, she had no protection from the sun. I watched as her face began to blister and burn.

"Stop it!" I shouted in vain.

Despite the difference in their sizes, Becca's supernatural strength allowed her to go toe-to-toe with the Hunter. She parried another blow, and another! They were evenly matched! But he was applying enough pressure that Becca didn't even have time to pull the enchanted cowl over her head.

The fight was so intense, neither could afford to take their eyes off the other for even a moment. I wasn't a fighter by any means, but even I could tell a single slip-up would be a fatal mistake.

"Gah!!" Becca went stumbling backwards after receiving a sharp kick in the chest.

"Becca!"

I was wrong. They weren't evenly matched at all... With each parry, the Hunter was driving her further and further back. She was losing ground! The daylight was sapping too much of her strength.

Wasn't there anything I could do? I felt so powerless! If I could just fire off a spell – any spell. All I could do was stand there and bitterly wish an Arcanus was on my finger.
"No." I thought to myself. I refused to just watch helplessly. I had to help Becca! Master Wis often said it wasn't magic a witch needed, but wits.

I looked around wildly for anything I could use to buy Becca an opening, and that's when my eyes settled on a sizable rock nearby. I snatched it up off the ground and flung it as hard as I could at the back of the Hunter's head.

It struck! Our enemy growled in pain. "You brat!"

He quickly turned around to face me and Becca took that opportunity to don her cowl just as I intended. But as he started for me, she shouted out to him, "Wait! Don't!"

The Hunter smirked and quickly whirled back around, thrusting his blade into her chest. "Got you!"

I screamed as I watched the blade pierce right through her body. I was in shock. I couldn't believe my eyes! It was a horrific sight, with the sun catching the point of his crimson-soaked blade. Becca's blood ran down the length of the sword and stained both her dress and the grass below. She just remained still in place. Motionless.

"No…"

And then…

"Hehehe… hehehe!" Becca began laughing, then dissipated into mist around his blade.

Her shadowy constitution traveled behind him and reformed once again. Only now the blisters on her face were healed, as well as the wound on her chest she had received just seconds before. In fact, her clothes were even repaired!

"That hood… some kind of night magic then?" The Hunter growled, throwing down his sword and reaching into his trench coat again. "That's okay. I have magic of my own!"

The monster slayer pulled out two blinding daggers. The small blades shined brightly, like they were radiating sunlight itself.

How many weapons does this guy have?!

He charged in again, and with incredible dexterity began unleashing a fury of blows. He moved so fast, trails of light followed each swing of his blades. And though Becca had no trouble keeping up with him now, she was still getting driven back.

No longer encumbered by the sun, shouldn't he pose no threat at all? Sure, he was a monster hunter. But wasn't she still at an advantage?

Then my eyes widened as I noticed something crucially important…

"Becca! Why aren't you fighting back?!"

Despite her renewed vigor and overwhelming speed, she hadn't counterattacked once. She continued to only parry and remained completely on the defensive!

"Becca—"

She started to answer, but the Hunter interrupted her by striking his daggers together. There was an explosion of light and Becca was sent flying backward. She crashed into a tree, slumping to the ground.

"No!" I stood up to run for her, but the hunter pointed one of his blades menacingly at me.

"Not another step." He warned sternly.

Becca struggled to her feet, using the splintered tree behind her as support. Her whole body was smoking and I watched in horror as her severely burned face began repairing itself. She looked like she was in a lot of pain.

"Becca…" She panted, as she slowly worked to regain her footing. "Becca promised, didn't she? You're giving Becca blood… so… she won't attack anyone!"

"What? You mean…" Tears welled in my eyes. "… you're suffering just for that?"

"Enough of this." The Hunter readied another attack.

"Becca, I'm sorry. I misunderstood you. But... you're not a monster!" I shouted. "So you can forget that promise! I trust you, okay? Instead, just promise me you'll do the right thing when it matters. And your *life* matters!"

"Bel-Bel..." Becca smiled softly to herself. "I pinky promise."

"Die!" The hunter charged in with his blades.

Becca lifted her parasol, and shadows swirled around it like snakes, completely enveloping it. When they dispersed, she was no longer holding a parasol, but a crimson rapier with a jet black hilt.

He slashed at her, but she disappeared and quickly reappeared behind him. A wicked smile spread across her face. "Yay! Looks like Becca gets to play after all!"

She slashed him across the back and he cried out in pain, stumbling forward. He swiftly turned around, but she was gone again. When she reappeared, it was to cut him across the right shoulder.

"Gah!"

It continued like this. The left shoulder. The right leg. The left leg. Her speed was incredible! She was clearly holding back, only going for quick, shallow cuts. Still, I tried to avert my eyes. It was hard seeing her like this...

"DAMMIT!" The Hunter raised his right dagger, preparing to strike it against the other one again.

But Becca wasn't going to let him get another radiant blast off. Taking advantage of her smaller size, she appeared beneath him. She then leapt straight up, flipping her sword in her hand and driving the pommel straight into his chin!

The Hunter was hit with so much force, he was lifted off his feet, and as he fell, so did several teeth from his mouth. He collapsed on his back, barely conscious.

"Becca wins!" She declared proudly, pointing her sword at his throat.

I was relieved. She wasn't going to kill him.

"Like... hell..." He grunted, as blood ran down his chin. His hand fumbled around clumsily at his side, but he managed to grab a hold of his discarded crossbow and direct it towards Becca.

"Don't be a sore loser, mister." She smirked. "You won't hit me."

"No?" It was his turn to smirk.

He quickly rolled over on his side and pointed the crossbow at me! Before I could so much as flinch, he pulled the trigger. The bolt went flying!

"Bel-Bel!"

Everything happened so fast, my eyes couldn't even follow what happened. The next thing I knew, Becca was crashing into me and we both fell backwards.

"Nnnn..." I groaned, rubbing the back of my head as I sat up.

My entire body ached! Otherwise, I seemed unscathed.

"Becca?"

She was lying near me, and remained still on the ground. I slowly crawled over to her side. "Becca?"

"Bel-Bel? Good... You're okay..." She whispered weakly.

Before I could respond, the smell of something burning caught my nose. I looked around frantically for the source. And then, to my horror, I found it.

"Becca! Your stomach!"

The crossbow bolt was protruding from her abdomen, scorching her skin and causing it to fume. Even worse, the wound wasn't healing! The blood loss was significant.

"Becca! Hey, stay with me!" I pulled her close and tried to apply pressure to the wound before directing my tearful gaze at the Hunter. "What did you do to her?"

"Heh..." He rolled back over and let go of the crossbow. "That's a holy water-soaked bolt for you."

No! This couldn't be happening!

"Bel-Bel..." Becca coughed. "Becca remembers... Becca remembers everything now."

"Shhh!"

"And... Becca is sorry..."

"For what?" I cried. *What could she possibly be sorry for? I was the one sorry!*

"Last night... Becca snuck into the lab... and drank the dragon blood."

"What?" I choked.

At a time like this, how could I be mad over a little blood?

Wait... Blood!

"Becca! That's it! Drink my blood!" I shouted frantically, thrusting my wrist in front of her face.

"What?" The Hunter grunted. He began trying to push himself up. "Stop!"

But Becca refused.

"No..." She muttered, turning her head away from me. "Becca... couldn't do that."

"Becca! You have to! We just made a *new* promise. Your life matters!"

"That's why... Becca can't... Hurting you... wouldn't be doing the right thing."

"Don't be silly!" I sobbed. "Come on!"

She just shook her head weakly.

"H-Hey, I made a promise too, remember?" I sniffled. "I said we'd play together! I don't want to break that promise."

"But..." Becca started, tears now forming in her eyes.

"You don't have to be alone anymore!" Once again, I thrust my wrist out in front of her face. "Please."

Becca hesitated, but reluctantly opened her mouth. I brought my wrist even closer and she sank her fangs into my skin, biting down as if it were an apple. White hot pain coursed through my body. I didn't want to worry her, so I tried my best not to scream, but it proved impossible. Tears formed at the corner of my eyes as my vision spun, though stifled shrieks still managed to escape my lips.

"Stop!" The Hunter was slowly managing to get to his feet, once again holding the crossbow.

I began feeling lightheaded and sluggish. It wasn't just my blood, it was like she was sucking away my life force itself.

Soon, I didn't even have the energy to sit up. I collapsed on my side as my vision grew fuzzy. I could feel my consciousness fading away.

My arm dropped and I watched as Becca stood to her feet.

Everything began spinning faster. How much time had passed? The last thing I saw was Becca sinking her teeth into the Hunter's neck.

"Becca... don't..."

When I came to, I found myself looking up at a familiar sight: my bedroom ceiling. I was buried underneath blankets, and I could feel Cloud's weight on my legs. A cool breeze touched my face, as moonlight poured in through my open window. The draft caused the candle burning nearby to flicker madly, which cast the warped shadow of a pointed hat along the walls. Its source was sitting in a chair to my right.

"Master Wis…"

"You're awake. Good." My teacher smiled warmly and spoke gently. "How are you feeling?"

"Weak…" I muttered, lifting up my left arm with some difficulty. My wrist was wrapped in bandages, and even now it ached.

"I have some medicinal tea here. Can you drink?"

"Wait! Where's Becca?" I asked, sitting up a little too quickly. My entire body was sore and I winced in pain.

"Here. It's a mild analgesic. Drink."

I accepted the warm cup of tea from my teacher, but repeated my question. "Where's Becca?"

My teacher didn't reply, instead averting her gaze. The expression on her face caused my breathing to stop.

"Master?" My voice quivered.

"Isabel… Becca's in pretty bad shape."

"Wait. What?"

"I don't know if she's going to make it."

"No. That's… no!" My body began trembling. "She fed on me. I gave her my blood!"

"She carried you all the way here. On her back. In the middle of the day." My teacher explained. "She must not have wanted to hurt you too badly. Whatever she took... it wasn't enough."

I can't even explain what I was feeling. I just shrieked and threw my cup of tea against the wall. It shattered, startling both Cloud and Master Wis. Steam rose from the hot liquid as it pooled on the ground.

"Isabel..."

"I couldn't do anything." I sobbed, burying my face in my hands. "I couldn't do anything at all!"

My heart throbbed. At that moment, I was suffering on the inside just as much as I was suffering on the outside. No, it was an even greater pain.

I was just some stupid apprentice. What was the point of wanting to help people if I couldn't actually do it? Becca was right in front of me and I was unable to do anything meaningful for her. And now...

Without warning, Master Wis wrapped her arms around me and pulled me close to her chest. She was warm and smelled like lavender, but I still tried to pull away. She didn't let me, continuing to hold me until I lost the strength to struggle anymore.

"I'm sorry." She whispered. "I should have been there. But I'm here now."

"I don't want to have to rely on you for everything." I cried. "Isn't there anyone I can save on my own?"

"Isabel, you're capable of so much more than you give yourself credit for." She pulled away from me and tucked some loose hair behind my ear. "There's no doubt about it. You *did* save Becca."

She couldn't be serious. "How?!"

"Do you think just any vampire would carry someone twice their weight for miles, through sunlight and a city full of onlookers? Why did she do that?"

165

I didn't reply.

"You meant something to her, Isabel. For maybe the first time since she was alive, she was thinking about someone other than herself. You helped her find her humanity again."

"Who cares? She's dying!" I snapped.

"Listen. We're going to do everything we can for Becca, okay? You fought really hard for her, and while I can't promise much else... I promise I'm going to do the same."

"Can... Can I see her?"

"Not yet. She's still a wanted vampire, so I've taken the necessary steps to ensure she stays hidden while I care for her."

"But she's safe?"

"She's safe." Master Wis assured me.

I looked down at my bandaged wrist and gently rubbed the wound with my thumb. The itch felt like it would never go away.

I had to become a witch. No matter what.

***

Several lifetimes ago, Becca lived in a small house with her mother and father in a tiny community now known as Old Aramore. The area was largely abandoned as Aramore continued to grow and people resettled, but a magnificent grove of trees now stood in place of her family home.

It was her father who carved the face into one of the grove's earliest trees, to create a guardian to watch over their family. And while she grew up happy and with loving parents, her story was one with a tragic ending.

A traveler was passing by late one night. This traveler asked if he could spend the night and leave first thing in the morning. Her father was opposed, but her mother was a kind and generous woman.

She invited him in and even gave him food. But that very night, they were attacked as they slept...

Becca woke up to find the vampire feeding on her parents. She fled from the home, and tried to get as far away as she could. It goes without saying a child was no match for a vampire. She didn't make it past Mr. Tree.

Though she died, she ended up waking several days later in a coffin at some strange castle. She spent the next century and a half as this vampire's thrall, imprisoned there until she managed to feed on him and escape. That's when she returned to Aramore on nothing more than instinct.

Rebecca Collier was Becca's true name. And it was this name that brought us to a butcher's shop on the west side of the city two weeks after our 'treasure hunt' together.

"This is the place?" I asked my teacher, as we stood out front.

"This is the place!" Master Wis replied cheerfully.

"Hmmm... it feels like I've been here before?"

"Shopping for dinner, perhaps?" Master Wis conjectured, as she opened the door to the charming, little shop.

The brick exterior was unassuming, with a sign out front that listed prices and the daily cuts of meat. Inside was just as quaint, with a display table and a large counter. A scale, cutlery and other tools of the trade lined the counter, while the table was filled with cuts of goat, bird, cow, and even wyvern.

The carcasses of animals and other beasts hung from meat racks behind the counter, with some to be dried and others to be later carved. The stench of raw meat wasn't very pleasant and the thick smell of the pepper and other spices used to prepare the meat didn't help much.

"Madame Wis, welcome!" An older man bellowed cheerfully from behind the counter.

He was in the middle of cutting a piece of meat, but set his cleaver down as we entered. He looked to be middle aged, with a heavy beer gut and a thick, blonde beard. His eyes were a sea foam green and seemed to smile above his rosy cheeks. This was in contrast to his grim attire: a blood-covered apron, speckled with varying shades of red.

"Good afternoon!" Master Wis replied. "I brought Isabel with me today."

"Welcome!" A young girl, perhaps his daughter, echoed from our side of the counter. She held a broom in her hands and was clearly doing chores around the shop.

"I know you!" I exclaimed, when my eyes met hers.

"You do?" Master Wis asked.

"Yeah! We met a couple weeks ago!"

This girl was pretty cute, and like her father, had eyes like sea foam.

That's why this place looks so familiar!

"Yeah, you were with Becca that one time, right?" She smiled. "I'm Avelina!"

"And I'm Bertram." The butcher introduced himself. "I'm guessing you're here to buy some of my extraordinary meat?"

"You know that's not why they're here!" Avelina groaned, rolling her eyes. "Ignore him. I'll go get *her.*"

She ran off into the back, while Bertram roared at his own joke.

But it really wasn't that funny…

As I waited for Avelina to return, excitement welled up within me. I looked at Master Wis anxiously and she returned a comforting smile.

I hadn't seen Becca even once since our encounter with the Hunter. The days passed with me in constant worry, so distressed that I couldn't even stomach food half the time. But as promised, Master Wis fought really hard – and Becca did too. Miraculously, she was able to make a full recovery!

And as Becca healed, Master Wis was able to use her connections in the city to see if there were any surviving kin of the Collier bloodline – which led her to this store, Collier's Cuts.

Apparently, Becca's father had a brother who lived in the city. And the man bellowing before us was a descendant of that man. In other words? Bertram was Becca's *very* distant cousin.

Master Wis tracked him down and explained the entire situation. It took some convincing, but at the end of the day, Bertram was unable to turn a blind eye to family. He came to see the kind of person Becca was with my teacher's help, and he graciously took his vampire cousin in as one of his own.

And wasn't a butcher's shop the perfect place for a vampire?

There were a lot of logistics to work out, and it took time to get Becca settled. Between that and her recovery, there wasn't any time to see her. This would be our grand reunion!

I heard her footsteps first, coming down on wooden steps so quickly it sounded like a stampede. Already I was grinning like an idiot.

"Bel-Bel!" Becca came barreling into the storefront, and in her haste turned into mist to phase through the counter. She reconstructed and nearly knocked me over with a hug around my waist.

"Becca." I couldn't take it. Immediately I broke down in tears and clung to her with all my strength. "Thank goodness… I'm so happy."

"Becca! You can't use your abilities like that!" Avelina chastised, re-entering after her. "What if someone saw?"

"Hehe…" Becca giggled from my arms.

She pulled away and looked up at me with a bat-like grin. She looked healthy and as happy as ever. I never would have guessed she was fighting for her life just a week before. I was so relieved.

Despite her new home, Becca was still donned in all black and looked largely the same. Except now a shiny bracelet dangled around her wrist, a gift from the apothecary. It was a simple piece of jewelry, with a plain, leather cord supporting a round, translucent ivory crystal on each end. The mineral was called Satin Spar. It shimmered like Luna.

That was an appropriate aesthetic, given the accessory allowed Becca to be standing here in the middle of the butcher's shop with us at lunchtime. It functioned like the Night Hood, but was more discreet, practical and fashionable. I even got to help Master Wis enchant it!!

"I like your bracelet." I giggled, though tears still flowed freely down my face.

Becca jostled her hand to show it off. It was like the crystal was dancing, the way it sparkled in the light.

"Becca missed you, Bel-Bel!"

"I missed you too." I choked, with a tearful smile.

"Don't cry Bel-Bel."

"I can't help it!" I pulled her in for another hug.

"Becca wants to apologize."

I pulled away and looked at her in confusion.

"Becca didn't want to hurt you. Becca... is so sorry."

"Don't you dare apologize." I hiccuped, wiping my eyes.

"But look..." Becca grabbed my wrist and turned it upward, revealing two perfectly symmetrical puncture marks.

"This? It's nothing. Master Wis could have prevented it from scarring... but I want it as a reminder of my resolve."

I would *become a witch.*

Becca looked at me in confusion, but I just shot Master Wis a big smile.

"You've been studying so hard these last couple of weeks." Master Wis praised. "Keep it up!"

Slightly embarrassed, I turned my attention back to Becca.

"Thank you. What you did for me... I've felt so terrible. If you had died..." I nearly started crying again.

"If that happened, Becca never would have gotten to see you again. And Becca wasn't going to let that happen!" She grinned. "Besides, Becca wasn't going to lose to that meanie."

"Oh! What even happened to that Hunter anyway?" I asked, stunned I hadn't brought it up sooner.

"Becca used some blood magic to erase his memories of us." Becca happily replied.

"He probably woke up with a nasty headache and a sore neck, but I heard from the Guild he's okay." My teacher added, to reassure me. "He left the city a few days ago."

I didn't want to talk about that horrid man any longer than I had to, so I quickly changed the subject. "So how do you like it here, Becca?"

"Soooo much!" Becca twirled around on the balls of her feet, her dress dancing with her. "Avelina and Becca play every day! And Berty is super funny!"

"See? At least my new daughter thinks so!" Bertram laughed, playfully shaking Avelina by the shoulder.

Avelina just rolled her eyes and wrested away from his grasp.

"And how's the food?"

"Well, the blood here doesn't taste as good as yours..."

"Becca!"

"Becca's only-half joking!" She snickered mirthfully. "Becca is just glad she isn't hurting anyone anymore."

"Well, I am too." I smiled.

"I am three." Master Wis added.

And then Bertram facetiously chimed in, "I am four!"

"Dad!" Avelina groused, though this time, everyone couldn't help but laugh. Once the laughter settled down, Becca lightly grabbed my hand.

"By the way, Becca never thanked *you* Bel-Bel."

"No, thank Master Wis. Or Bertram! They both did way more for you than me."

"Nuh-uh!" She argued. "Of course Becca is grateful to them, too. Becca wouldn't even be here if it weren't for you. You saved Becca…"

I scratched my cheek in embarrassment. "But you saved me too, so… call it even?"

"Not even close." She shook her head.

"Well, enough of the sentimentality." I coughed, straightening my hat on my head. "I think our reunion means it's time to finally fulfill my promise."

"You mean…?"

I just nodded my head, a big grin splayed across my face.

"Yay!" Becca began jumping up and down. "And can Avelina play too?"

"Of course!" I grinned.

"Can I, Dad?" Avelina asked eagerly.

Bertram nodded in approval.

"Yay!" She ran to the other side of the counter and gave Becca a high five.

The three of us then went outside to have some fun, because Becca didn't have to fear the sunlight—or being alone—anymore.

Betrayal

"Cloud?"

I got down on my hands and knees and peeked under my bed to see if that's where my missing cat was hiding, but he was nowhere to be found.

"That's odd…" I muttered to myself.

Just moments before, I was settling into bed for the night when I noticed he wasn't there to curl up between my legs. Sure, Cloud was a nocturnal creature. But even if he ultimately scurried off to chase mice or play in the rafters, he always came to bed with me until I at least fell asleep. So it was strange that, come this particular bedtime, he wasn't nearby.

"Cloud?" I called again, peering outside into the hallway from my room. Again, no sight of him.

So I then began checking his favorite places around the apothecary.

The comfy, worn-out loveseat in the den? Nope.

On top of the window-side bookshelf of the laboratory? Nope.

Tucked inside one of the empty cauldrons? He wasn't in any of them, but you'd be surprised how often I found him nestled in one.

How about the windowsill down in the shop, or the counter? Nothing again!

I threw my hands up in frustration. "Cloud?!"

I was starting to get a little worried, though I tried to calm down by reminding myself that cats were pretty sneaky creatures. And if Cloud didn't want to be found, there was a good chance I wouldn't find him.

I decided to head back upstairs, to see if he was blending in on a pile of my dirty clothes, or a pillow or something. He was a white cat, after all. And that's when I noticed the door to Master Wis' room was slightly ajar. This was odd, because usually she kept her door shut.

Surely not...

Moving quietly so as to not disturb her in case she was asleep, I pushed the door open just wide enough to stick my head through. And I audibly gasped in shock due to the sight inside. I couldn't believe it!

There I found Cloud, sleeping happily on Master Wis' lap!! She was in her armchair, reading a book and enjoying a cup of tea. She saw me peek my head in, and the sight of my face must have been quite amusing to her. She smirked at me and mockingly put a finger to her lips.

It was as if she was trying to say, "Shhhh, he's sleeping."

A sharp pang of jealousy coursed through my chest. How could he?? Never before had I felt so betrayed!

"Traitor!" I pouted, before retreating to my room in defeat. Alone.

The Troublesome Twins

With the brew at a rolling boil, I felt pretty good about myself! The liquid was a bright yellow, as it should've been. And there was a sweet fragrance hanging in the air, just as the grimoire said there would be.

"Hmph!" I nodded triumphantly.

But then...

"Uh-oh!!"

The contents of the cauldron began smoking profusely! The fumes were thick, and purple! This was an unexpected development, to say the least.

Cloud cried out from my feet and backed away from the cauldron cautiously.

"I know it's not supposed to be doing that!" I told him anxiously, quickly trying to adjust the flames underneath.

But it didn't do any good. Next thing I knew, the surface of the liquid erupted in flames.

"Ahh!" I shouted in surprise, tearing the pointy hat off my head to fan away the smoke, liberating my peachy hair from underneath.

My apple-red eyes frantically scanning the lab for anything that would extinguish the flames. The smoke was beginning to fill the room and was getting in my lungs, causing me to cough. I made my way to our cabinet of components, madly tossing the various vials and bins aside until I found something useful.

"This will work!"

I scooped some white algae out of a wet jar full of the strange plants and tossed the clump into the cauldron. Immediately, the fire was extinguished with a long sizzle and the smoke began to disperse.

"Phew…" I sighed in relief.

Those plants were aptly called Fire-Eating Algae, and well… they were effective at what they did at least.

I wandered back over to the cauldron and moaned in despair. Seeing the algae floating on top of the – now dull-orange mixture – was quite the depressing sight. It bubbled pitifully and smelled like burned hair. Yet another failure…

I was attempting to conjure up a *Sundrop Potion*, which was supposed to make whatever you added even a small amount to taste like "that which made you happiest." In my case, I was hoping to please my palate with the sweetness of apple pie, croquembouche or even dark chocolate for many meals to come. Or, I wonder what cracking open a new book would've tasted like?

I guess I would just have to continue enjoying my morning porridge the old, boring way…

I knew I overdid it on the fire salt!!

It was a silly mistake, reminding me how far I still had to go. I was no Master Wis… yet!

Once again, she was away on business, which gave me free rein of the laboratory. Of course, she didn't like me experimenting on my own—this was probably *exactly* why, butttt...

"Hello?" Someone called out from the storefront.

Great. We're slow all afternoon, and now somebody comes in?!

"Coming!" I roughly shoved my hat back on my head and adjusted it as I entered the store. The lingering remnants of smoke followed me out, and the burning smell continued to stubbornly cling to my nose.

Standing in front of the counter was a young woman, maybe just two or three years older than me. Her hair was tucked away underneath a tattered flat cap, but it appeared to be a shiny black. She was wearing plain, tomboyish pants and a faded-blue vest shirt.

She was tall and had a lovely figure, with a beautiful, tawny beige complexion. Most striking were her eyes! Her left pupil was bright yellow like the morning sun, and her right was a deep red like mine.

"Um, fire?" As I appeared, she made the statement like she was asking a question.

"No, don't worry. I put it out." I replied.

"No. Fire!" The girl pointed to the sleeve of my robes.

I looked down and, sure enough, she was right – the end of my sleeve was still smoldering!

"Oh no!" I hastily patted away at my sleeve until the small embers were no more.

How embarrassing...

"Sorry about that." I chuckled nervously. "Welcome to Wis' Apothecary! How can I help you?"

I didn't like the look my customer was giving me... like I was an idiot or something.

"I'm looking for something to help with a fever." As she spoke, pointed fangs peeked out from inside of her mouth.

"Are you not feeling well? I'm sorry to hear that!" I replied, sympathetically. "We have several herbal remedies, as well as more complex tinctures. Do you have a preference? Or are there any other symptoms? Maybe you actually have a cold, or a summer flu?"

"No, it's only a fever! Just give me the best you have, okay?" She gruffed.

"Well, I'm no doctor... and I'm not an experienced-enough apothecary to diagnose you. Without knowing what's causing the fever..."

"I said just give me your best, didn't I?"

"S-Sure. Though..."

"What?" She snapped.

I didn't want to profile based on appearance, but given her ragged clothes... *can she really afford the best we have?*

I quickly dismissed the nasty thought and told her, "Nevermind!" with a nervous chuckle. It wasn't any of my business, and if I couldn't diagnose her, our most powerful was naturally the safest bet anyway.

I retreated back towards where our anti-inflammatory medications were shelved and browsed the selection. After a quick search, I spotted our most powerful antipyretic – which notably used ginger root and the rare but wondrous venom of a white snake.

I had to stand on the tips of my toes to retrieve the orangish-brown mixture, which was just a shelf too high for my reach, and dutifully brought it up to the counter. "That will be 120 gold pieces."

But my customer quickly snatched up the potion and began pouring it down her throat, after crudely uncorking it with her teeth.

"Hey, you've gotta p— ..."

The customer shot me a dirty look, then slammed a fat pouch of coins down on the table. But then...

"What's with this potion? I feel kind of... funny..." She staggered backwards, grimacing and tossing the potion onto the counter. It toppled to its side and its remnants began spilling.

"Are you okay?!"

She clutched her chest and her face contorted in pain. "This..."

She fell to her knees and I scrambled to the other side of the counter to help.

"What's wrong?" I asked, getting down to try and help her back up. Was this some kind of allergic reaction to the potion?

But as I reached for her...

Poof!

A white puff of smoke enveloped the girl, but when the smoke cleared, I found myself looking at a cat! A completely ordinary-looking calico, save the same discolored eyes, had fallen right to my side!

What the heck?! I was as confused as I was panic-stricken. Before I could even wrap my mind around what was going on, the cat (or rather, my customer?) bolted out the door of the apothecary – which was always left open when the weather allowed.

"Wait!" I called out, chasing after her.

She darted around the corner of our shop, and I was quick to follow. I was worried I might lose sight of her, but by the time I rounded the corner myself, the girl was back to normal!

She once again looked perfectly human, leaning seated against the wall to our neighboring shop while clutching her forehead in confusion. I thought I saw the flash of a spotted, orange tail disappear back behind the apothecary. Was it just my imagination?

"Are you okay?" I asked, helping her up to her feet.

"What was that?" She muttered. "How did *that* happen?"

"I… I don't know…" I reluctantly admitted, biting my bottom lip.

"You don't know?!"

It was true I didn't know what was going on, but I also didn't want her thinking poorly of my master's shop. "Let's just get you inside for now, okay?"

"Fine. Whatever that was, it seems to be over now…"

The girl began to follow me back around the front, but then made a grunting noise.

"Oh no…" She groaned, placing her hand up against the wall to support herself.

"What?" I quickly spun around to find…

Poof!

How was this happening?!

"Woof!"

This time she was a *dog*! My customer had now transformed into some kind of adorable spaniel, with a coat of tawny gold fur that was reminiscent of her human features. And just like she did as the cat, she retained the odd colors of her eyes, except…

… wasn't her right eye red before? Now it was her left eye that was red, and her right eye that was gold. Or did I have it wrong earlier? I felt pretty mixed up right now…

This time, she didn't run. She just stared at me blankly while wagging her tail.

What was I going to do? How did this happen?!

"Please forgive me!!" I cried out in distress, getting on my knees and hugging the dog tightly.

Poof.

"Um, I enjoy hugs as much as anyone, but... could you please not touch me so familiarly?"

"Eh?" I pulled my head back and, to my embarrassment, found she was back to her human self.

My face turned bright red. It was one thing to have your arms wrapped around an adorable dog, but to have your arms wrapped around an adorable stranger?

"Ah! S-Sorry!" I exclaimed, quickly ripping my arms away from her.

"What kind of apothecary are you running?" She scoffed, standing up and dusting off her legs. She glared at me as she adjusted her hat.

"No, this shouldn't be happening!" I quickly retorted. "It's just a potent antipyretic. What's happening is impossible!"

"Then you must have given me the wrong potion!"

"That's..."

... not possible, right?

I hurried back inside the shop and ran behind the counter to double check. The girl followed me back in with her arms crossed over her chest.

I grabbed another one off the shelf and examined it closely. I checked it against the original potion and Master Wis' labels. There was no doubt about it, I gave her the correct potion.

My confusion was only growing—I wasn't sure how to resolve the issue.

"It doesn't look like it was the wrong potion…" I told her, in my bewilderment.

"So what are you saying? I turned into an animal on my own?" She barked.

"No… Of course not!" I stammered. "Master Wis is away on business right now, but I'm sure I could get her back here and we can resolve this!"

"Look, I'm not feeling well. And I'm trying to hurry back home. I'll trust you, okay? Just give me *that* potion and we'll call it even."

"Huh? But what if you transform again? I really think I should involve the owner here…"

"Like I said, I really don't have time for that. But I don't feel strange anymore, and nothing has happened since, right? I think I'm okay."

"But…"

"Please don't make me go somewhere else in my condition." She insisted.

"I really don't think that's a good idea, but…"

I placed the potion on the counter anyway. If that's what the customer wanted, was there anything else I could do? Nothing like this had ever happened while I was watching the store before. I was completely baffled… and embarrassed.

The customer picked up the potion and her bag of money and put them both back in her pocket.

But wait, she didn't give me the coins yet! I opened my mouth to protest, but she cut me off with a sharp look.

"Sorry, but you don't still expect me to pay, do you??"

"Um—"

"You should just be thankful I don't report your business to the Merchant's Guild."

I hung my head, so my wide-brimmed hat covered my eyes. I couldn't really argue, could I? Master Wis was going to be so upset. It was such a rare and expensive elixir... and I lost two!

I know it's childish, but I was so frustrated I was on the verge of tears...

I couldn't even bring myself to properly say goodbye to my guest as she left the store. I just sank into my stool and pouted, staring blankly at the spilled potion as its contents ran off the edge of the counter and dripped onto the floor.

What was I going to tell Master Wis? I probably needed to reach out to her...

She kept a vial of aquacanus on her person whenever she traveled, a special kind of water which allowed me to scry her—or vice versa—in case of emergencies. It was our way of communicating with each other over a long distance. It's companion was in the laboratory; a shallow, ceramic basin filled with the same type of magical fluid.

She would probably be upset about the lost money, but I think she would agree that a potion turning someone into pets was a bigger problem! As I stood up and headed towards the back to contact her, I was interrupted by my own misbehaving cat! Cloud sneakily jumped up onto the counter and began lapping up the elixir that had pooled on the smooth, wooden surface.

"Ah! Cloud! Don't!" I lunged at the counter and scared him off. "You know better than getting into our potions!"

Was he going to be okay? I was pretty worried. Would he transform into a dog? Or a different cat? There was also venom in that potion, mostly harmless to humans. But to cats?

I picked up the fallen vial, which still had about half of its contents still inside, and hurriedly wiped up the mess with a nearby towel before following him back into the lab. He had leapt up onto his

184

favorite bookshelf, looking down at me in irritation. I looked back at him, anxiously.

Several moments passed; nothing happened. In fact, he got tired of looking at me and just curled up on his back.

It was so cute when he did that! Thankfully, it looked like he was going to be okay. I sighed in relief. It would've been quite the ridiculous scene if Cloud transformed into a different animal!

In fact, wasn't the whole thing utterly ridiculous in the first place? My heart rate had calmed and my emotions were beginning to settle, so I began thinking about the situation with a more collected mind.

How was it even remotely possible that an anti-inflammatory medication caused someone to transform into an animal? Transformation was a particularly difficult branch of magic! The most logical explanation would have been that I accidently mixed up the potions while stocking the shelves, but I already confirmed that wasn't the case.

Another explanation, then, was something went horribly wrong when the potion was being brewed. That's certainly not a mistake Master Wis would have made, and even if I happened to brew that particular elixir, could I really have bungled it so badly? Sure, my knowledge was pretty limited, but I couldn't think of a single component—snake venom or otherwise—that I might have accidentally introduced to the concoction that would've produced such an outrageous effect.

And didn't she make quite the show of drinking the potion right in front of me? I had dealt with many sick customers before, and never did any of them drink the medicine right then and there in the store! And then how quickly and calmly she was trying to leave the store after… Wouldn't a normal person be really freaked out?

The more I thought about it, the more suspicious everything seemed. A bad feeling formed in my gut…

I marched right back into the store and picked up the potion off the counter. I would have to drink the potion myself! If I was right,

I wouldn't have to embarrass myself in front of Master Wis... but then I'd have to figure out how to deal with the thief.

But if I was wrong? Well... worst case scenario? At least the transformations didn't seem permanent. And even if they were, maybe Cloud and I could still be friends?

I chuckled at my own dark humor. No, I felt confident I was right! Something was definitely off about this whole situation.

I swallowed my apprehension and uncorked the vial. It wasn't like I hadn't done experiments before.

Here goes nothing! I really hope I'm right...

I washed down that apprehension with the rest of the potion. I winced, and my lips puckered. The elixir had a bit of a pungent taste thanks to the ginger, but like most medicines, it was mainly bitter and just a tad sour. Perhaps because of the venom?

I set the empty bottle down and clenched my fists nervously. Now it was a waiting game...

A quiet 15 minutes passed, but I thankfully didn't transform into any animals. In fact, nothing interesting happened at all. I felt a bit nauseous, but otherwise, I was entirely myself! I ran upstairs to look in my bedroom mirror. Not even a whisker on my face.

Sorry Cloud.

At first, I was relieved. Not only was I not an animal, but the store's reputation was in the clear. And it didn't seem like I made any stupid mistakes.

Well, maybe I did make *one* mistake. And that thought had me mortified for a completely different reason. I totally just got scammed, didn't I?! Nothing had changed – Master Wis was still going to be *totally* upset with me!

I growled. That girl... She tricked me. She *lied* to me. But worst of all, she stole from my teacher!

But... *how* did she do it?

186

I thought back to something she said, *"So what are you saying? I turned into an animal on my own?"*

Is that exactly what happened?

More importantly, *why* did she do it? Sure, it was an expensive elixir. But she sure went through extraordinary lengths for it. Was she really not feeling well?

My initial relief had turned into humiliation and anger. I needed to get our money back! Or otherwise, I would *still* have to embarrass myself in front of Master Wis...

***

I'll be honest, at first I was worried about being able to find her after she disappeared from my store. Turns out, it's pretty easy to pick up on the trail of a troublemaker – even in a city as big as Aramore.

I was walking in the direction that I had seen her leave the apothecary, when I noticed a commotion between a merchant and his wife.

"That damn brat!!"

"Dear, enough! You'll scare away customers!"

The wife was trying to calm the burly man down in front of a small produce stand. A variety of fruits and vegetables were scattered across the ground, many of them crushed or flattened.

"I bet that dog was hers!" He growled.

My ears immediately perked up.

"Excuse me sir." I said, approaching the couple. "Can you tell me what happened here?"

"Some girl just stole a bunch of fruit and vegetables from me." He gruffed.

His wife was reluctant to have him sharing any details with a stranger, but luckily he was in a foul mood and ready to vent to anyone who would listen. Apparently a girl carrying a bag of food was walking by his stall as he was restocking some vegetables. A dog appeared out of nowhere under his feet and he tripped. He fell into the girl, causing her to drop her bag of food onto the ground. So he offered to replace the food she lost, but...

"Look! It's all rotten! It's like she pulled it out of the trash or something!"

"Ewww..." I examined the fruits and vegetables, and sure enough, none of them were any good. They were discolored and mushy, and assaulted the nostrils.

"I was nice enough to replace her food, but now it's clear she was only out to con me."

"Was the dog a spaniel by chance? With gold fur?"

The merchant looked surprised. "Yes, as a matter of fact!"

"And the girl... she had discolored eyes, correct?"

"Wait, do you know this person?"

"Can you tell me which way she went?"

He had other questions for me, but I didn't have time to answer them. I hurried in the direction he pointed, trying to catch up with the crafty con artist.

Now I was even *more* confused. I watched her transform into the dog, right? But the merchant saw both the dog *and* the girl at the same time. How was that possible?

As usual, the streets of Aramore were a mess. People everywhere. At times like these, I thought how nice it would be to be able to fly on a broom. No traffic, and looking down at everything with a bird's-eye view... catching the thief would be a cinch.

I continuously scanned the crowd as I pushed my way forward, anxious to find her quickly. She had darker skin and was taller than your average girl, but that didn't mean she would be any easier to find.

I was almost at the end of the street, and now I began to worry that perhaps I had already passed her. Then the swishing of a golden dog tail managed to catch my eye from up ahead.

I watched as it vanished around the corner, with an all too familiar face following closely behind. She was clutching a bag of fresh produce.

There she was, my scheming customer! Anger began bubbling in the pit of my stomach.

"Good job, sis! We'll be able to cook an excellent dinner with this!" I heard her say as she cleared the corner.

I growled and dashed after her. I haphazardly rounded the corner and frantically looked around, but this time I didn't have any trouble spotting her. I found her stopped in front of another market stall, chatting pleasantly with the owner. But, where was the dog?

"Looking for me?" A cool breath on the back of my neck accompanied the whisper.

It startled me and I yelped, nearly jumping out of my skin! I whirled around on the heels of my feet and found a pair of gold and red eyes glaring at me.

"Y-You!" I stammered. "But how? Weren't you just...?"

I turned my head back towards the stall, but found myself facing a pair of red and gold eyes again.

"... Over here?" She finished.

"Ah!" I yelped again. "How are you doing that?"

I did a double take... but wait, was I *seeing double*??

Two sets of laughter rang out, and I watched as the gold-and-red-eyed girl in front of me high-fived the nearly identical red-and-gold-eyed girl behind me. They stepped away from me and clung to each other as they laughed.

I had to rub my eyes, just to make sure I wasn't seeing things.

"Wait! You're twins??"

From their tawny skin, to their shiny black hair, the two girls were identical in almost every way. There were some noticeable differences, though. For starters, their eye colors were opposite of each other. They had both changed and were no longer wearing ragged hats, so an even bigger difference jumped out: animal ears were sticking up from their heads!

They weren't just twins, they were Hybrids, too!

"Duh! About time you caught on, idiot!" One of the twins cackled.

She had cat ears, with blotches of black, gold and white, and a spotted cat tail swishing at her waist. Her left eye was the gold one, her right eye the red one. She was wearing a cropped, white blouse and a pair of baggy, yellow pants. Her black hair came down to her shoulders and was even messier than mine. And when she laughed, a pair of fangs protruded from her mouth.

"We got you so good!" The other twin laughed.

This one had golden brown dog ears that flopped down against her long, black hair. Her hair was braided over her shoulders but the rest flowed down freely to the waist. *Her* left eye was the red one, and her right eye was the gold one. She chose to wear an ordinary, white blouse with a long, yellow skirt that split at the sides of her legs. Her tail wagged excitedly, which caused the patterns on her dress to dance. And her laugh only revealed a single fang.

"Knock it off!" I bellowed, as the two continued to snicker. "And give me the money you owe me!"

"What are you talking about?" The cat twin asked, playing dumb.

"For the potion you stole from me!" I snarled.

"Hey, I didn't steal anything! Are you trying to pick a fight?"

"Yeah, your potion made us sick!" The dog twin chimed in.

"Us?" I countered. "Are you even hearing yourselves? You clearly scammed me!"

"Do you have any proof?" The cat huffed defiantly.

"Your animal ears!"

"Ahh! Oh no!" The dog twin shrieked. "Your potion gave us animal ears! What should we do, sis?"

"Good question. Maybe we need to report her to the Guild after all!"

I wouldn't be intimidated by that farce this time.

"You're obviously Hybrids, who transformed into animals willingly. I can't believe you tricked me into thinking it was the potion that did that!"

"Dummy, everyone knows Hybrids can't transform into animals." The cat twin snappily replied.

I thought back to a lesson I had with Master Wis on transformation magic. I remember her telling me that Hybrid Mages had an easier time adopting animal forms than their human peers.

"Not true!" I argued. "Some Hybrids *can* take animal form... *if* they have a strong enough affinity for magic."

The twins seemed stunned that I knew this. Who did they think they were dealing with?

"Look, no one has to get in trouble. If you can't pay for it, then just give the potion back, okay?" I pleaded. "Why do you even need it? Clearly, neither of you are sick. Are you just planning on using it to scam someone else?"

The cat twin snarled and opened her mouth to retort, but at that moment, a trio of scary looking men approached us. They varied in height, and looked rough with scars and tattoos. There were only five eyes – and not a full set of teeth between the three of them.

"Ailu. Kyon. There you are! We've been looking for you." A bald-headed man leading the pack spoke.

His voice gave me the creeps!

"Oh great, it's the Brainless Threesome." The cat twin hissed. "What do you want?"

"Now, now Ailu. Is that any way to treat your new landlords?" He replied coolly. "The boss is growing impatient. It's time to pay up."

The dog twin shrank nervously behind her sister.

Who were these guys?

"We... need a little bit more time..." Ailu muttered, though she didn't cower like her sister.

"What's that?" The bald man asked. "Even though you have a bag full of food?"

He snatched the produce from her arms.

"Hey! That's ours!"

Well, it wasn't but...

"Turin, check her messenger bag."

"What are you doing? Stop!" I couldn't help but defend the twins, as the tallest thug tried to wrest her bag away from her.

I may not have been fond of them, but I didn't like watching them get bullied either. I tried to interject, but the third thug held me away with his arm.

Ailu tried to hang onto the bag with all of her might, but she was no match for Turin. He towered over her like an orc, and ripped the bag out of her grasp. And without considering the contents inside, he turned it upside down and let them all spill out onto the ground.

Among those contents was her coin purse and the potion, which shattered as soon as it hit the sidewalk.

"No!" Ailu yelled. "Why you—"

She raised a fist, but Kyon held her back. "Don't! Stop Ailu!"

"What did you do that for?" I shouted angrily. Now the twins couldn't return it to me even if they wanted to.

"Hey now, what's this?" The bald man crouched down and picked up the bag of coins.

He undid the purse string and looked inside, but his lip curled into a snarl. "Seriously?"

Like the messenger bag, he turned it over and a flood of pebbles spilled out from inside. The pouch was just filled with small rocks.

Seriously?!

"Man, you really do need more time." He laughed, and his two cronies joined in. "Well, you better come up with something quick. I'd hate to think of your poor, sick mother sleeping out on the streets."

I gasped and looked at the twins, who ignored my sympathetic gaze. Their mother was sick? I clenched my fists... I was aware of that pain too well...

"You've been warned." The bald thug callously raised a hand and turned away to leave.

"Thanks for the food!" Turin added, and the three of them cackled until they disappeared into the flood of people out in the street.

The three of us remained solemnly in place, standing in silence. I think all three of us were looking at the potion, its orange-brown fluid pooling out across the hundreds of glittering shards of glass on the ground.

I broke the silence first.

"Was... that elixir... for your mom?" I asked quietly.

"It's none of your business!" Ailu snapped.

"Please!" I spoke so emphatically, it startled the twins. "Was that elixir for your mom?"

I took the twins' silence as a yes. So I continued in a softer voice, "I just want to help."

**

"Here we are." Ailu announced bashfully.

We had arrived at a narrow, wooden house wedged between two other rundown homes. It leaned slightly, the siding worn with age, some boards broken or missing altogether.

"It's not much, but it's ours!" Kyon added cheerfully.

"Well, not exactly..." Ailu sighed as she opened the door to their home. "Ma, we're home."

We stepped inside, which consisted of only a single room. A fireplace was at the center, next to a kitchenette. The flooring was made of straw and packed dirt, and the walls on the inside looked just as worn as those on the outside.

A bunk bed was in the far corner, opposite the door. A frail-looking woman was laying in the bottom bunk, wrapped in blankets. A damp cloth was on her forehead and bindings covered her eyes.

"Oh, hi girls." The woman greeted weakly from the bed. "Is someone with you?"

"Excellent hearing, as always Mama!" Kyon praised. "Mama, this is Isabel. Isabel, this is our Mama!"

Like them, their mother was a tawny gold – though her complexion was a bit more pale due to her illness. Her black hair also didn't have the same sheen as her daughters'. Ailu must have taken after her dad, because like Kyon, their mother had dog ears.

"Welcome to our home." She turned her head towards me and smiled. "I'm sorry... I can't get up... to properly greet you."

"Oh no, please don't worry about it." I insisted nervously. "Thank you for having me."

According to the twins, their mother fell suddenly last winter. Since the fall, she hadn't been able to see and didn't have the energy to be out of bed for long. Often, she became feverish and couldn't leave the bed at all.

My own mother was bedridden for most of my life, and it made me remember how tough those days were. My heart panged in sympathy.

"How are you feeling, Mama?" Kyon asked, approaching her side with Ailu.

"I'm okay." She fumbled for Kyon's hand, and when she found it, she squeezed it reassuringly.

"I see the fever still hasn't broken." Ailu muttered, grabbing the towel off of her forehead and replacing it with another.

"I'm sorry you have to spend so much of your time taking care of me. If your father was here..."

"But he's not!" Ailu hissed angrily. "When will you stop mentioning that dirtbag?"

"Ailu..." Her mother said mournfully.

Kyon lowered her ears and turned her head away from her sister. An awkward silence filled the room. I just heard something deeply personal, standing there unsure of what to do.

Then I remembered a patch of purple coneflowers nearby we passed on the way here, and thought of a way I could help. "I'll be right back!"

The twins watched in bewilderment as I ran out of the home, then returned out of breath a couple minutes later with an armful of flowers. "Can I use your kitchen?"

195

"What do you think you're doing?" Ailu asked distrustfully.

"Helping." I replied.

"You can use our kitchen, Isabel." Their mother answered with a smile.

"Thanks!"

Their kitchenette didn't have much, but I was able to make do with what they had. They had water stored, and I even found honey, the only other ingredient I needed. There was also a cheese cloth I could use as a strainer, and though the pot was a bit rusty, it didn't matter.

It was no Wis' Apothecary, but for the next hour, their small kitchen was my personal laboratory. As I worked, Kyon watched from right over my shoulder (which was a bit annoying), while Ailu looked on warily from a distance.

When I was finished, I smiled proudly and turned to face the twins. In my hand was a standard herbal remedy, echinacea syrup, which was another store-favorite when it came to treating fevers. I had personal experience treating someone with it, too. It was a much more simple remedy than the elixir from before, but that didn't mean it wouldn't be effective.

"This doesn't mean I forgive you or anything, but here... for your mom." I handed a cup of the syrup to Kyon, who was still right behind me. "I still expect you to pay for the elixir you stole of course, but this one's on me."

"We don't need your pity." Ailu scoffed.

"It's not pity. It's just... the entire reason I'm studying to be a witch."

"Isabel!" Kyon embraced me in a big hug.

"Hey... c-could you not touch me so familiarly?" I muttered in embarrassment, echoing her words from earlier.

Kyon shook her head. "Nope. We're friends now!"

"No we're not!" I stubbornly refuted, still rather upset about their scam...

"It sounds like... you two... found a good friend." Their mother sighed happily. "Thank you so much... Isabel. You're... sweet."

Kyon passed the syrup to Ailu and while she administered the medicine, Kyon made some tea for everyone. There weren't any chairs, so we sat on the floor beside the bed to drink.

"Sugar?" Kyon asked, handing me a small dish.

"Thanks." I replied, taking the dish from her. I dropped a couple spoonfuls into the hot liquid and stirred. I put the chipped, ceramic cup to my nose and inhaled deeply.

"Ah..." Since living with my teacher, I had grown to really like tea. I eagerly took a sip.

"Pffft!!" I didn't want to be rude, but... it was nasty! I couldn't help but spit it back into the cup.

When Ailu and Kyon started cracking up, I had a rough idea of what happened.

"Nice one, Kyon!" Ailu laughed, giving her sister a high-five.

"Haha! Got you!" Kyon laughed, as I glared at them. "That was actually salt!"

"Can you not?" I growled in annoyance.

"Girls, be nice!" Their mom chastised from the bed. "I'm sorry, Isabel. They're always... playing jokes like that."

The twins just continued to laugh, but managed to settle down after several more moments.

"Here. You can have mine." Kyon handed her cup to me, as she wiped tears from the corners of her eyes.

I looked at her distrustfully, but accepted the cup anyway. This time I wasn't going to take any chances, I was just going to drink it black.

We chatted idly and enjoyed the tea until their mother fell asleep a short time later. Already, the remedy appeared to be working and she felt cooler to the touch. Now, with their mother sleeping, I summoned the courage to ask a difficult question.

"So... are you all facing some kind of money problem right now?"

"Again, it's none of your business." Ailu didn't speak to me as sharply as before, but she was still firm.

"You know Ailu, I've been thinking..." Kyon started softly. "You know that trick you've been wanting to try, the one that requires a third person?"

"Huh?" Ailu looked at Kyon, then looked at me. "You don't mean...?"

"Why not? If we pull the trick on *him*, it could get us out of debt! Our house could be ours again!"

"What are you talking about?" I asked, confused by the back and forth. "You're not suggesting I help you steal from someone?"

"Not just anyone." Kyon replied. "A bad man."

"Kyon!" Ailu snapped.

"Tell me."

Despite Ailu protesting, Kyon told me about their situation. A few years ago, their father stole a large sum of money from a man named Laurent Desmarais and fled Aramore. Laurent ran a seedy bar in the city and used it as a front for all kinds of illegal operations. And with their father gone, he looked to his family to settle the debt.

He coerced their mother into working at the bar in exchange of paying down the amount the family owed, but her work barely covered the exorbitant interest he was charging. In the end, their mother worked herself until she collapsed. Without an ability to pay, Laurent took their house as collateral. And now that it's coming up on five years of debt, he's threatened to sell the house if they don't pay him back soon.

Even worse, their mother still believed their father would one day come back.

"That's terrible…" It was a hard story to listen to. I couldn't even imagine…

"We'll manage, somehow." Ailu said defiantly.

"How much money do you still owe?" I asked.

"50 plats."

"50 plats?!" I asked in shock. That was the equivalent of 50,000 gold pieces!

Kyon smiled softly and raised her eyes sardonically.

They were in an awful situation and it wasn't even their fault. It must have been so tough… I looked at their mother sleeping in the bed, and I shifted uncomfortably on the ground. The fang-shaped scar on my wrist began to itch and my eyes drifted to it thoughtfully. I gently massaged it with my thumb as I made my decision.

"Okay…"

I certainly didn't approve of stealing from anyone, but… Laurent really did sound like an awful man. And if they could escape their crushing debt, then maybe Ailu and Kyon wouldn't have to steal from anyone else! To me, they just seemed backed into a corner.

"… if you agree to pay me back for the elixir you stole, I'll help you with your plan."

"What?"

"Really?"

"Really."

"Oh, Isabel!"

"Hey!" I gruffed, as Kyon tackled me. "So… what's the plan?

Laurent's Dive.

Even in the morning like this, it was the kind of bar where you could always count on finding someone passed out somewhere. I followed my sister inside and carefully stepped over a man sprawled out on the floor. Several of his teeth were lying near his mouth in a dried spattering of blood.

Light struggled to trickle in through the boarded up windows, which were all broken or missing. But the handful of creatures that dwelled here preferred the dark anyway. It allowed them to gamble noisily at a table in the corner, or conspire quietly while passing around a pipe filled with who knew what. Tobacco? Dragon's Breath? Dreamroot? A persistent haze of smoke clung to the air at all times, and the floor was perpetually sticky.

Because I was currently a dog, I had the misfortune of smelling everything else too, to an excruciating degree. Like the urine-soaked pants of some slob at the bar top, clearly too drunk to bother with the restroom. Or the three-week body odor of the one-legged man sitting at a table by the door. How did the woman entertaining him tolerate it? Even with my circumstances, you couldn't pay me enough!

The man we were looking for was behind the bar, cleaning mugs with a soiled rag (I don't think an ocean of soap could properly clean anything in this place…) He was tall, with dark gray hair and broad shoulders. His eyes were a dull blue and a small patch of hair warmed his upper lip.

"Laurent." My sister approached the bar and greeted him. I sat at her heels obediently, like a good dog.

"Well, well, well. Ailu." He spat, placing his hands menacingly on the bar top. "Come to finally pay up? Did your sack of rocks magically turn to gold?"

"Save it Laurent. I've got some money for you." Ailu replied coolly. "Or rather, I will soon."

"Soon? What the hell does that mean?"

"I've gotta do a quick favor for someone first, then I get paid. It won't take long. But do you think you could watch this dog in the meantime?"

"Huh? Do I look like a dog sitter to you?" He snapped. "What's your ditsy sister doing? Have her take care of the mutt."

Hey, not nice!

"She's taking care of Ma today and this dog is too energetic to keep around with her condition." Ailu replied. "The mutt just started following me around a couple days ago, so I'm trying to look after her until I can figure out what to do."

"That's not my problem."

"Please?" My sister pressed her hands together and batted her eyes. "I'll only be an hour or two! And besides, won't watching my dog ensure I have to come back here to give you the money?"

Laurent grumbled to himself, but ultimately succumbed. "Fine. But I'm not responsible for anything that happens to it. You see the company I keep around here."

"Thank you, Laurent. I'll be back with a payment soon!"

Ailu knelt down to me. "Okay Sandy, I've gotta step away for a little bit. But Mr. Laurent here will take care of you in the meantime. Behave, okay?"

I barked while circling in place. It wasn't enough to just look the part. Ailu pet me on the head and waved goodbye to Laurent, before hurriedly heading out the door.

Laurent sighed deeply, then looked at me. "Those good-for-nothing twins are always taking advantage of my kindness."

Is that what you call it?

He stepped out from behind the bar and picked me up under my front legs.

Oof!

I was so tiny and helpless, my legs flailed underneath me as they dangled. I squirmed uncomfortably, though there wasn't much I could do held in his strong grip.

"If Ailu can't figure out what to do with you, maybe I'll turn you into stew." He chuckled maliciously.

I gulped nervously.

"Huh... Those eyes..."

Uh-oh. I barked loudly, which surprised him and caused him to drop me. Then I scurried away before he could inspect me any closer.

"Be quiet, dammit! Don't disturb my customers!" He growled, standing up and dismissing me with a wave of his hand.

Phew. It wasn't like he knew I was Kyon, but why take the chance of him figuring it out?

See, the fact that we could take on our animal forms was a secret my sister and I shared with very few people.

When we were little, we watched a Hybrid street performer who could transform. He told us his secret, and we practiced and practiced for years until we got it right! We could only transform into our Hybrid animal, no other magic, but it was a useful trick all the same.

Laurent went back to cleaning and a boring fifteen minutes passed. I spent the time pacing around the tavern aimlessly. I would've laid down, but the floor was too filthy and I cared about my beautiful coat of fur too much. But to my frustration, some pipe ash somehow managed to stick to my fur anyway.

"No!" I cried.

Then an adorable, young girl entered the tavern. Spotting her caused my tail to wag back and forth excitedly. She was wearing fine robes and a pointed hat rested on her peach-colored head. She was right on time!

***

From the moment I stepped foot inside the dank and horrid bar, I was immediately filled with regret. It was the seediest place I had ever visited and it gave me the creeps. To be honest, I was a little scared...

There were about half a dozen or so people in the tavern, and I couldn't help but feel sorry for them. Didn't they have anything better to do at 10 a.m. than drink? But they weren't my concern. The golden spaniel pattering around near the bar was.

I took a deep breath. *I hope my acting is convincing enough...*

"Um... e-excuse me..." I cleared my throat and approached the bar. Based on the description Ailu and Kyon gave me, the fierce-looking bartender was Laurent.

Scary!

"I'm looking for my teacher. She's a no-good drunk, so I've been checking the local bars. I was wondering if you may have seen her?" I recited the lie I practiced the day before with the twins.

Forgive me, Master Wis!

"Is she a witch?" Laurent asked, noticing my hat.

"That's correct."

"Sorry young lady, no witch has passed through here."

"Oh. Well, thanks anyway."

I turned to leave, but at that moment Kyon jumped up on me and placed her paws on my legs. She barked happily, as she clamored for my attention.

"Aw! What a cute dog!" I smiled, petting her behind the ears. "Hey, wait a minute! Whose dog is this?"

"None of your business." Laurent replied gruffly.

"Oh my goodness!" I got on my knees and held Kyon's head in my hands. "There's no doubt about it, this is the royal family's missing dog!"

"What the hell are you talking about?"

"You haven't seen the posters?" From within my robes, I pulled out an official looking bulletin and handed it to Laurent. "Take a look at this."

The twins and I created a couple of fake missing dog flyers, as if they came from the castle. They detailed how the queen's dog, "Estelle," ran away, and that the royal family was offering a 150 gold reward for her safe return. We described the dog as a golden spaniel, with a red eye on the left, a gold one on the right.

I used a potion I was familiar with to animate a quill, so the calligraphy looked neat and official. I was quite proud of myself!

Laurent read the poster over, pursing his lips. He shrugged and roughly shoved the poster back towards me. I couldn't tell if he was actually disinterested, or just feigning so. I continued.

"Of course, what the royal family doesn't want you to know is that this dog is actually a carbuncle." I said casually.

Okay, I was putting on a pretty good performance if I do say so myself.

"What the hell is a carbuncle?" He grunted.

"Well, it's a mystical kind of dog. But that's not really important." I explained. "See this golden eye? It's a really, really, *really* rare alchemy ingredient that can be used to turn lead into gold!"

To be clear, while carbuncles actually existed, their eyes held no such ability. That was made up.

"Really?" *Now* Laurent sounded intrigued.

"Of course, it makes no difference to me where it came from. Would you be willing to sell it?" I asked innocently. "My teacher would pay an absolute premium for this creature!"

"How much are you talking?"

"Hmmm… 100 plats? And I mean, that's *at least.*"

"100 plats?!" Laurent started coughing to hide his surprise. "Well, if you're willing to pay that much, I'll sell you the eye right now!"

Laurent pulled a blade from his pocket, causing Kyon to yelp and retreat backwards.

"No!" I shouted, perhaps too quickly. Laurent looked taken aback. "I mean… my teacher obviously needs the dog alive and in good health. To, uh, preserve the integrity of the eye's alchemical properties."

"I suppose that makes sense." Laurent put his knife away.

Phew…

"In that case, how about once you find your teacher, you both come back with the money? And then I'll gladly sell you the dog."

"Really? Are you sure you don't want to try and keep the creature around? They're supposed to bring prosperity to those around them."

"I may not be willing to let her go for 100 plats, but I'm willing to negotiate."

"Wow, my teacher is going to be thrilled! I'll be back soon then! Thank you!"

"No, thank *you*!" Laurent chuckled greedily.

I pet Kyon on the head, then waved goodbye to Laurent. I once again promised to see him soon and left the bar. I stood on the steps outside, exhaling in relief. My nerves were fried!

Hopefully I played my part well...

Now the rest was up to Ailu.

"Well, if it isn't Patches!"

I let out a charming meow and rubbed up against the fisherman's leg.

The smell of sea salt filled the air, as the restless ocean sprayed against the myriad of ships docked at the port. Their wooden gangways creaked as sailors and merchants scrambled back and forth, shouting to one another and loading or unloading various kinds of cargo.

I was at the fish market set up a little ways down the pier, where fishermen were getting their stalls filled with that morning's catch. I had a little time to kill, so I thought I'd ham it up to try to get some dinner for the night.

Many merchants were pretty protective of their goods and were quick to chase me away. But this particular person, who had nicknamed me "Patches," was a pretty nice guy. Maybe because he had a young daughter who *loved* me.

"Patches!!" The little girl appeared from behind a cargo crate and scooped me up in her arms.

I didn't really like being picked up, but...

"Meow!" I purred.

The young child was probably eight or nine years old. She had a dark and rich complexion, with curly locks that played across her shoulders. She was a little rough with me as her hand ruffled my ears, but I tolerated it.

"Can I give her a fish, Daddy?"

Bingo!

"Alright Patches, salmon or halibut?" The fisherman laughed from his gut.

"Meow!"

Salmon, of course!

"Halibut it is! Go ahead and give her one of the small ones, Mide."

Damn. Well, they say beggars can't be choosers...

"Yay!" The girl cheered, carefully dropping me at her feet before running over to the stall. She perused the fish, and the moment her father wasn't looking, she went ahead and picked up a particularly large halibut.

"Shhhh!" She winked, setting it down at my feet.

I cooed in thanks and went to pick up the fish. But, ugh, it was a struggle! After managing to get it situated in my jaws, I disappeared behind a bunch of crates and assumed my human form.

"Score!" I smirked, admiring the large fish in my hands.

I rushed home with it, checked on my Ma and then left for Laurent's. The sun was close to reaching its highest point, so Isabel had hopefully left a long time ago. It was almost time to close the deal, but there was one last thing I needed.

I scanned the streets for a particularly wealthy-looking mark, when I spotted a portly merchant with a thick beard and a soft, emerald tunic made of fur coming towards me. He looked mean and was scolding a young apprentice trailing behind him, who was struggling to balance a stack of boxes.

"You idiot! Keep up, will you?" I heard him shout.

Bingo.

I put myself in their path and once I was close enough to the merchant, stumbled over myself. The merchant and I collided and my hands moved swiftly.

"Hey! Watch where you're going!" He growled, though his face softened when he saw I was just a young woman.

"I'm so sorry. Are you okay?" I flashed him my best disarming smile and put my hand on his shoulder to balance myself.

"Just be more careful."

"Yes sir. Sorry again! Have a great day." I stepped behind him and helped straighten the boxes his apprentice was carrying.

"Th-Thanks..." The apprentice muttered with a smile.

"Hurry up!" The merchant shouted, and the two went along on their way.

But I clutched his coin purse in my hand, and he was none the wiser. Now I was ready to make Laurent pay. That bastard, I couldn't wait!

I arrived at the tavern a short time later. Now that it was lunchtime, there were even more unsavory individuals scattered inside. The man that had been knocked out across the entryway was gone, though his teeth were still on the ground...

Kyon spotted me as soon as I entered, immediately running to my side. She yipped repeatedly with joy and ran circles around me.

"Enough Sandy! I'm happy to see you, too!" I laughed, crouching down and ruffling her face between my hands. "Did you behave yourself?"

"Woof!"

"Thanks, Laurent." I said, standing back up and approaching the scumbag at the bar. "Here's your payment, as promised."

I tossed him the coin purse I lifted just minutes before. He opened the pouch and counted its contents. "That's it?"

"That's it?" I scoffed. "It's money, isn't it?"

"This is barely enough to even cover this month's interest!"

"It's not my fault interest is so high!" I retorted.

"Dammit, Ailu! Stop screwing around!" Laurent yelled. "I'm *this* close to just selling your house. Do you know how patient and generous I've been?!"

Right, sooo generous...

"I'm *so* sorry, Laurent!" I tried to look as pitiful as possible. "I promise I'll figure something out, really! When I think... about my poor Ma... *sniffle*..."

I began to tear up, and cracked my voice on purpose. No one could garner sympathy like Kyon but I could put on quite the performance too!

"Save your tears for someone who cares." He scoffed. "How about I hang on to this dog until you bring me my money?"

We figured he'd try and use the dog to extort more money from us, which meant it was time for me to act panicked. "No! Wait... You can't!"

Laurent narrowed his eyes, then smirked. "Why do you sound so desperate? It's just some dumb mutt, right?"

"Well..." I stammered.

"Spill it, Ailu."

"Fine. You got me." I groaned. "I can't fool you, Laurent."

From my pocket I withdrew a folded up missing dog poster, identical to a second poster Isabel had. Based on Laurent's facial expression, I was confident Isabel did her job and he had already seen it. Of course, I wasn't supposed to know that, so I handed him the poster with a look of defeat on my face.

"I saw this poster while I was out." I explained. "I was going to return the dog to make a little coin. But if you let me keep enough for groceries, I'll give you the rest — promise!"

Right now Laurent held all the power, so I had to grovel. That wouldn't be the case for long.

"Get out, Ailu. I'm keeping the damn dog."

"Why do you even care? The reward isn't even that big!"

"None of your business!" He spat.

"Laurent, if you don't give me Sandy back, then... I'll tell the royal guard you've kidnapped Her Majesty's dog!" I puffed my chest and crossed my arms smugly.

"So? I'll just tell them you're some lying brat and that I planned to return the dog myself."

"And *maybe* they'll believe you—though with your record I'm not so sure." I retorted. "Either way, do you really want the King's Guard poking around? We both know what goes on in here."

Laurent gritted his teeth. "You'd really dare cross me like that, Ailu?"

"I need the money." I lowered my voice and looked at him gravely.

"Tch." He snarled. "I'll take 150 gold pieces off your debt, okay? Just forget about the dog."

Hook. Line. And sucker! Now we could negotiate.

"No way, Laurent. That's not the same as actually getting 150 gold. Besides, what if I'm able to leverage the favor later? Maybe the royal family will be so grateful I could get a job at the castle. Or maybe even meet the king and queen!"

"You should be worried about *me*! Forget about that childish nonsense."

"Come on, Sandy. Or... Estelle." I turned to leave and Kyon scurried over to me.

"I'll forgive your debt for the next three months then!" Laurent was starting to sound desperate. "Come on kid, I'm trying to do you a favor."

"Seriously, why do you care about this dog so much? It's just some pampered pedigree." Now it was my turn to leverage some pressure. So I narrowed my eyes and spoke softly, "Unless... there's something you know that I don't?"

"Of course not! It's just a dumb mutt. Look, I'm trying to be nice here, okay?"

Clearly, Laurent was trying to keep me from getting too suspicious. But this was the pivotal moment of our scheme!

I laughed. "Come on Laurent, tell me the truth. What's going on? I know you better than that! You're seriously going to forgive our debt payments, for three months, just so I "forget" about this mutt?"

"Fine, you ingrate. Take the stupid dog and leave. See what I care!"

But I could see Laurent sweating. He was getting nervous!

"Hmmm... you know, I didn't consider running off with the dog before now, but I bet the right buyer would pay quite the sum for the queen's dog. Maybe I could get enough to erase our debt entirely! That would work out nicely for you, wouldn't it?"

I was laying it on thick!!

"No one is going to pay you more than what I'm offering right now, I promise you that. Think how much your family owes me, Ailu."

"You might be right. But I'll take my chances." I continued heading for the door.

"Ailu, if you walk out that door I'm not offering you a cent later!"

"Goodbye Laurent." I placed my hand on the door and pushed it open.

"Wait!" He roared. I stopped, but didn't turn around.

Laurent was in a tough spot. He couldn't afford to let me leave with the dog, but he couldn't risk the consequences of taking her from me either. I held all the cards, and his next words confirmed it.

"… I'll clear your entire debt." He sighed in defeat.

I was turned away from him so he couldn't see, but I shot Kyon a devilish grin.

Jackpot.

I closed the door and returned to the counter, pretending to act like I was thinking deeply. "Hmmm… You really mean it? I just have to keep my mouth shut about the dog?"

"That's the deal."

I had to be careful. Deliberate. Like any good negotiation, I couldn't be too quick to show my hand.

"Then… As a sign of good faith, hand over the deed to our house right now."

***

I sat behind the counter of the apothecary, tapping my foot anxiously. Cloud had tried to jump up on my lap several times, but I was too restless, so he ended up hopping off in frustration each time.

I couldn't help it. The suspense was *killing* me! I mean, where were they? It was well past noon and they should've been here by now!

What if they got caught? What if I got in trouble? What if my lie came back to hurt the apothecary? Maybe I had made a big mistake…

There weren't any customers to distract me from my worries, so I was a bit of a mess. I even tried studying, but it was impossible to focus on the text. So the grimoire was uselessly splayed open across the counter, doing nothing more than wasting space.

To make matters worse, Master Wis was supposed to be back from her business trip at some point this evening. What if she came back and I was in jail? Would that be the end of my apprenticeship? That would mean nearly two years of hard work would all be for nothing!

I groaned and pulled my hat down over my eyes. What had I done?

At that moment, the shop door flew open.

"We did it!!"

I lifted my hat and peeked out from under the brim, to see Ailu in the entryway, triumphantly holding a piece of rolled up parchment over her head.

"Ailu!" I stood up and slammed my hands on the counter. "I was so worried! Where's Kyon?"

"Do you think she would have been able to escape immediately? Calm down. She'll give Laurent the slip and be here soon." Ailu approached the counter with a sinister grin on her face, accented by her sharp fangs. "More importantly, looky looky!"

She roughly threw aside my grimoire...

"Hey!"

... and rolled the parchment out across the wooden surface.

"We're officially free of Laurent!" She cheered.

"I'm so happy for you, Ailu!" I clapped my hands together and smiled brightly.

"Oh, and here." She tossed a small bag into my hands; it jingled as I caught it. "Don't worry, it's really money in there this time."

I undid the string to the purse and looked inside. By a rough count, all 120 gold pieces appeared to be in there!

"It's called a closing fee." Ailu smirked, proud of herself. "I squeezed a little extra out of Laurent for some medicine on my way out."

Note to self: Never cross Ailu. She can be scary...

"You have a cat?" Ailu asked. Down at her feet, Cloud was rubbing against her ankles affectionately, but Ailu looked less than thrilled and was shying away from him.

"How do *you* not like cats?" I asked.

Ailu scowled and muttered something I could barely hear, "...remind... my Pa..."

Several moments of awkward silence passed. I wasn't sure what to say exactly. It seemed like a really sore subject.

"Geez, what's taking Kyon so long?" Ailu laughed nervously, trying to diffuse the tension. "That klutz! It's rude to keep us waiting!"

"Yeah..." I stiffly chuckled, going along with her.

Five minutes passed. Then half an hour turned into an hour and a half! Still, no sign of either "Sandy" *or* Kyon!

"Something's wrong!" Ailu declared, sitting on the windowsill of our shop. "She should be back by now."

"..." Ailu just stared out the window. "I'm going to go check it out."

"Wait! I'll go with you!"

"No offense, but you'll just get in the way. I can transform—slip in and out."

"But what if Kyon really *is* in trouble? I want to help!"

Ailu thought for a moment. "Fine. But you do exactly as I say, got it?"

"Got it."

So we headed back for Laurent's Dive. We took a route that put us across the street hidden in an alleyway, giving us full vantage of the tavern, which was attracting more traffic now that it was later in the afternoon.

"Okay, I'm going to go around the back and enter through the kitchen. Hang tight for a minute." Ailu told me, looking at the bar from over her shoulder.

"Be careful!"

Ailu nodded, then... *poof!*

A calico cat sat where Ailu was just moments before, and I watched as she quickly made her way across the street before vanishing behind the building.

I was so focused on the tavern that I didn't even notice the footsteps that approached from behind me.

"Look boys, it's the little witch!"

I turned around, but a heavy fabric was immediately thrown over my head. My vision went dark, and then suddenly, I was hoisted into the air.

***

"Dammit Kyon, just tell me where the dog is!"

I heard Laurent's angry voice, as my assailants roughly dropped me on the ground. When the hood was ripped off my head, I found myself in the cellar of what I could only assume was the bar. Casks of alcohol lined the walls, as did large pieces of distilling equipment and crates of grain.

My hands were bound behind my back. To my left, the lost dog twin was in a similar situation. Laurent had her by the scruff of her neck, screaming in her face. When she spotted me, her face fell in shame.

"Boss, we found the witch girl." It was the bald thug from earlier, and he was with Laurent's other two cronies.

215

"And as I thought, she's the same girl we saw running with Ailu and Kyon earlier." He continued.

"I see… So *that's* what's going on." Laurent growled. Suddenly, he smacked Kyon across the face with so much force she was knocked to the ground. She whimpered in pain.

"Hey!" I tried to stand up and protest, but the bindings wouldn't let me.

"So this is one of your damn schemes, Kyon?!" He shouted. "Do you idiot twins really think you can pull one over on me?"

He kicked her in the stomach, causing her to cry out again.

"Stop it!!" I yelled, tears forming in my eyes.

"And *you!*" Laurent turned his attention towards me.

This was bad. This was an unbelievably terrible situation. My entire body was trembling in fear, and it was becoming hard to breathe.

At that moment, a cask of alcohol came crashing to the ground from one of the upper racks! The wood went flying like shrapnel, ale surging and splashing everywhere as the smell of malt and yeast filled the air.

My nerves were already on end, so it nearly scared me to death. But it caught everyone else unawares too.

"Kyon, now!"

Ailu was up on the rack, pressed against the wall. She must have braced herself and pushed the cask down with her feet.

With everyone's focus elsewhere, Kyon used the opportunity to transform into her dog form. The ropes that had been holding her fell uselessly to the floor, and she bolted for the stairs.

"What?!" Laurent couldn't believe his eyes!

Ailu leapt off the rack and transformed in mid-air. She hit the ground as a cat, then sprinted after Kyon.

"But... How? Grr, after them!" Laurent yelled out violently.

The three cronies looked at each other dumbly, just as surprised as Laurent, until the bald man began shoving. "Go! Let's go!"

The trio quickly ascended the stairs, scrambling to catch up with Kyon and Ailu.

Was I being left behind?

Moments passed, still just Laurent and I down in the cellar. The hope that I had begun to feel at Ailu's appearance quickly turned into frustration and despair.

They really did... leave me...

Why did I ever get involved with them? Why did I even agree to this plan? Even worse, I practically volunteered! Too many emotions welled in my chest, and I could no longer hold back my tears. They steadily began falling down my cheeks, glistening as they rolled off my chin.

Laurent was absolutely steaming, closing his eyes as he let out a frustrated exhale.

"You're probably regretting getting mixed up with those two right about now, huh?"

I couldn't say anything, but tried to calm my tears. I must have looked so pathetic...

"Unfortunately for you, we still have business." He lifted me by my collar and hoisted me up off my feet. "I'm going to teach you a lesson. And then, I think you owe me some money."

He raised his hand and I shut my eyes to brace for the impact.

I was so stupid...

The hit never came.

"Argh!!"

Laurent yelled out in pain, and I found myself falling to the ground. I opened my eyes...

"Gotcha!" Warm hands caught me by the shoulders, and their owner gave me a reassuring smile.

"Ailu!"

I looked over at Laurent to find him trying to shake canine-form Kyon off his arm, but her jaws were locked tightly around his wrist. In fact, though she probably only weighed 30 pounds or so, she was able to throw her weight around in a way that had him on the verge of falling over.

"And Kyon, too... I thought you abandoned me..."

"Will you shut up? We've gotta go!" Ailu exclaimed, as she undid the ropes binding my wrists.

My tethers fell to the ground. My arms were free! Ailu pulled me to my feet and we ran for the stairs.

"Kyon!"

With one last good tug, Kyon managed to successfully pull Laurent to the ground. She released her grip on his wrist, then chased after us. But as we made our way up the stairs, Laurent scrambled to his feet and made a clumsy pursuit.

"Oh no you don't!" He dove across the steps, managing to catch Kyon by a back leg. She yelped as he began dragging her backwards.

I saw the commotion over my shoulders and ran back down after her. "Let go!"

I thrust my foot into Laurent's face and heard something pop as it connected with his nose.

"Gah!" He let go of Kyon and tumbled backwards.

"Nice one, Isabel!" Ailu cheered.

Kyon darted ahead of us, and we chased after her before Laurent could regain his bearings.

He shouted after us, "Stop them!"

But his fury was left unheard, muted in the cellar as we made our getaway.

"What about Laurent's men??" I asked the twins, as we ran down the street.

"Are you talking about the Brainless Threesome? Yeah, like it was hard giving *them* the slip!"

The three of us barreled into the apothecary a short time later, but at that moment, I wasn't sure who was more surprised. Was it us, who didn't expect to find such a lovely witch fiddling with a ledger behind the counter? Or was it the said lovely witch, who didn't expect to see her apprentice storming in like a crazy person, completely out of breath and accompanied by two total strangers?

"M-Master Wis!"

What was she doing back so early?

She gazed at us through her chic spectacles, her violet eyes filled with visible confusion. It was clear she had just gotten back moments before. Her broom was still nearby, as was her travel bag, and her hat was perched comfortably on the counter, her wisteria-like hair liberated but wind-whipped.

"Isabel! What's going on? Why is the shop closed?!"

Though I was certain a punishment was just around the corner, I couldn't help but feel a sense of immense relief at the sight of my teacher. I was safe. My bottom lip began to quiver, and tears once again began forming in my eyes.

"Isabel…"

Before I could address her, I had something else to address first. I turned around and threw my arms around the twins, pulling them into a hug. Then came the waterworks!

"Hey! What are you crying for, dummy??" Ailu stammered in embarrassment. Then Kyon joined in. "N-Not you too!"

"I was so scared!" I cried. "You idiots! I can't believe I went along with your dumb scheme!"

And though I was chastising them, I couldn't help but hold them close. "But... Thank you. Thank you for not leaving me."

"You big cry baby!" Ailu chuckled in embarrassment. "You actually thought we'd leave you there?"

"Kyon, are you okay?" I sniffled.

She shook her head.

"I'm sorry, it's all my fault!" She wailed. "If only I had been more careful sneaking out that window..."

"Come on, get a grip you two!" Ailu growled. "Everything worked out in the end, didn't it? We still have the deed!"

"Are you talking about this?" Master Wis asked, holding up the rolled up piece of parchment we had left on the counter. "Will someone tell me what's going on?"

I pulled myself away from the twins and turned around to explain the situation. But before I could even introduce Ailu and Kyon, the door to the apothecary burst open!

"There you are! You rats!" It was Laurent, backed by his three thugs.

Dried blood was plastered across his face, which had spread from a now crooked nose. And a towel was wrapped around his wrist like a makeshift bandage. Needless to say, he looked downright awful, but he also looked absolutely furious, and I didn't like the venom I saw in his eyes.

"H-How did you find us so quickly?!" Kyon stammered, as the three of us backed away from the door, fearfully retreating towards the counter.

"Um, excuse me. Can I help you gentlemen?" Master Wis stepped out from behind the counter with a guarded expression on her face. She then got between us and Laurent.

"Step aside. This doesn't concern you. It's those girls I have business with." He growled.

"This is *my* shop. And one of those *girls* happens to be my apprentice. So I'd say it very much concerns me."

"Ah, so you're the no-good drunk? Or was that just another lie?"

"Sorry?" Master Wis looked at me in confusion, but I could only avert my eyes.

"Out of the way!" Laurent demanded. His three goons pushed forward aggressively.

Master Wis looked from them, to us cowering behind her, and narrowed her eyes.

"If my apprentice caused you any trouble, I sincerely apologize. She's my responsibility, and... I know she can be a bit misguided at times." She adjusted the glasses on the brim of her nose. "Still, if she upset you, I expect you deserve it. As her teacher, why don't you try taking your complaints up with me?"

Master Wis had a very scary look on her face that I had never seen before. Even though her glare wasn't directed towards me, I couldn't help but feel a chill crawl down my spine.

Laurent and his men flinched, but just when it looked like they might all turn tail and run, his eyes drifted down to the document still in Master Wis' hand. "The deed!"

"Yes, I think I'll be hanging on to it for a little while."

"I will not be made a fool of!" Laurent roared stubbornly. "I want that deed!"

His men charged in. Idiots. They should've run when they had the chance.

All Master Wis had to do was lift her hand and chant a few, simple words.

***

Ailu and Kyon were in debt again.

Not with Laurent of course—that issue was settled—but with the apothecary. To help pay that debt (I was just in trouble...), the twins and I were in the attic of the shop, reorganizing boxes and throwing out the junk Master Wis no longer needed. It was a dim, dusty space with lots of cobwebs.

"Isabel!" Kyon gasped. "There's a spider on your shoulder!"

"What?" I shrieked. "Where?!"

The twins watched me dance around in horror for several moments, before they both burst out in laughter.

"You're so gullible!"

"You should've seen the look on your face!"

"Ugh! You guys!" I snarled, throwing a dingy pillow at them I found lying nearby.

"We better not be fooling around up here!" Master Wis said sternly, peeking her head up into the attic.

"Yes ma'am!" Ailu and Kyon replied in unison, stiffening up at the sound of her voice.

"Once you've moved the last couple of boxes, come downstairs. "You have a visitor."

"Yes ma'am." This time, we all replied in unison.

Once she retreated back down the ladder, we exchanged curious glances. A visitor?

"Well, we better finish first." Ailu peeked down the stairs quickly and whispered, "She *still* scares me."

"But she's so cool, right?" Kyon gushed.

Needless to say, the way Master Wis handled Laurent and his men the week before left quite the impression on them. Don't get the wrong idea, it's not like she hurt them or anything. Let's just say it wasn't likely Laurent would ever bother the apothecary or the twins' family again.

We finished moving the boxes as instructed, and I exhaled deeply as I wiped away the sticky sweat that had accumulated on my forehead. My hands were filthy and my back was starting to hurt from all the lifting. It was hard, dirty work. But besides the stern lecture and loss of my next couple of weekends, I suppose I got off relatively easy...

"Yay! We're done!" Kyon cheered. "Now let's go see who's here!"

We hurried downstairs, finding Master Wis in our eclectic den, sharing tea with our new guest.

"Ma!" Kyon gasped happily, running and giving her mother a big hug.

"What are you doing here?" Ailu asked in an almost challenging way, but even she couldn't help but smile at the sight of her.

Not only was their mother up and moving around on her own, but the bandages had been removed from her eyes too. She could see again! She still wasn't back to a healthy weight yet, but she wasn't pale anymore, and her hair had regained its sheen.

And *that's* why the twins were back in debt. Their mother was healthy again thanks to a powerful mandragora tonic, supplied, of course, by Wis' Apothecary. Such a cure wasn't exactly cheap. Master Wis cut them a deal on the price and told them they could work it off with odd jobs around the apothecary every now and then.

"Hi girls." Their mother greeted cheerfully. "I knew you'd all be working hard today, so I brought lunch! There's enough for Madame Wis and Isabel too, of course."

"You're too kind, Miti." Master Wis smiled, accepting the basket of food their mom picked up from her feet.

"Yes Miti, thank you so much!" I added heartily.

Cloud poked his head into the common area to see what all the commotion was about. But he didn't go unnoticed by Kyon.

"Cloud!" She rushed over and reached out to pet him, but naturally this just scared him off. Actually, he didn't even really like Kyon to begin with.

Cloud darted behind Ailu and hid behind her ankles. Ailu scowled, but didn't try and move him. Kyon got on her knees and tried to reach out to him one more time, but my fussy cat just hissed at her.

"That's cruel..." Kyon whined.

We all had a good laugh at her expense, but Kyon couldn't help but join in herself.

Miti had prepared us all simple yet tasty sandwiches with chicken, cheese and spinach. And as we all sat around eating together, chatting and laughing about nothing in particular, it dawned on me how lively the apothecary had suddenly become. We never had this many guests over at once, and we didn't really even have the space. But it was really nice nonetheless.

After the meal, the twins offered to clean up and disappeared into the kitchen together. Minutes later they called for me—I looked at Master Wis inquisitively. What could they want? I just shrugged and got up to see.

I approached the kitchen, but found that the door was closed, though I heard them giggling from the other side. They were up to something...

Maybe they didn't think I could hear them, or perhaps they thought I wouldn't come to the door so quickly. Either way, I wasn't just gonna stand here and let them have their fun. I quickly opened the door hoping to interrupt their shenanigans, but... *Splash*!

I gasped as a douse of cold water shocked my entire system! A bucket fell to the ground next to me with a clatter. It was now empty, its contents having been poured out all over me. My clothes were heavy and water continued to run down from my hair and onto my face.

I was so stunned, I couldn't even move!

Kyon and Ailu stood at the other end of the kitchen, doubled over and clinging to each other in a fit of hysterical laughter.

"After all that work, we thought you could use a bath!" Kyon cackled.

"Oh man, what a mess!" Ailu gasped for air.

My face contorted in rage and I emitted a deep rumble from my throat. "Grrrr…"

"Run!" Ailu laughed, transforming into a cat. Kyon followed suit and they both went sprinting past me for the stairwell.

"KYON! AILU!" I shouted angrily, taking off after them. "I'm going to get you for this!"

They really were the worst! But… all things considered, I suppose having them around wasn't so bad.

Cloud Chronicles #1

Is there anything more wonderful than sleep?

A morning nap. An afternoon doze. An evening respite. How can I choose a favorite? All I need is a surface, any surface will do, and...

"Cloud! You can't sleep here! Move!"

Oof! Don't touch me!

I was just starting to drift off when my human suddenly scooped me up off the cool, wooden chest I had made my bed, then rudely dropped me to the ground. I hissed to let her know my displeasure.

"I know, I'm sorry!" She groaned, opening the chest and rummaging around inside. "But there are plenty of places for you to sleep! Why do you have to be *here?*"

We were in the coolest and quietest room of my domain. The walls were made of stone and lined with shelves filled with strange devices and glass containers of this or that. A small window near the ceiling let just enough light in for it to not be too cold. And in the afternoons, on top of that chest was the only place to catch it.

The better question was, if the contents of that chest were so important, why put them inside my bed? She *knew* I liked to sleep there. Instead of going in and out, and having to move me each time, wouldn't it be easier for everyone to keep them somewhere else?

Besides, I didn't wake *her* up. Well, unless my bowl was getting close to empty, or if I was feeling like a morning jog across the bed. But otherwise, I tried to be considerate. The poor thing got less than eight hours of sleep a day as it was.

"Here it is!" My human smiled, withdrawing something from the chest before hurriedly returning back to the shop where she was spending the afternoon. "If that's all, your total is going to be..."

My human was always running somewhere. Honestly, it was exhausting just to watch. That's why I slept so much. Unlike where I lived last, tending to this home was a lot of work! Some stranger was always coming or going, and if I was going to watch over my human, I needed proper rest.

But it was hard to get quality rest around here. Case in point? Before I even had a chance to consider where I was going to nap next, my human's human came rushing into the laboratory. She had a broom in one hand and a jar filled with dancing lights in the other.

Why were humans always in such a rush? It must have been their needless reliance on time. Time was such an odd human construct. I slept when I was tired. I ate when I was hungry. And I played when I needed to burn off some energy. It was simple. So why did everything require a schedule with them?

She set the jar down on a nearby table and took off her glasses to rub her eyes. She seemed tired. I rubbed myself against her legs sympathetically, but to be honest, I was also just trying to get a closer look at the jar.

What was going on in there? It was like three, small blue balls of flame were dancing around inside. They circled one another and bounced off the glass like they were trying to get out. But the purple-haired witch must have noticed me staring, because she placed her hand defensively on the jar.

"No Cloud, these Will o' Wisps aren't for you! I promise, you wouldn't even taste them." And as if she didn't trust me, she pushed the jar further away from the counter's edge and back towards the wall. "Now shoo!"

I quickly retreated to the stairs as she waved her hands in front of my face. For now anyway. Her capriciousness, of course, just made me even more curious...

"Isabel, Mr. Landry will be here later this evening to pick up the Friar's Lantern." She returned to the shop and began addressing my human. "I'm going to run out for a quick errand. I should be back well before he arrives."

"Actually, can I come with you? I have to grab some things for dinner."

"If you're quick. I don't want to leave the store closed for too long."

"The rush has died down. I think we can leave the store alone for just a little bit."

"Hmmm..."

My human's human was always concerning herself with another strange human construct: money.

"Alright then. Let's hurry." She finally decided.

"Coming!"

Moments later, I heard the door to the shop close behind two pairs of footsteps, and iron twist as it locked. Now was my chance!

"*Was this the Friar's Lantern?*" I thought to myself, as I approached the counter once more.

Without effort and with much grace, I jumped up on the counter and cautiously approached the jar. My eyes had to adjust to the bright light the jar was putting off, as the formless little flames bounced around energetically. But the flames were icy, blue like a shining star in the night sky.

I could only learn so much with my eyes. I lowered my head and brought my nose to just a hair's breadth away from the glass. It didn't *smell* hot. It didn't really smell cold either. No, it smelled *magical.* These little balls of flame were alive!

What in the world?

I touched the jar with my paw and it inched forward ever so slightly. The movement disturbed the creatures inside, who began swirling around even more erratically. I moved the jar again.

Ha. What a rush! This was kind of fun...

I continued to bat at the jar, each swat of my paw bringing the container closer and closer to the edge. Before long, it was there. Hmmm... what would happen if I gave it one final push?

I couldn't help myself. Oops.

Crash!

I didn't know what I was expecting, but the sudden shattering of glass startled me! I backed away from the edge of the counter and watched in horror as the balls of ethereal flame rose into the air.

Oh no! The Willy Wisps! (Or whatever.)

I tried to knock one out of the air before it exited my reach, but my paw passed right through the creature! The hell?!

I leapt up on my hind legs and tried again, this time with so much force that I knocked myself off the counter. Of course, I had no trouble landing on my feet.

As if to mock me, the three Willy Wisps descended and began circling my head. I snapped at them and swatted at them, but nothing seemed to work! How was this even possible?

But I was a mighty hunter! I wasn't going to let these strange insects best me! I chased after them as they ducked under one of the nearby shelves for cover. I was able to squeeze my front paws underneath, but watched helplessly as they emerged from the other side.

They were quick. But I was up for the challenge!

We zipped across the lab and back up onto the counter. In my haste, I knocked over something ceramic, which also fell to the ground and broke. That was hardly a concern at the moment.

Next, they headed for the stairs, but I was quick on their heels. I was able to make it onto the steps with just two quick pounces. But it didn't matter how fast I sprinted after them if I couldn't touch them! What was I going to do?

As they zeroed in on the open window upstairs at the reading nook in the den, it quickly dawned on me: there was absolutely nothing I could do except watch from the white, cushioned bench as they fluttered out the window and disappeared happily into the horizon of Aramore's tiled roofs.

Damn. They got away. I *had* been bested.

I yawned and ritualistically began washing my face. Oh well. Nothing could be done now, I suppose. How exhausting! It was most certainly time for a nap.

I jumped down from the bench and made my way to my human's room, where I nestled myself in a thick pile of blankets on the bed. I yawned again and tucked my chin on my front paws.

Perhaps I'd have better luck catching the Willy Wisps in my dreams.

Like I said, quality sleep was hard to come by here. Not much time passed before my ears were flickering. The humans had returned home—my peace was ruined...

"Isabel!"

...

"Cloud!"

Ugh. Can't a cat just get some rest around here?

230

Birthday Wish

A chilly breeze carried a crimson leaf through my window, gently and delicately. The frond landed on my cheek, tickling me awake. It was the perfect time of year, where I could keep my window open and sleep under a mountain of comfy blankets without being too hot.

And it practically guaranteed Cloud would cuddle with me, whom I awoke to find nestled between my legs in a makeshift nest of sheets.

"Good morning, Cloud!" I greeted happily, sitting up and scratching his head.

"Meowww…" My snowy white cat replied said with a yawn.

"Aw, you remembered!" I joked.

I carefully lifted him from my legs and jumped out of bed in excitement.

This time of year was perfect for one other reason…

I looked at my circular wall calendar just to double check what I already knew to be true: it was Octoria 13th! My birthday!

I swiftly brushed my messy hair and got dressed as quickly as I could. No need for robes today, Master Wis had promised we'd have the day off! I was really excited!

After all, it wasn't every day a girl turned 15. Wasn't I basically a woman now? Well, close enough anyway.

Maybe I'd have Master Wis take us to get crepes for breakfast! After all, *I* certainly wasn't going to cook.

To be honest, I was really just looking forward to spending the day with her. We had a *big* fight the other day and things had been a bit awkward since. I didn't think I was wrong then, but I still felt bad…

I ran down the stairs, giggling as I imagined what else I could guilt her into doing for me on my special day, and erratically threw the kitchen door open.

"GOOD MORN—"

But Master Wis wasn't in her chair drinking tea like usual. Instead, a note was waiting for me on the table, along with a few gold coins. I apprehensively picked up the note…

Isabel,

First and foremost, HAPPY BIRTHDAY!

I'm sorry, some urgent business came up that I absolutely must take care of. However, I left nice and early so I can be back as soon as possible.

In the meantime, why don't you buy yourself some breakfast? Perhaps those crepes you like? I promise I'll be back in time to treat you to whatever kind of lunch you would like!

I'm looking forward to celebrating your birthday.

Love,

Wis

I read the letter through a second time, in complete shock. Unbelievable! I crumpled up her note and angrily threw it across the room.

Ugh!! This was exactly what we had been fighting about!! How could she?

Lately, she had been so absent. Even *if* she was at the apothecary, her mind was still away on business. I understood that a witch of my teacher's caliber was always in high demand, so I tried to be patient. But how was I supposed to become a proper witch myself if Master Wis wasn't there to teach me? I could only learn so much from a dusty, old book!

And now she was absent on my birthday too? I fell pitifully into a nearby chair and let out a deep sigh.

The truth was, this time of year was perfect in a lot of ways. But since coming to study under Master Wis, this season also made me feel a little extra lonely.

The changing leaves always reminded me of apple picking season; how busy it would be around the orchard back home. Or the apple pies my mom would make, especially for my birthday. Even if she wasn't feeling well, there was always a pie waiting for me on my big day.

I wrote to my parents regularly, but it had been a while since I had actually seen them in person. I missed my mom's smile and my dad's deep laugh…

I shook my head and stood up. No! It was my birthday! I wasn't just going to spend it moping around and feeling sorry for myself! I'd just have to keep myself busy until Master Wis returned.

I wasn't in the mood for crepes anymore, but I was still hungry. So I scooped up the gold coins and decided to visit Heidi at her family's bakery around the corner.

It was a bit cool outside, so I grabbed my traveling cloak on the way out the door and wrapped it tightly around my body. An autumn palette of leaves crunched beneath my feet with each step I took, as I sucked in the chilly, morning air through my teeth.

It wasn't a very long walk and soon I stepped inside the rustic little bakery. Unfortunately, it appeared I came during a rush, and there was a long line of people to the door.

"We're going to need more loaves of rye up here soon!" Heidi, who was busy behind the counter with her mother, shouted to her father in the back. "Hi, good morning! How can we help you?"

As she was helping the customer, she spotted me at the door and gave me an enthusiastic wave. I waved back with a soft smile on my face.

"Next!"

I waited patiently, despite the tantalizing smells of the bakery torturing my empty stomach. Before long, I was up at the counter.

"Isabel, it's so good to see you! How have you been?"

"Well, I'm having to eat breakfast on my own on my birthday, so..." I bashfully admitted with a chuckle.

"It's your birthday? Wow! Happy birthday, Isabel! Though, I'm sorry to hear that..."

"Thanks Heidi." The corner of my mouth flickered upward.

"Breakfast is on me! What do you want?"

"Oh no, I couldn't." I tried to politely decline.

"No, I insist! Get whatever you'd like!"

I blushed. "That's so nice. I really appreciate it. If you insist, do you have any breakfast baguettes available?"

"As a matter of fact, a rack just came out of the oven a short time ago."

As the baker's daughter scurried away, she looked like a floppy rabbit with her long, braided pigtails. She returned moments later with my savory bread.

"Thank you again!"

"Hey, I've gotta do *something* for your birthday! We're friends, right?"

"Yeah." I grinned stupidly. "Hey Heidi, actually, by chance do you want—"

"Order up!"

"Sorry to interrupt Isabel, but I've gotta get this."

I scanned the room and noticed the crowd of customers wasn't letting up any. I shook my head, it was a silly idea. Heidi was far too busy.

"No, of course. Nevermind." I smiled weakly. "See ya later."

"Bye! And again, happy birthday!" She waved me off, as she hurried to help her father with the bread that just came out of the oven.

I pouted as I left the shop, quietly taking a bite of the baguette. At least it was pretty tasty. I walked around aimlessly, munching on my breakfast as I took in the sights of my fall-soaked city. I still had a majority of the morning left, what was I going to do now?

If Heidi wasn't available to hang out, maybe Becca would be? She was always super happy to see me. So I headed for her butcher's shop, except...

"Sorry Isabel, Becca is sleeping right now." Her cousin and adopted father, Bertram, told me when I arrived at his store. "Though you and Madam Wis were nice enough to provide her with that lunar bracelet, being up during the day to help with the shop all week can still be tough on her. So I let her sleep in on the weekends."

"Oh…"

The portly and cheerful butcher must have watched my face fall, because he said, "But you know what, let me go wake her up for you. I know she'd love to see you."

"No, that's okay." I quickly replied. "I don't want to be a bother."

I was sure she was probably really tired after working all week in the daytime. She deserved the rest.

"Are you sure? It would be no trouble."

"Yeah, it's totally fine." I faked a big smile and giggled. "Tell her I'll come by again soon."

"Wonderful. Will do. Have a great day, Isabel!"

Yeah, really great so far...

I shut the door behind me and my fingers wistfully lingered on the doorknob for just a moment before I stepped back out onto the street. Perhaps I should've had him wake Becca? But that would've been selfish...

There were other people I could still see. Like the twins. Of course, hanging out with them meant subjecting myself to a morning of teasing and pranks, but even that was preferable to spending my birthday alone. And it wasn't as if being with them wasn't fun.

So I decided to make my way over towards the wharf near where the twins lived. It wasn't the most scenic part of the city, but the walk there was rather enjoyable. And that wasn't just because everything looked so pretty, but also because the streets themselves seemed even more excited than usual.

It was harvest season, which meant everyone was looking forward to the festivals right around the corner. A majority of people were busy trying to get their affairs in order before winter. There was an influx of traffic as a result, not just of farmers and merchants, but also artisans eager to wrap up work for the year. And the scholars and mages from across the kingdom were doubling down on coursework so they could return home for the holidays.

The walk took me alongside the river and I could see the castle standing majestic and proud in the distance. It made me think of Fleur—I wondered how she was enjoying married life with Reynard. I needed to write to her soon.

And speaking of letters, I also needed to check in on Jonah. Tragic circumstances forced him into an entirely different kingdom, but he seemed to be genuinely happy these days. I hope that was still the case. He was surrounded by a loving family now, after all.

My walk to the twins had become a walk down memory lane, and by the time I had polished off the last of my breakfast, I was at their front door. I knocked three times, then took a step back.

Usually, you could hear Kyon noisily sprinting for the door. That wasn't the case this time. Instead I heard a gentle, "One moment, please!"

The latch on the door came undone and a very pretty woman stuck her head out and smiled at me. It was Miti, Kyon and Ailu's mother.

She looked remarkably like the twins, though as a dog Hybrid like Kyon, *that* resemblance was a bit more uncanny. Unlike the twins, both of her eyes were the same color, a palatable gold. Not too long ago, she was bedridden and blind. Now, she looked as healthy as could be.

"If it isn't Isabel! What a pleasant surprise! How are you?"

"Hi Miti! You look well."

"All thanks to you and Madame Wis!"

"No, I didn't do anything." I chuckled, scratching my cheek.

"Nonsense! You did more than I think you'll ever realize."

"Hehe... um, are the twins home?" I asked, quickly changing the topic. I couldn't help but feel awkward when receiving gratitude.

"Sorry Isabel, they're out at sea right now."

"Out at sea?!" I staggered backwards. "When did they leave? When will they be back?"

"Relax, Isabel." Miti laughed. "They're just out with a fisherman. They'll be back by the evening."

"Oh." I exhaled in relief.

At least they were trying honest work now...

"Why don't you stay and have some tea?"

"Erm, no. I don't want to trouble you." I waved a hand at her and turned away to leave. "Thanks for the offer though!"

"Please? I'm bored here all alone... I would love the company."

I smiled tenderly and turned back. I certainly understood the feeling.

***

"I see..." Miti muttered, after hearing about my morning and the recent fight with my teacher. "I'm sorry Isabel. I know that's not a fun start to your day."

She handed me a cup of tea and sat down next to me on the edge of her bed.

"What can you do?" I chuckled weakly. "I suppose I should feel fortunate to be the apprentice to someone so widely regarded."

"Absolutely. I know at your age it's hard to be patient, but don't be too tough on your teacher. She's a remarkable woman and is no doubt doing a lot for you behind the scenes. And that's probably something you'll never truly understand, until you have a child or student of your own."

"Maybe..." I couldn't help but smile a little.

"Of course, I'm sorry you're having to spend your birthday getting lectured by an old, boring woman like me!"

"Not at all!!" I argued. "And in what world are you old?" She didn't even look much older than Master Wis!

Miti just laughed in response. "You're sweet, Isabel. But you could still stand to learn a thing or two about Hybrids."

The time passed quickly, chatting with Miti. The tea was soothing, and she was surprisingly funny, though not in a malicious way like her daughters. We talked about working at the apothecary, Cloud and then the conversation drifted to my life before becoming a witch's apprentice.

"You're not from Aramore, right Isabel?"

"That's right."

"Do you come from far away?"

"No, not really." I laughed softly. "I grew up on an orchard in Pommeseed, which is less than a day from here by carriage."

"So do you visit home often?"

"Not as much as I should..." I admitted.

"Isabel! Shame on you." She scolded playfully. "Speaking as one, I'm sure your mother misses you."

"Yeah... I really missed her too..."

"Be sure to visit her soon."

"I will." I promised, draining my second cup of tea. And then I noticed the sunlight pouring into the house. "Wait, what time is it?"

"It must be getting close to noon. Are you hungry?"

"No, thanks for the offer. But I should get going! Master Wis will be back soon."

"Ah, good! Get her to take you somewhere nice for lunch." She winked.

I laughed. "Definitely!"

She offered to take my cup, then we stood up together. After she set the dishes down in the kitchen, she walked me to the door.

"Again, happy birthday! 15 is a very special age," She placed a hand on my shoulder as she opened the door. "You're blossoming into a young woman, so be sure to treasure this time."

"Thanks Miti! And for the tea, too. I feel a lot better."

"Anytime."

We waved goodbye and I hurried back to the apothecary with lifted spirits.

Unfortunately, my reinvigorated attitude didn't last long. When I climbed up the stairs and entered the apothecary, I found Cloud waiting for me... but not Master Wis.

For a moment I started to get angry, but I remembered to breathe instead. Master Wis herself taught me to do that once when I was feeling overwhelmed, and it always seemed to help.

"*Relax.*" I thought to myself.

I looked at the enchanted dial mounted in the kitchen to confirm the time. It wasn't quite noon yet. I should just give her the benefit of the doubt.

But the dial on the wall continued to spin, and Master Wis remained absent. There wasn't even a sign of her broom in the sky! Before I knew it, a whole other hour had passed.

Even worse, I wasn't even surprised...

I shouted in frustration. I couldn't take it anymore! What was she doing?

Frustrated, I stomped my way down the stairs and into the laboratory. I approached our scrying basin and angrily gripped its ceramic sides. Runes etched into the stone lit up at my touch.

I looked into the mirror-like water and chanted, "Crystal Pool hear my plea. Reveal to me who I want to see."

The reflective water became almost silver, then rippled gently. Right about now, the vial Master Wis kept on her person would be shaking and quivering to catch her attention. It was filled with the same liquid, aquacanus, which allowed for a magical link to be established. I could scry her, and she could scry me right back.

And she noticed. Moments later, Master Wis' visage began to materialize in the water. The image was murky at first, but continued to become more and more clear until it was like we were looking at each other through a window.

Master Wis forced a gentle smile, but wore a complicated yet sympathetic expression on her face. "Isabel, I am so, so—"

But I was out of patience and became immediately combative. I didn't even let her finish her apology before I interrupted her. "Where are you?!"

"Well, um... There's been a slight problem." She was speaking loudly. In fact, she was nearly shouting. Her voice was competing with an intense roaring sound, like a raging river or bonfire, but I couldn't really get a good look at her surroundings.

And was something clanging in the background? Like metal? Frankly, I didn't really care.

"So what does that mean? Are you coming back soon?" I growled.

"I'm sorry Isabel, it seems I'm going to be here another hour or two."

"What? Why?!"

"I promise I'm trying to return as quickly as possible."

Unbelievable. Absolutely unbelievable. At that moment, something inside of me just snapped.

"You know what? Don't bother!" I shouted. "I'm going home."

"What? Wait, Isabel –"

Before she could reply, I furiously slapped the surface of the water to break our magical connection. A tear rolled off my cheek and fell into the basin.

I wasn't even really thinking as I marched into my room and began stuffing clothes and belongings into my messenger bag. I was so furious! I was *not* going to spend my birthday at the apothecary alone. And if business was more important than her apprentice, why would I waste my time waiting around for Master Wis?

In a blind rage, I placed Cloud in the bag on top of my things and stormed out of the apothecary. I slammed the door behind me, but at least I remained courteous enough to lock up.

Cloud cried from my bag.

"Are we coming back? I don't know." I replied simply. As I began walking away from the shop, I couldn't help but turn and look at it one last time.

A sign above the door read *Wis' Apothecary*, and the sight of it made my heart ache. The truth was, I loved my teacher. But...

"Hey Cloud," I spoke softly. "Do you remember when we first met Master Wis?"

A sudden, sharp pain in my finger caused me to drop the knife I was gripping with my left hand.

I winced, sucking air in through my teeth.

The apple I was holding together with my right hand fell apart, as I lifted it to inspect the damage. I watched a streak of crimson run down the length of my finger.

"Careful!" My mother, Ariana, chided. She rushed over to me at the cutting board and knelt down. "Let me see."

We were in the kitchen of our home, and I was helping my mother bake an apple pie. I wanted to learn so I could eat one every day! But I had been a bit careless with the knife.

I think the sight of blood panicked me more than the brief pain, as tears began to form in the corners of my eyes.

"You're okay, Bella. It's just a tiny nick." She reassured me, my hand held gently in hers. Her hazel gray, sympathetic eyes shimmered at me.

Despite our different eye colors, she was still unmistakably my mother with her peach-colored hair, right down to the cowlick with a mind of its own. It came down past her shoulders in beautiful waves. I thought it was really pretty, but I hated managing my ill-tempered hair and couldn't imagine letting it grow out as long as hers.

"I'm not crying." I insisted.

I was 12 — much too old to be crying!

"Bless your tender little heart." My mother chuckled softly and ruffled my hair. "Let me get you a bandage. And then I'll show you how to make the dough."

But as she gripped the counter and went to stand back up, her legs began to wobble and she fell back down on her knees.

"Are you okay?" I asked, reflexively reaching out and supporting her by the shoulder.

She was a frail woman and unfortunately this kind of thing happened often. That didn't mean I was any less concerned.

"I'm fine." She smiled weakly. "I'm just suddenly feeling... a little light-headed."

She tried to stand up again but instead slipped right out of my fingers. I tried to catch her, but I wasn't fast enough. She had fallen over and collapsed on her side.
My lungs seized.

"Mom?!" I gently shook her by the shoulder, but she didn't respond.

I scrambled to my feet and dashed outside to the orchard in a panic. "Dad! Dad!!"

***

My mom spent a lot of time in bed. Not because she was lazy, mind you. In fact, cheerful and restless, her true nature was the exact opposite. But she was terribly sick, and her body wouldn't let her tend to her family the way her heart wanted to.

Sure, she'd have good days — even good weeks, but her mysterious illness was fickle and unpredictable. She could put in a long day out in the orchard one day and be just fine, but collapse during a simple task like washing dishes the next. Even a sudden drop or spike in the weather could put her down for days.

This time, she had been bedridden for an entire week, with no signs of getting better. I had been outside foraging all day, and now I was at her bedside showing her my haul. My snowball of a cat, Cloud, a once-sickly kitten we recently found abandoned in the orchard, rested comfortably atop her thighs.

"And *this* is a purple mushroom I found growing underneath that sprite's nest! They swarmed me so fast!" I laughed.

Luckily, even angry sprites were pretty harmless.

"Very neat... sweetheart."

"Bella." My father's stern voice came from behind me. He was carrying a tray of tea. It was time for my mother's medicine.

"Sorry." I quickly scooted out of the way, making room for my father.

His name was Bosc, and he towered like a magnificent tree with broad shoulders and muscular legs. A heavy, black beard covered the majority of his face, and extra bushy eyebrows covered his eyes. He was so strong he could lift me with a single arm, which was fun when I was younger — but now I was getting a bit too old for it.

Even though he tended to trees now, my father had spent a majority of his life felling them as a woodsman. He had always dreamed of opening an orchard and spent years collecting seeds and saplings while in the forest. He inherited this land from his uncle, which he even cleared himself! Or so my mom told me. He never really talked about himself, or much of anything for that matter.

Though quiet, he could still expertly communicate his feelings with a simple sentence or light body gesture. And really, he was a big softie! My mom called him her mighty oak.

My father propped her up, causing Cloud to scurry down to my side, and helped her drink the medicinal tea. One of his large, calloused hands held the cup to her lips, while the other rubbed her back tenderly.

My mom smiled in relief after draining the small cup.

"That should help with the fever." He said, gently laying her back down.

"Is she... arriving today?" My mom asked him with haggard breaths.

"Yes."

Huh? Who?

"Is another doctor coming?" I asked, tilting my head.

Lots of doctors had come and gone from our home, even ones from the capital of Aramore, but none had been able to tell us what was wrong with my mom.

"Not exactly." My father smiled and squeezed my mom's wrist tenderly. He looked oddly hopeful.

And at that moment, as if our guest had just been sitting outside waiting for the perfect entrance, there came a knock at our door.

"That must be her." My father began to stand up, but I was much more agile.

"I'll get it!" I announced, running out of the room and for the door, my father not far behind.

"Stop." He scolded, as I reached for the door handle. My hands froze in their tracks.

He brushed me aside and opened the door himself. "Hello?"

"Good afternoon. Are you Mr. Pirige?"

"You must be Madame Wisteria."

"Just Wis is fine." She replied pleasantly.

It took me a moment to make my way around my father's large frame, but when I did, I peeked out from behind him to take a good look at our guest. The sight of her caused me to gasp. She looked absolutely magical!

I was drawn first to her eyes, which rested behind a pair of thin and stylish glasses. They were soft pools of purple that seemed to gaze at a different world than the rest of us. And her hair was a matching lavender, with ribbons of curls cascading past each shoulder, a pretty bow holding the rest of it loosely together at her back. Her hair reminded me of the vines for which she was named.

Her complexion was lively and flawless, her figure just as healthy. She wasn't terribly tall, but she carried herself with such elegance and poise that you may not have noticed.

She held a broom at her side in one hand, a green-jeweled ring sparkling on her finger. On her head sat a pointed hat adorned with a lovely, amber-colored ribbon. And she wore robes of a quality so fine she seemed to shimmer, her smile every bit as bewitching.

She was almost as pretty as my mom! No wait, was she prettier? I couldn't admit to something like that...

"Wis Amberfinch, owner and proprietor of Wis' Apothecary, at your service."
For some reason, I was intimidated. I cowered behind my father's legs and gazed at her. That only caught her attention.

"Who is this?"

"Bella..." My father pushed me forward.

"Um, hi. I'm… I-Isabel. Isabel…"

She didn't wait for me to finish the introduction before dropping to her knees and suddenly enveloping me in her arms! The gentle scent of lavender filled my nose.

"You're so cute!" She squealed.

What?

I was stunned! No stranger had ever just grabbed me like that, certainly not during an introduction. Was she allowed to behave this way?

"Uh…" Is all I could manage to sputter out of my mouth.

"Sorry! I'm making you uncomfortable." She quickly pulled away and tenderly straightened my now-ruffled clothes. "My apologies, I just couldn't help myself."

She flashed me a smile before standing up again, and after clearing her throat, she turned to address my father. "Now then, can you show me to your wife?"

As I watched my father walk her back to my mother's room, a single thought crossed my mind: *What a strange woman.*

***

"You don't have to stare from a distance, you know."

Busted!

Cloud at my ankles, I had been peeking my head into my parents' room, silently watching Madame Wis work at the bedside. She had a small suitcase of ingredients and glassware she had conjured, seemingly out of nowhere, and was swirling some mixture together in a beaker. At her urging, my father had returned to tending to the orchard, so she was alone with my mom.

After reflexively ducking my head back behind the wall, I sighed and lifted Cloud into my arms before shifting uncomfortably into the room. No point hiding now…

How did she know I was looking?! She hadn't even turned her head...

"Want to see what I'm doing?" She asked me.

I meekly nodded.

"Come on then." She gestured toward her side. "I don't bite... hard!"

As I sat next to her, she playfully snapped her teeth at me.

"Stop." I growled, shying away from her. She just laughed in reply.

"Is that your kitten?" She asked me, after a moment of silence.

I nodded.

"He's really cute. What's his name?"

"... Cloud."

"Cloud? I like it. It suits him!"

I didn't reply, but continued to watch her work in fascination.

"Isabel... isn't normally this quiet... even with strangers." My mom observed, chuckling weakly.

"Is that so?" Madame Wis laughed.

"Th-That's not true!" I quickly refuted in embarrassment.

"If you have a question, just ask it." She reassured me with a smile.

I gulped. "Then... what are you doing?"

"I'm mixing a solution that will hopefully help me see what in her body is making your mother sick."

"And... are you... a wizard?"

"Not quite. I'm a witch!"

Woah! I had never met an actual mage before. Those that could use magic were really rare. It took years of training and not just anyone could do it. No one like that existed in my small town.

"What's the difference?" I asked curiously.

"A wizard uses magic to bend reality and warp the elements, but a witch uses magic to *harness* reality and the elements we've already been provided."

"So... why did you decide to be a witch?"

"Hmmm..." Madam Wis thought for a moment. "Because it seemed like a fun, easy way to make money?"

That's all?! It was a surprisingly simple and straightforward answer.

"But then... doesn't being a wizard sound like more fun?"

"Isabel!" My mom chided, with a weak breath.

Madame Wis just laughed at my candor. "But I think if something as incredible as magic exists, it should be used to help people. Don't you?"

My heart thudded. For some reason, those words struck at something deep within me. I was moved. And at that moment, Madame Wis seemed really cool!

After that, I took an extreme interest in this witch, Wisteria Amberfinch. I asked her about every step she took and every ingredient she used. And though my mom scolded me for being annoying, Madame Wis was patient and answered every single one of my questions.

Finally, she finished the potion. She had shown me glow moss and boiled willow bark were the main components. My mother winced in disgust as Madam Wis helped her drink it.

"Pretty gross, huh?" Madame Wis smirked sympathetically.

"What now?" I asked.

"We wait." The witch replied.

"For how long?"

She laughed. "For a while."

"And—"

But my mom interrupted me before I could ask another question. "Bella, why don't you put Cloud down… and show Madame Wis around?"

She was tired. Perhaps she was just trying to get rid of me… I frowned. But Madame Wis seemed delighted by the idea.

"Oh, yes!" She exclaimed, clasping her hands together. "Show me where to find the best fruit, Isabel!"

I began by showing Madame Wis around our home. We weren't rich or anything, but I suppose we were pretty well off due to the orchard and my parents' modest lifestyle. I always wore new clothes, never went hungry and had plenty of room to run around and explore.

We lived in a plain, log cabin that my father, of course, built himself. It was only one story, but had several rooms and a spacious living area. A fire was often crackling in the fireplace, and furs lined the walls. I loved the way it smelled, especially when my mother was baking.

We were twenty minutes from town by cart and lived on the edge of a small forest. A trail led from our house to the orchard, which was enclosed by a wickerwork fence. My father had hundreds of trees, harvesting peaches and pears in the summer, then apples in the fall. Which is exactly what they were busy harvesting right now.

That made for an especially scenic walk down the trail, with the leaves on fire with every shade of red, orange and yellow imaginable.The ones that had already fallen crunched pleasantly beneath our feet as we chatted idly.

"Wow! How pretty!" Madame Wis admired, as we approached the orchard.

It cast a lot of shade, but sunlight always stubbornly fought its way through. And falling leaves from the nearby forest scattered in the wind and played amongst the trees.

It was an especially busy time of year and my father, along with about half a dozen helpers, were scattered about the orchard pruning trees and collecting apples. I usually helped, too—so did my mom if she was feeling well enough.

I spotted my father at a tree at the edge of the far fence and waved enthusiastically at him. He smiled softly and waved back. He was holding a bucket as one of his helpers up on a ladder dropped apples down into it.

"So, which tree produces the sweetest fruit?" Madame Wis asked, rubbing her hands together. "Surely you have a favorite!"

"Well, Dad doesn't like me taking fruit from the trees, so I have to be sneaky." As I told her this, I put a finger to my lips.

"Of course." Madame Wis nodded seriously.

I took her to the back edge of the orchard, which bordered the forest. There, we approached my favorite tree. I don't know if its apples were actually any better than the others, but this tree was out of sight and had lots of low branches that made it easy to climb.

I reached out to grab one from the low hanging limbs, but before I could touch it, an invisible force gently tugged it off the tree and carried it into Madam Wis' outstretched hand. I watched in awe! It was my first time ever seeing magic!

She winked at me, putting her finger to her lips in the same exact fashion that I had. I chuckled and went to grab another. This apple also plucked itself off the tree, but zoomed high into the air out of my reach.

"Hey!" I growled.

Madame Wis laughed before waving her hand and releasing the magic. The apple ended up falling right into my hands.

"I'm terrible! A guest at your home, helping you steal apples from your father." She clucked her teeth.

"I didn't steal anything! You're the one that pulled the apples from the tree!" I grinned devilishly.

"True. But if you take a bite of the apple then we're accomplices."

I shrugged and took a big bite of the fruit. She smirked and raised her fruit, "To accomplices then!"

She then returned in kind, taking a bite from her apple.

It didn't take us long before we had whittled the fruit down to their cores, which we both audibly enjoyed.

"And to get rid of the evidence?" I tossed the remainder of the apple into the forest as far as I could throw it.

"The perfect crime." She tossed her apple after me, then licked her lips. "That *was* a really sweet apple!"

I watched as her discarded apple landed near mine, but directly in my line of sight something shiny at the edge of the forest caught my eye. I quickly ran over to investigate and picked up quite the unusual rock.

"What did you find?" Madame Wis asked curiously.

It was a glassy stone, which was interesting enough. But what made the rock truly special was the hole bored through the center of it! The stone easily fit in the palm of my hand, and with the hole looked like it could be a ring for a giant.

"Look at this cool rock!" I presented it to her in my outstretched palm, proud of my discovery. It may have been one of my most unique finds yet!

"Oh, wow! An adder stone!" Madam Wis remarked.

"An adder stone?"

"Actually, it's also nicknamed a witch stone." She smiled mirthfully and her eyes twinkled. "That's because, like certain crystals, it's a great conduit for magic. These types of rock are often enchanted and made into necklaces or talismans to ward off certain spirits or harness energy."

"Wow. That's awesome!" I couldn't believe I found something so rare. "It's going in my collection for sure!"

"Your collection?" I had piqued the witch's interest.

🍎

Because we lived outside of town and because I was an only child, often I was left to my own devices when it came to finding entertainment.

I liked to read, and now that I had a cat, playing with Cloud was a fun pastime too. But my all-time favorite activity was exploring the nearby forest.

It wasn't super large, but to a 12-year-old child, it might as well have been Aramore's fabled Pinnella Forest – named for its golden-leafed trees that could grow to be 300 feet tall!

This made for some fun expeditions. And whenever I went out to explore, I always brought back trophies of my adventure. Over the years, I amassed quite the collection of interesting odds and ends, which I kept displayed on a blanket in my room. I was really, really proud of it!

So when Madame Wis asked to see it, of course I jumped at the chance to show it off.

"Wow, Isabel! This is impressive!" She lauded, after we had made it back to my room.

I had pulled the blanket out into the center and straightened its contents so they were neat and orderly. Everything was organized by size, color and category. For example, the mushrooms were kept separate from the rocks, which were kept separate from the flowers. (I pressed them in books, something my mother had shown me how to do.)

"Hawthorn branch, orris root, shed scitalis skin... you have a collection that would make any apothecary jealous!"

"Really?" I chuckled nervously.

It wasn't like I knew anything about what I was picking up. I just picked up the stuff I thought looked cool or interesting. To think some of this was valuable, even if just in the eyes of an apothecary like Madame Wis, was like learning I'd been holding onto treasure!

"Really! You... have an exceptional eye." She muttered, glancing at me curiously. "And... oh wow!"

She picked up the purple mushroom I was showing off to my mom earlier. I had since added it to the collection.

"I found that this morning!" I declared proudly.

"Did you find it with others?"

"No, only the one."

Madame Wis frowned, looking disappointed. "I thought so."

"What is it?" I asked, leaning forward.

"A pixie cap mushroom. They're *really* rare, because the growing conditions have to be so exact. In certain potions, they can have near-miraculous healing effects."

"Oh wow, no way."

"I almost want to steal it from you." She laughed.

My face fell, and a bit conflicted I muttered, "Well, if it would help you..."

"You're a sweet child, Isabel. Don't worry, though!" She pinched my cheek. "Hang on to it for your collection."

She carefully returned the mushroom to my hands, smiling at me. "Thanks for showing me all this! You'll have to see *my* collection sometime."

"Really?" I gasped happily. "That would be amazing!"

"We'll definitely arrange something. For now, how about we check on your mother?"

"Yeah!"

My father must have been done with work for the day because we found him in the bedroom, sitting in a chair beside my mom. She seemed to be sleeping, and Cloud had returned to napping on her lap.

"How's she doing?" Madam Wis asked, as we entered the room.

"She seems okay." My father said quietly, as to not wake her.

"May I?"

My father got up and offered his seat to Madame Wis. But the witch declined, instead kneeling down at her bedside. To remain out of the way, he picked up the chair and moved to the foot of the bed.

"I'm going to undress her now." Madam Wis announced clinically. "Sorry Cloud."

With first my cat, then the blanket, and followed by my mother's clothes, she gently and carefully pulled away each layer. But she didn't need to go any further after removing my mother's shirt. She had, quite obviously, found what she was looking for.

My father quickly stood from the chair, and I gasped. Like branches, the veins around my mom's heart were radiating brightly through her skin. The icy blue glow looked both unnatural and ethereal, and made for a shocking sight.

"Don't worry, the glowing veins are just an effect of my potion, but... this is still pretty serious." Master Wis remarked grimly, tracing along my mom's skin with her fingertips. "It seems there's some kind of abnormality with the heart... her blood isn't flowing properly."

"Is my mom going to be okay?!" I ran over to Madame Wis' side.

As panicked thoughts raced through my mind, my chin quivered and my chest tightened. My father also appeared to be pretty disturbed by the news, grimly stroking his beard.

Madame Wis didn't reply right away, which was equally frightening. Instead, she looked lost in thought. She reached for her nearby suitcase and began rifling through the various components stored inside.

"Garlic cloves... Hawthorn berries..." She began muttering to herself. "But not *that*... and even if I did..."

She bit her lip and adjusted her glasses.

"Um, Madame Wis?"

Madame Wis looked at me and her eyes widened. "Unless..."

"What?"

She cleared her throat and smiled up at me. "Isabel... can you help me help your mom? It's going to be a big favor."

"Anything!" I readily replied, without hesitation.

"In that case, can I steal that pixie cap mushroom after all?"

"Isabel, wake up." A voice gently stirred me awake.

"Hm?"

As I sat up, a crick in my neck caused me to wince in pain. I rubbed the back of my neck.

So I fell asleep in the chair, huh?

I found myself seated at the kitchen table, with a blanket draped over my body and a sleeping kitten curled up on my lap. The sun outside was just beginning to peek out from behind the trees—the early morning light that filtered through the windows tenderly kissed everything inside.

"It's ready!" Madam Wis was standing beside me proudly, a bright red potion in her hands.

She must not have slept at all. Her hair was a mess, her hat nowhere to be seen and dark circles under her eyes. Her glasses were also dangerously close to falling off her nose.

The kitchen was just as messy. Components and beakers were scattered across the table and counters, and powders and leftover bits of flora were strewn everywhere. Sitting on the stovetop was a complicated-looking device, complete with scales, a flame and mystical looking runes. Madame Wis told me it was her portable cauldron set, which magically fit at the bottom of her suitcase.

Needless to say, but the kitchen had become Madame Wis' makeshift laboratory overnight. And I was with her because I had insisted as much. My father didn't want me to be in the way, but it was my condition for handing over the pixie cap. And Madame Wis didn't mind one bit.

She even let me help! I mean, I mainly just grinded up ingredients. A couple of times she did let me add a couple portions to the concoction that she, of course, measured out. It helped keep me from worrying about my mom too much, and it was actually a lot of fun! But I guess I wasn't able to make it to the end…

"Don't sulk. I said it's ready! Let's go!"

Madame Wis was right, and I felt hopeful. I grinned, excited for my mother. *Could this really be it?!*

I followed Madame Wis to my parent's room and she gently knocked on the door. "May we come in?"

"Please do," came my father's voice from the other side.

We entered to find my father still by my mother's side. Like Madame Wis, he looked like he hadn't gotten any rest. My mother, on the other hand, was sleeping soundly, though her cheeks were flushed and her face was damp with sweat.

"Madame Wis, good morning. I hope Bella wasn't too much of a bother."

"Not at all! She couldn't even keep her eyes open past midnight." Madame Wis chuckled as she teased me.

"Hmph." I pouted.

"But don't worry, Isabel was a lot of help!" She put her arm around me and placed her hand on the outside of my shoulder. "I literally couldn't have done it without her."

She then pulled me into a tight side squeeze, but this time I was in no mood to resist; a big, stupid grin was plastered across my face.

"We really are accomplices now, huh?" She whispered in my ear, and I couldn't help but giggle in reply.

"So this is it?" My father asked, taking the potion from me. "This will cure her?"

"Well, I don't like to make promises, but..." Madame Wis gingerly took the potion from his hands and got down on her knees beside my mom.

"Good morning, Ariana." She said quietly, softly shaking my mother awake.

My mom groaned, but her eyes fluttered open. She smiled at Madame Wis and muttered a reply I couldn't hear.

"Can you drink this?"

My mother nodded weakly, and propping her head up with her hand, Madame Wis helped her drink the potion. My father and I stood behind her, anxious, as the medicine was consumed.

For the next several moments, no one uttered a word. Then I watched, in real time, as a healthy color returned to my mom's face.

Her visage brightened, like she was waking after a long afternoon nap. And she sat up with a wondrous look on her face.

"I can't believe it…" She muttered, swiveling her feet to the edge of the bed. Her feet touched the ground and she began to stand up. "I can't explain it, but… suddenly, I feel… I haven't felt this good in a very long time!"

"Ariana!" The corners of my father's mouth were pulled so high, they even managed to lift up his thick beard.

"Does this mean she's all better?!" Without waiting for a reply, I threw myself at my mom and wrapped my arms around her waist.

"Bella…" She smiled, and squeezed me in return.

"Only time will really answer that question." Madame Wis answered, standing up and dusting off the hem of her dress. "But it looks like the elixir is already doing its job."

Tears began to fall steadily down my cheeks. "I'm so glad."

"Are you crying?" My mom asked me, running a hand through my hair.

"N-No…"

I was 12 now. I was too old to be crying.

"Bless your tender little heart."

My father pulled us into his arms, holding the back of our heads with his hands. His grip was strong and warm, and he smelled like firewood. It was such a beautiful hug. It was truly a tremendous moment for our family, absolutely beside ourselves with glee.

"I don't know what to say…" My mom coughed through wet eyes, looking at Madame Wis, struggling to find the words.

Perhaps my dad said it best: simply.

"Thank you Madame Wis. Truly." My father emphasized his gratitude with a poignant pause.

"Really, you should be thanking your daughter. If it wasn't for her sharp eye, I may never have been able to brew up a potion this powerful. Or, at the very least, certainly not this quickly." And then she quickly added with a wink, "She was also quite the little helper."

"That's my girl." My mom hugged me from behind and kissed me on the cheek. My father placed a hand proudly on my shoulder.

"But I didn't really do anything!" I protested, stepping forward. "Magic is incredible! No. Madame Wis, *you're* incredible!"

"You're right on both accounts." She laughed, ruffling my hair with her hand. "So how would *you* like to learn *magic* from *me*?"

Wait, come again?

"Do you mean it?!" I asked excitedly, before looking at my parents to receive their blessing, but they both looked thrilled by the idea.

"Of course. We're accomplices, after all."

Was I dreaming? I could be just like Madame Wis? She was so incredible! And she used magic to help people. I mean, she just saved my mom! Sure, she was a little strange. And I barely knew her. Even so... Madame Wis was my hero!

"You really think I could do it?"

"I can just tell. You're going to be a wonderful, compassionate witch someday."

I couldn't even utter a reply. Of course the answer was yes, a million times yes, but...

I must have been quite visibly processing the information, because Madame Wis just laughed and conjured up a piece of paper in her hand.

"Why don't you think about it? You're not quite old enough yet anyway. But when you turn 13, if you're still interested, write me." She then extended to me the piece of paper with her address written on it. The address to Wis' Apothecary.

And so I did. I wrote to her every week for a year. And when I turned 13, as promised, she officially asked if I wanted to be her apprentice. And well, I don't have to explain the rest, right?

***

By the time I reached my family home, the sun was already beginning to set. The orange of the leaves faded into the orange of the sky, and the little warmth this time of year offered began to fade away too. The wheels of the carriage that took me here rattled and churned, as they unsteadily made their return to the main road across dirt and rock.

I waved goodbye to the carriage driver and faced the thick, wooden door. Even from outside, the log cabin still smelled the same. I was home!

I eagerly opened the door, which creaked loudly due to its age and weight, and stepped inside. Immediately, I was welcomed by the wonderful aroma of baked apples and pie crust. My stomach rumbled in excitement.

"Mom? Dad?"

I heard light footsteps running towards the entryway first, which meant...

"Isabel?!"

"Hi Mom."

Joy overcame my mother's face. She ran to me, grabbing me by the shoulders and pulling me into an enthusiastic hug. "Oh my goodness! What a surprise!"

Since that day three years ago, my mother hadn't collapsed once. And she was quite possibly healthier than ever before. Her wonderful hair still came down in waves, and her face was full of life and energy.

Just seeing her made me realize how much I truly missed her. I began to tear up, though I tried to choke them back. As of today, I was 15. When was I going to stop being such a crybaby?

"Bless your tender little heart." She smiled, holding one of my cheeks in her hand. "I swear, you look more like a woman every time I see you. Happy Birthday, Bella!"

"Is that apple pie I smell?"

"It's an annual tradition, whether you're here or not." She grinned.

I licked my lips hungrily. But before I could insist on a warm slice, heavy footsteps came next. My father leaned into the entryway like he was unsure if he had imagined my voice or not. When he saw me, his face lit up and he lumbered over to me with his arms outstretched wide.

"Bella!"

"Dad! Oh…" I grunted, as he embraced me. The death squeeze…

My father only seemed to get bigger with time, or at least, his belly did. His beard was now speckled with silver, but his brow was just as heavy as ever.

"Happy birthday, little one!" He said, kissing me on the top of my head.

My mom took my traveling coat and helped Cloud out of my messenger bag. He scurried off, probably to one of his favorite spots to find mice, and my mom hung the bag nearby on the wall.

"Are you alone? Where's Madame Wis?" She asked.

"Who cares?" I scoffed.

My mom exchanged concerned glances with my father. "Um, okay. Well… How about some pie?"

"Yes please!"

We went to the kitchen and my dad and I sat at the table, while my mom began cutting into the pie. Its tantalizing fragrance still hung fresh in the air, like she had finished baking it not too long ago.

I only visited once or twice a year, but things never seemed to change. Not just the oak table or the cabinet where my mom kept the nice plates, but the spot where my dad took his boots off for the day, and the painting on the wall that always seemed to tilt no matter how often my mom straightened it.

Maybe that's exactly what a home was?

"So what's going on?" My mom asked, setting a piece of pie down in front of me.

"What do you mean?" I asked, as she served my dad and then sat down for her own piece.

"Bella, we're so happy to see you. But… usually you only visit for the holidays. Is something wrong?"

I didn't immediately answer the question, instead ravenously tearing into the apple pie. The flakey, buttery crust. The cinnamon apples that just melted in your mouth… It was a recipe that also never changed!

"Mmmm!!" At that moment, I could have died happily.

"Bella." My father's stern voice brought me back to the kitchen table.
"What? Can't I just miss you guys? Do I need a reason to visit my own parents?"

"We missed you too." My father replied, squeezing my hand.

"But I'm sure Madame Wis is also missing you right about now." My mother added.

I scoffed again.

"So something *did* happen."

"No. Nothing happened, and *that's* the problem." I grumbled, setting my fork down. "She hasn't been around much lately. But worst of all, she wasn't around today. And after she had promised we'd spend the day together…"

"Well honey, she's quite the renowned witch. I'm sure she's busy."

"I know!" I groaned. "But how am I supposed to become a great witch myself if she's never around?!"

My father and mother looked at each other again, then my mother leaned forward with a frown. "So, what? Are you giving up? I thought you wanted to help people."

"No!" I replied quickly. "I mean, I do. But... I don't know."

I looked down at my wrist, forever marked, and let out a frustrated exhale. "What am I supposed to do?"

"Be patient." My father responded.

"That's right. Have faith in your teacher."

"But it's been two years! And I can't even cast a spell yet!"

"You're not a greenhorn anymore, Bella." My father argued.

"Huh?"

"He means your teacher is leaving you alone *because* she trusts you." My mother explained. "When your father hires someone new on the orchard, he's with them every step of the way in the beginning. But eventually he has enough faith that they can do their job without him, and he gets to spend more time doing his."

"I... I guess..." I had never really thought about it that way.

"Besides, can you really say you're learning nothing?"

No, I knew that wasn't true. I was learning something every day. Not just from Master Wis, but from the people I was lucky enough to meet through the apothecary. And they were all lessons way more valuable to me than notes in a grimoire.

I gulped. I may have just turned 15, but... maybe I was still acting pretty childish.

"She writes to us too, you know." My father continued.

"And until you have a child of your own, I don't think you'll realize how much she cares about you." My mother finished softly. "You mean the world to her."

I had heard something like that before.

"Master Wis... means the world to me too." I replied quietly.

"Bella." With just a look, I knew exactly what my father was trying to say. What was I even doing here?

I had made a huge mistake...

"Sorry guys, I've got to go. I love you!"

"Wait!"

"How are you getting back?!"

To be honest, I didn't even think that far ahead. I just grabbed my travel cloak and snatched my bag off the wall and began searching wildly for Cloud...

Knock. Knock. Knock.

"Are you expecting anyone else?" I asked.

"Get the door, Bella." My parents didn't even bother getting up.

I shook my head in confusion. That was so unlike them! But, whatever...

"Hello?" I opened the door and found myself standing face-to-face with the one person more than anyone else I had wanted to see for my birthday.

Her expensive robes were wind whipped and her pointed hat was nowhere to be seen. As she leaned on her broomstick like a staff, hobbled over, her glasses came dangerously close to sliding off her nose. But even now, even after all this time, she looked absolutely magical. She was my teacher, the great witch Wisteria Amberfinch.

"Master Wis!" Before I could say anything else, she lifted her hand.

"Isabel, I am so, so sorry. I messed up." She rubbed her forehead, with a pained look on her face. "I wanted to be there for your birthday, I really did. But there was a problem with your gift, and then I got back but you weren't home, so I looked everywhere, and –"

"Wait. Birthday gift?? I thought we agreed you wouldn't do presents anymore!"

She was an awful gift-giver... Last year, she got me an enchanted chest that tried to eat Cloud!!

"I think you're really going to like this one." She smirked.

She reached into her robes and withdrew a small jewelry box from inside. And as she handed it to me, she smiled brightly and said, "Happy birthday, Isabel!"

It was a small, black ring box.

Is this what I think it is??

I opened the box. From inside, a crimson-red stone sparkled at me. It was set in a soft pink metal, inscribed with runes of powerful origin. Even a novice like me could feel the magic radiating from the ring! There was no doubt. It was an Arcanus!

I looked up at Master Wis, my breath caught in my lungs. What could I possibly say? *This* was why she wasn't there this morning?

"I'm sorry Master Wis." I finally managed to choke out. "I'm not ready."

I had been such a jerk! I didn't deserve the Arcanus at all!

I closed the box and started to hand it back to her. But she held her hand out to stop me. "You *are* ready."

"You don't understand."

"Your left hand?"

"Master Wis!" I protested.

"Your left hand, Isabel." She demanded.

I reluctantly held out my hand. But she didn't place the box in it like I was expecting. Instead, she went one step further. Holding my hand in place, she withdrew the ring from the box and slid it onto my ring finger.

Immediately, I felt a mysterious force surge through my body. I felt it resonate deep within my soul, a strange and great power which I knew too little to understand. I was speechless and could only helplessly stare at it on my finger.

"You're ready." My teacher repeated.

"Master Wis…" My eyes began to water. "I'm the one who really messed up!"

And without any warning, I threw myself at her, giving her a hug I think even my dad would be proud of.

"You're not the little girl anymore I met all those years ago." She spoke softly, patting the back of my head. "I'm so proud of the woman you've become."

"I probably don't say it enough, but… thank you. Thank you for everything!" I sobbed. "I know I can be selfish, and ungrateful, and lazy…"

"Shhh…" She soothed me. "You're my accomplice, remember? For every bit you're grateful for me, just know I'm ten times more grateful for you."

I didn't want to let go. We held each other as the sun continued to sink down below the trees, silently appreciating one another. It was a wonderful moment—I looked forward to many more.

"Alright, enough of that." Master Wis finally said with a cough, before pulling away and tenderly straightening my clothes. "You've already come all this way, so I don't want to get in the way of family time. I'll just see you back at the apothecary in a couple of days, okay?"

She flashed her usual mystical smile and turned to leave, but I grabbed her by the sleeve of her robes. "Wait. Master Wis?"

She turned back towards me and tilted her head. "Yes?"

"There's still some apple pie left. Would you... like to come in for some?"

We had only known each other a short three years, but pie with family wouldn't have been as sweet if she wasn't there.

"I think I'd like that very much."

As I stepped out of the way so this strange witch could enter our home, a single thought crossed my mind: I couldn't wait to return to the apothecary!

Afterword

Let me first start by saying thank you for picking up *Welcome to Wis' Apothecary*! I've always considered myself a storyteller, and got into journalism for that reason. To write an impactful piece, you need to first find a real person the audience can relate with, and share their story. And though this is my first time publishing a fictional story, with characters that only exist in my mind, my goal was the same: tell compelling stories with even more compelling characters. I appreciate you giving me a chance, and I hope you enjoyed following Isabel along on her misadventures.

For me, Isabel was a bright light during a pretty dark time in my life. The pandemic has been challenging for probably every person on this entire planet, and I'm no exception. I was dealing with isolation, big changes at work, heartbreak and a brutal winter. But I suppose what they say is true, out of adversity comes opportunity. I wanted to find something beautiful during that difficult time, and Master Wis, her young apprentice, and all their new friends, are the result. If I did my job right, perhaps you found some beauty within this book too.

I also want to take a moment to thank my illustrator Eduardo, who has so much raw talent, it blows my mind. And my editor Bob, who really whipped this novice author into shape. The apothecary simply wouldn't have been the same without either of them.

As you can probably tell, Isabel's adventures are far from over. So please look forward to the second volume, and all the characters we still have to meet. Until then!

Andrew Freeman

About the Author

Andrew Freeman is a journalist and author living in Rochester, NY. He studied Broadcast Journalism and Communications at the University of North Texas before going on to report in the Texoma region, and Upstate New York. When he's not writing stories, he enjoys spending time outdoors, practicing martial arts, and doting on his cat. You can follow his future endeavors @WisApothecary on Twitter and Facebook.

Made in USA - Crawfordsville, IN
10263_9780578307862
09.12.2022 1454